GINNY MOON

BENJAMIN LUDWIG

ONE PLACE. MANY STORIES

HQ
An imprint of HarperCollins*Publishers* Ltd.
1 London Bridge Street
London SE1 9GF

This edition 2017

1
First published in Great Britain by
HQ, an imprint of HarperCollins*Publishers* Ltd. 2017

ISBN: HB: 978-1-84845-542-9
TPB: 978-1-84845-661-7

Printed and bound by
Printed and bound by CPI Group (UK) Ltd, Croydon CR0 4YY

A lifelong teacher of English and writing, Benjamin Ludwig lives in New Hampshire with his family. He holds an MAT in English Education and an MFA in Writing. Shortly after he and his wife married, they became foster parents and adopted a teenager with autism. *Ginny Moon* is his first novel, which was inspired in part by his conversations with other parents at Special Olympics basketball practices. His website is available at www.benjaminludwig.com

For my wife, Ember,
whose heart was open.

GINNY MOON

The plastic electronic baby won't stop crying.

My Forever Parents said it's supposed to be like a real baby but it isn't. I can't make it happy. Even when I rock it. Even when I change its diaper and give it a bottle. When I say *ush, ush, ush* and let it suck on my finger it just looks dumb and screams and screams and screams.

I hold it close one more time and say, *Nice and gentle, Nice and gentle*, in my brain. Then I try all the things that Gloria used to do whenever I went *ape-shit*. After that I put my hand behind its head and move up and down on my toes. "All better. All better," I say. From high to low like a song. Then, "So sorry."

But still it won't stop.

I put it down on my bed and when the crying gets louder I start looking for my Baby Doll. The real one. Even though I know it isn't here. I left it back in Gloria's apartment but crying babies make me really, really anxious so I have to look. It's like a rule inside my brain. I look in my drawers. I look in the closet. I look in all the places a Baby Doll might be.

Even in the suitcase. The suitcase is big and black and shaped like a box. I pull it out from under my bed. The zipper goes all the way around. But my Baby Doll isn't inside.

I take a deep breath. I have to make the crying stop. If I put it in the suitcase and put enough blankets and stuffed animals around it and push it back under the bed then maybe I won't hear it anymore. It will be like I put the noise away inside my brain.

Because the brain is in the head. It is a dark, dark place where no one can see a thing except me.

So that's what I do. I put the plastic electronic baby in the suitcase and start grabbing blankets. I put the blankets over its face and then a pillow and some stuffed animals. I'm guessing that after a few minutes the noise will stop.

Because to cry you need to be able to breathe.

I'm done with my shower but the plastic electronic baby is still crying. It was supposed to be quiet by now but it isn't.

My Forever Parents are sitting on the couch watching a movie. My Forever Mom has her feet in a bucket of water. She says lately they have been *swollen*. I walk out into the living room and stand in front of her and wait. Because she is a woman. I'm *a lot more comfortable with women* than I am with men.

"Hey, Ginny," my Forever Mom says while my Forever Dad presses the pause button. "What's up? It looks as though you might have something to say."

"Ginny," says my Forever Dad, "have you been picking at your hands again? They're bleeding."

That was two questions so I don't say anything.

Then my Forever Mom says, "Ginny, what's wrong?"

"I don't want the plastic electronic baby anymore," I say.

She brushes her hair off her forehead. I like her hair a lot. She let me try to put it in pigtails this summer. "It's been almost forty minutes since you went into the shower," she says.

"Did you try to make it stop? Here. Hold this until we can get you some Band-Aids."

She gives me a napkin.

"I gave it a bottle and changed its diaper three times," I say. "I rocked it and it wouldn't stop crying so I s—" Then I stop talking.

"It's making a different sort of sound now," my Forever Dad says. "I didn't know it could get that loud."

"Can you please make it stop?" I say to my Forever Mom. And then again, "Please?"

"It's great to hear you asking for help," my Forever Mom says. "Patrice would be proud."

Far away down the hallway I hear the crying again so I start looking for places to hide. Because I remember that Gloria always used to come out of the bedroom in the apartment when I couldn't get my Baby Doll to stop. Especially if she had a man-friend over. Sometimes when it cried and I heard her coming I used to take my Baby Doll and climb out the window.

I grab the napkin tight and close my eyes. "If you make it stop I'll ask for help all the time," I say and then I open them again.

"I'll go have a look," my Forever Dad says.

He stands up. When he walks past me I *recoil*. Then I see that he isn't Gloria. He looks at me funny and walks into the hallway. I hear him open the door to my room. The crying gets louder again.

"I don't know if this idea is working," my Forever Mom says. "We wanted you to see what it was like to have a real baby in the house, but this is not turning out like we planned."

In my bedroom the crying gets as loud as it can get. My Forever Dad comes back out again. One of his hands is in his hair. "She put it in her suitcase," he says.

"What?"

"I had to follow the sound. I didn't see it anywhere at first.

She crammed it in there with a bunch of blankets and stuffed animals, zipped it shut and then forced it back under her bed," he says.

"Ginny, why would you do a thing like that?" my Forever Mom says.

"It wouldn't stop crying," I say.

"Yes, but—"

My Forever Dad interrupts her. "Look, it's going to drive us all nuts if we don't put an end to this. I tried to make it stop, but I couldn't do it, either. I think it's at the point of no return. Let's just call Mrs. Winkleman."

Mrs. Winkleman is the health teacher.

"She said she gave the emergency phone number to Ginny this morning," my Forever Mom says. "It's on a piece of paper. Check in her backpack."

He walks into the hall and opens the door to my bedroom again. I cover my ears. He comes out holding my backpack. My Forever Mom finds the paper and takes out her phone. "Mrs. Winkleman?" I hear her say. "Yes, this is Ginny's mom. I'm sorry to call so late, but I'm afraid we're having a problem with the baby."

"Don't worry, Forever Girl," my Forever Dad says to me. "This will all be over in a few minutes, and then you can get ready for bed. I'm sorry this is so intense and nerve-racking. We really thought—"

My Forever Mom puts the phone down. "She says there's a hole in the back of its neck. You have to put a paper clip into the hole to touch a button and shut it off."

He goes into the office and then he comes out again and walks down the hall into my bedroom. I start counting. When I get to twelve the crying stops.

And now I can breathe again.

When I was in Period Four which is social studies Mrs. Lomos came into the classroom to give me a message. She is my guidance counselor. She has big circle earrings and wears lots of makeup. "Your parents are coming to school for a meeting," she said. "They're going to bring you home afterward, so when we hear the afternoon announcements and the bell rings, just stay in Room Five with Ms. Dana. You can work on your homework for a little while. They'll call you in at some point. They want you to be part of it."

So right now I am in Room Five which is where I go for part of language arts with all the other special kids. Because I have *autism* and *developmental disabilities*. No one told me yesterday that there was going to be a meeting today. I'm guessing it's about the plastic electronic baby.

Ms. Dana is at bus duty. I see her out the window wearing her orange vest. She is standing next to Bus Number 74. Which is my bus. Behind it and in front of it are other buses. Lines and lines of kids are getting on them. In the hallway all the sports kids are getting ready for practice. Alison Hill and

Kayla Zadambidge are already gone. They are the other two kids who go to Room Five with me and Larry.

The buses usually leave by two-thirty but three minutes is not enough time for me to get on the internet. I've been trying for a long time to get on by myself but I'm not allowed to use it without an adult. One time when I was with Carla and Mike I put Carla's laptop under my sweater and brought it into the closet. I was typing *Gloria LeBla*— in Google when the door opened and Carla found me. She took the laptop and when I stood up she *got in my face* and yelled and screamed.

And that made me scared, scared, scared.

So once at school when I was doing a report about big cats I tried to Google *Gloria mostly sells Maine coon Cats* because that is what Gloria does to make money. But my teacher caught me and when I came to this new school at my new Forever House my new Forever Parents said I can't go on the internet, ever, because they need to keep me safe. Then Maura said that both she and Brian love me and that the internet *just isn't safe. Just isn't safe because we know you're looking for Gloria* is what she really meant even though she didn't say that last part.

And my Forever Mom is right because Gloria is back at the apartment with my Baby Doll. I don't know what town the apartment is in. I need to know if she found my Baby Doll or if it's been too long and now I'm *too late*. If I'm not too late I need to pick it up out of the suitcase fast and take excellent care of it again because Gloria sometimes goes away for days and days. Plus she has a lot of man-friends come over. And she gets mad and hits. Plus Donald, when he's in town. *I really wish I could be here more often, but I can't,* Crystal with a C used to say to me when I told her the things Gloria was doing. *So make sure you take excellent care of your Baby Doll, just like your mom says. She'll always be your little baby, no matter what.*

I come up out of my brain and start picking at my fingers.

Larry walks in. He puts his backpack down on a desk and leans his arm braces against the wall and sits. Arm braces are like crutches except they attach to your body. They make Larry look like a grasshopper. Larry has brown hair and brown eyes. My eyes are green. Plus he sings all the time and doesn't like math the way I do. "Hey, babe," he says.

So I say, "Larry, I am not a babe. I am thirteen years old. Don't you know that yet? This is *tedious*."

Tedious means when you say something over and over and people get irritated like when Patrice used to tell me all the time that I was *a little like a baby doll myself* when I was in the apartment with Gloria. That was what she said when I tried to tell her that I needed to go check on it. She didn't understand at all.

Larry stretches out his arms and yawns. "Man, am I tired. It's been a long, long day," he says. "I have to stay until my mom picks me up to go to my sister's volleyball practice."

"You should do your homework while you wait," I say because that's what Mrs. Lomos told me to do. I take out my language arts book and turn to page 57 which has a poem on it by Edgar Allan Poe.

"Nah," says Larry. "I'm going to check my Facebook. I just got one yesterday."

He gets up and puts his arms in his arm braces again and goes to the computer. My eyes follow him.

"Do you have a Facebook?" Larry says when he gets to the computer. Without turning. He types.

I look down at my hands. "No," I say.

"Then, babe, you've got to get one." He looks at me. "Here, let me show you. All the cool kids are on it, you dig?" Larry says *you dig?* all the time. I think *you dig?* is mostly an expression.

"I'm not allowed to use the internet without an adult," I say.

"Right. I remember," says Larry. "Why won't your parents let you?"

"Because Gloria is on the internet."

"Who's Gloria?"

"Gloria is my Birth Mom. I used to live with her."

Then I stop talking.

"Is she easy to find?" says Larry.

I shake my head. "No," I say. "I tried to find her three times on the internet when I was in different Forever Homes but I keep getting *interrupted*."

"What's her name again?" says Larry.

"Gloria," I say. I feel myself stand up. I feel excited and ready because I know Larry is going to help me.

"Gloria *what*?"

I lean forward and look at him sideways over the top of my glasses. I push my hair out of my face but it falls back. I wish I had a scrunchie. "Gloria *LeBlanc*," I say. It's been a long time since I said the name *LeBlanc* with my mouth. Because that is what my name used to be. It's like I left the *original* me behind when I came to live with my new Forever Parents. With Brian and Maura *Moon*. My name is *Ginny Moon* now but there are still parts of the *original* me left.

So it is like I turned into the original Ginny Moon.

"Spell it," says Larry so I do. Larry types and then he steps away and points to the chair. I sit.

And I see her.

Gloria, who hit me and gave me hugs afterward and cried. Gloria, who left me alone all the time in the apartment but gave me fancy drinks when we sat on the couch watching monster movies, who said she was *a smart cookie no matter what anyone says* because she *passed the GED with flying colors* which in my brain made me see a parade of girls in pretty skirts twirling batons with streamers and cheering.

Gloria, the second-scariest person I know.

Gloria, my Birth Mom.

Gloria's shirt and hair are mostly different but at least she has pictures of Maine coons all over the page. And Gloria still has glasses and is really, really skinny like me. I haven't seen her or talked with her since I was nine years old. That was when the police came and she said, "I'm so sorry! I'm so sorry, Ginny!" I'm thirteen years old right now but I'll turn fourteen on September 18th which after today is in nine days because:

$$
\begin{array}{r}
\text{September } 18 \\
- \text{September } 9 \\
\hline
9
\end{array}
$$

Plus nine is how old I was when the first Forever started. The two months cancel each other out, mostly.

"Babe?" says Larry.

He is talking to me. I come up out of my brain. "What?" I say.

"Do you want to see if she's around to chat?"

I am excited. Because *chat* means *talk*.

Larry points to part of the screen. "Here," he says. "Just click here."

So I click and then I see a place where I can type.

"Type what you want to say to her," says Larry. "Just say *hi* and ask her a question."

I don't want to say *hi*. Instead I type the question that I keep asking everyone and that no one ever, ever, ever understands:

Did you find my Baby Doll?

And then I wait.

"You have to click Send," says Larry.

But I don't really hear him because the pictures of the police and Gloria and the kitchen are moving so fast that I can't see anything else. I am going deep in my brain again. I see Gloria with her face squished against the wall and the police holding her there. I see the broken-down door and the light coming in from outside and two cats running out. I don't remember which ones.

"Here," I hear Larry say. "I'll click it for you."

In front of me I see the arrow move on the screen. It touches the send button and then I start counting because when something might happen I need to see how high I can count before it gets here especially when it's the answer I've been waiting four whole years for.

Six seconds pass. Then some words appear on the screen under the ones I typed. The words say,

Is this you Ginny?

But that isn't an answer to my question. I want to pick at my fingers but I can't do that because there's a question on the screen and it's my turn to type. So I type, Yes this is Ginny. You did not answer my question. And click Send like Larry showed me.

Then one more word blinks onto the computer screen. It is in capital letters and it is screaming. The word is:

YES!

And then,

YES WE FOUND YOUR BABY DOLL WHERE THE HELL ARE YOU?!

I want to write *Are you taking good care of it?* but my hands are shaking so hard now that I can't make them do what I want. Plus Gloria asked a question. I open and close my hands three times and put them between my knees and take them out again and type, In Room Five with Larry.

And then she writes,

WHO IS LARRY WHAT IS YOUR ADDRESS?

Now I am picking at my fingers. I have to because I don't want to talk about Larry or what my address is. I only want to talk about my Baby Doll. Because even though Gloria said *YES!* and *WE FOUND YOUR BABY DOLL* I don't know if she's telling the truth or if my Baby Doll is okay. Because Gloria is *unreliable* and *inconsistent* and she's the one who lies. So I open and close my hands two more times and remember to breathe and then I type, Larry is my friend. 57 Cedar Lane Greensbor—

I stop typing because I hear Ms. Dana in the hallway. I hear her talking to someone else. Another teacher, I'm guessing.

Which means in a minute I'm going to get caught.

"Babe?" says Larry. He is standing behind me. His voice is *anxious*.

So I type, I have to go, but as soon as I click Send I want to go back and also say *Can you please, please, please bring my Baby Doll to me?* but my turn is gone and Ms. Dana will come in any second now.

I stand up fast to move away from the computer. Then someone touches my shoulder so I *recoil*.

I almost fall. When I see that it is just Larry and no one is hurting me I lower my arm and look at the screen again where I see another word. It says,

MANICOON.COM

Then,

THAT'S WHERE TO FIND ME JUST IN CASE.

Then,

FUCK IT I'M ON MY WAY I'LL BE THERE TOMORROW.

I look away. I don't see Gloria or the apartment or my Baby Doll. I see only Larry with one of his arms out of a brace and his hand up in the air. "Whoa, dude," he says. "Are you all right? Come on. We need to sit down and get our books out." Then he bites his lip and says, "I'm going to shut the computer. Don't freak out on me, okay?" He reaches and puts one hand on the mouse and clicks the words Log Out and then clicks the X up in the corner of the screen. He goes to his desk and sits. I push the chair back and get up and rub the dirt off my hands and look at the picture of Edgar Allan Poe.

Ms. Dana walks in. "Ginny, your parents are ready to see you," she says, "in Mrs. Lomos's office."

I stand up and take my backpack and leave the room. When I get into the hallway I start running. I run with my fingers touching the wall. I feel like I might fall if I don't keep touching something so I run and run and run. I am still excited but I am also scared.

Because Gloria is coming. Here to my school.

M y Forever Parents are outside the door of Mrs. Lomos's
tiny office. "Let's step into the conference room, Ginny,"
says Mrs. Lomos.

We take five steps to get to the conference room which is
across the hall. My Forever Parents sit at the table so I sit too.
"Hi, Ginny," my Forever Mom says.

"Hi," I say back to her. She sits with her hands on her big
round belly which is as big as a basketball. My Forever Dad's
belly is big too and his face is round but he doesn't have a white
beard or a nose like a cherry.

"Ginny, your parents came in to talk about what happened
last night with the electronic baby," says Mrs. Lomos.

I sit and wait for them to talk. But they don't.

"They let me know that you put it in a suitcase," says Mrs.
Lomos. "Is that true?"

"Do you mean the *plastic electronic* baby?" I say.

She looks at me funny. "Yes, of course," she says.

"Then yes," I say.

"Why did you put it there?"

I make sure my mouth is shut so no one can see inside my brain. Then I look at her over my glasses. "Because it was screaming," I say.

"So you decided to hide it under all your blankets and zip the suitcase shut?"

"No," I say. "I kept my quilt out." Because my quilt is the only thing I have left from the apartment. Gloria's own Frenchy mom helped her make it when she ran away to Canada with me after she had me in a hospital. They made it together for me and for no one else. I used it all the time to wrap my Baby Doll in.

"All right, but why didn't you try to comfort the baby?" says Mrs. Lomos.

"I did try to comfort the *plastic electronic* baby," I say. "I said *ush, ush, ush* like you're supposed to and I tried to give it my finger but the hole in its mouth didn't open. I gave it a bottle too."

"And that didn't work?"

I shake my head no.

"Did you do anything else to make the baby be quiet?" my Forever Dad says.

I make sure my mouth is closed again so no one can see inside. I shake my head a second time.

Because lying is something you do with your mouth. A lie is something you *tell*.

"Are you sure?" he says. "Think hard."

So I think hard. About keeping my mouth closed.

"Ginny, there's a computer inside the electronic baby," says Mrs. Lomos. "It keeps track of how many times the baby is fed and changed, and how long it cries. It even keeps track of strikes and shakes."

Everyone is looking at me. All of them. My Forever Mom next to my Forever Dad on the other side of the table with her hand on her big round belly. I don't know what *strikes and shakes* are but no one asked a question so I keep my mouth shut very tight.

My Forever Dad takes out a piece of paper. "The computer said the doll was hit eighty-three times and shaken four," he says. He puts the paper down. "Ginny, did you hit the baby?"

"The *plastic electronic* baby," I say even though it's a rule that *We do not correct.*

"It doesn't matter whether the baby was real or not," he says. "We asked you to try taking care of the baby. We can't—"

"Brian," says my Forever Mom. Then to me she says, "Ginny, it's not okay to hit or shake a baby. Even if the baby isn't real. Do you understand that?"

I like my Forever Mom a lot. She helps me with my homework every night after supper and explains things when they don't make sense. Plus we play Chinese Checkers when I get home from school. So I say, "When I was in the apartment with Glo—"

"We know what happened in the apartment," she interrupts. "And we're very, very sorry that she hurt you. But it's not okay to hurt babies, ever. So we need you to start seeing Patrice again. She's going to help you get ready to be a big sister."

Patrice is a therapist. An *attachment* therapist. I haven't seen her since the adoption in June. I lived with my Forever Parents at the Blue House a whole year before that. That was when I started going to my new school too.

Which reminds me again that Gloria is *on her way* right now. I don't know how long it will take her to get here. I don't know if she'll get here before I go to see Patrice. And that's important because I need to know when things are going to happen so I can count and check my watch and make sure everything works the way it's supposed to.

I pick hard at my fingers.

"When will I see Patrice?" I ask.

"We'll call her on the phone today and see when she's available," says my Forever Mom. "Probably early this next week, if she has some time in her schedule. I bet she'll find an opening, for you."

Gloria didn't come to school today. I waited and waited and then my watch and all the clocks in all the rooms said 2:15 and we had the afternoon announcements. Then the bell rang and I went outside with all the other kids to get on the bus.

So I am confused.

But right now I'm confused about something *more pressing*. Patrice says that *more pressing* means *something more important than something else*. The *more pressing* thing is that someone is angry here at the Blue House. I have to figure out who it is.

That's why I'm standing here on the front step of the screen porch. I'm still wearing my backpack and carrying my flute. I see that our mailbox is knocked over and there are tire tracks on the ground which means someone *peeled out*. *Peeling out* is what people do when they're in a car and they're really mad. I stand there wondering who made the marks and when I look up I see my Forever Dad's car in the driveway next to my Forever Mom's. Usually he's at work. He's the guidance counselor at the high school.

With one finger I straighten my glasses. I look at the tire tracks again. In my brain I remember that at 2:44 right before the bus stopped in front of the Blue House I saw two police cars coming the other way. They were driving slowly so I took a deep breath and held it until we were past.

I don't like police officers. They all have the same head.

Then I got off the bus and saw the mailbox and the tire tracks.

I open the door to the screen porch. Right away I smell cigarette smoke. No one at the Blue House smokes. The smell makes me think of Gloria's apartment.

I go inside. My Forever Mom is standing in front of the kitchen sink holding a glass of water in one hand and holding her belly in the other. Her hair looks like she didn't brush it and there are dark, dark lines under her eyes. Without looking she says, "Hi, Ginny. Come put your things down. We need to talk with you in the living room." Her voice is quiet.

I put my backpack and flute case in my room and come back out.

"Hello, Forever Girl," my Forever Dad says. He is standing near the window. "Did anything interesting happen at school today?"

"No," I say, "but I would like to know which one of you is angry."

They look at each other.

"Angry?" says my Forever Dad.

I nod my head yes.

"Why would one of us be angry?"

"Because there are tire tracks on the front lawn. Which one of you peeled out?"

"Wait," he says. "You think that because there are tire tracks on the front lawn, one of *us* is angry?"

I nod my head yes again.

My Forever Mom makes a little smile and then a long breathing sound. "Well, I guess this is going to be easier than we thought," she says. "Ginny, neither one of us made those tire tracks."

I am confused so I stand there thinking.

"Let's get back to the first question first," says my Forever Dad. "Did anything interesting happen at school?"

"No," I say again.

"Did you make a phone call?"

"No."

"Did anyone come to visit you?"

"No."

"Did anyone ask for your address?"

"Do you mean today?"

My Forever Dad looks at my Forever Mom quick and then looks back at me. "Yes. Of course we mean today."

"Then no."

"*Then* no?" says my Forever Dad. "What about yesterday, then? Did anyone ask for your address yesterday?"

But that was two questions in a row and I'm not sure which one to answer. Plus it's a rule that I can answer only one question at a time. Because I have only one mouth and I don't know which question is *more pressing*. So I shake my head and keep my mouth shut tight, tight, tight. Just in case.

My Forever Mom looks at my Forever Dad. She puts her hand on her chin. "Well, then, how the hell did she track us down?" she says.

So I say, "How the hell did *who* track us down?"

"The person who peeled out on the front lawn," my Forever Dad says. "But don't worry, she's gone. The police made her leave."

"So you're not still angry at me about the plastic electronic baby doll?"

He looks at me in a funny way again. "*Angry* isn't the right word," my Forever Dad says. "We're *concerned*, is all."

I wonder if they are lying. Gloria lies all the time. Then I start wondering if maybe they found out that Gloria is *on her way* because *angry* is what everyone would be if they knew. I pick and pick at my fingers and close my eyes and say, "Will someone please, please, please tell me which one of you is angry?" because you have to be careful around angry people. They get mad and hit.

Then my Forever Mom says, "Ginny, we already told you. No one here is angry. You're safe. We can talk about the tire tracks some other time. What's with the frowning face? Now, go wash up and get dressed. You're going to the apple cider farm next week, and you've got a birthday coming up! And you're going to see Patrice on Wednesday! We already talked with her and made the appointment. Maybe you should mark it on your calendar."

But that wasn't a question so I don't say anything. Plus what she said about the apple cider farm wasn't true. My class is going there on September 21st, not next week. And now I can't remember what I was worried about but when I look up I see my Forever Parents looking at me and smiling. I smile back.

"Ginny, would you like a hug?" my Forever Mom says.

I would so I let her give me one. She has to lean forward because her belly is so big.

"Now go change your clothes," she says.

I go into my room and change into my play clothes. I look out the window at the yard and see the tire tracks again.

And I remember.

It's hard for me to figure things out sometimes. I get distracted and forget to look at what I'm supposed to look at. Or I go so deep in my brain that I forget what I'm supposed to know. But I know now that no one here at the Blue House is angry. No one yelled and no one hit me. Someone else made the tire tracks but she's gone now so I can get ready for Gloria. When she comes to school I'll run out to the Green Car to see if my Baby Doll is with her. If it isn't then I'm going to have to get in the car and go back to the apartment. Even though I don't want to. Even though I know what will happen to me. Because I have to see if my Baby Doll is still in the suitcase. If it is and I'm not *too late* then I need to take it out and *take excellent care of it*. I can tell that Gloria *hasn't changed a bit*. I remember all the drugs and cats and the strange men at night. I remember what she used to do to me when I made too much noise. But the worst part is Donald. He's going to be really, really mad when he finds out what I did. He's going to make me dead. Gloria said so.

And I believe her even though she's the one who lies.

Whenever Gloria left to get more Maine coons or see her dealer I had my Baby Doll to keep me company but now my Baby Doll is there by itself. I don't know if you can hear anything when you're zipped up tight inside a suitcase. Waiting.

So I have to go back.

Maybe when I run out to the Green Car, Gloria will be *in a good place*. Maybe she'll get out and give me a big hug and say, "Holy shit, Ginny! You have really grown! Your eyes are still green? Even though you got adopted and changed your name, you'll always have green eyes. Just like us!"

I hope she is right.

It is 6:45 which means it is time for school. I have my backpack
on and my flute case and I am wearing my watch. I wear my
watch everywhere I go except the shower.

My Forever Dad is with me. Usually he stands in the screen
porch while I go out to get on the bus but today he wanted to
come along. We are walking across the grass to where the bus
comes which is at the end of the driveway. We pass the tire
tracks. On the ground near one of the tracks I see a white plastic box so I pick it up. It is a Tic Tac box with five white Tic
Tacs inside. I hold the box up and count the Tic Tacs two more
times. I shake them. They rattle.

"What's that?" my Forever Dad says.

I don't answer. Gloria always had Tic Tacs. She always smelled
like Tic Tacs and cigarettes. White ones were her favorite.

Then I remember that the curtains in the screen porch smelled
like cigarettes too.

I look at my Forever Dad and shake the Tic Tacs. I point to
them. "These are from Gloria," I say.

My Forever Dad makes a breathing sound with his mouth. He nods. "Yes, they probably are," he says.

Then he takes them because he says they might be dirty even though I promise not to eat any.

"How did they get here?" I say.

"Well..." he says but then he doesn't say anything else.

What this means is that Gloria came here to the Blue House. Yesterday. *That* was where the tire tracks came from. *She* was the angry person. She came when I was at school. Then she peeled out and left. Which means she came to the wrong place. Which means I won't be able to run out to the parking lot to see if my Baby Doll is in the Green Car with her. I won't be able to go back to the apartment and check inside the suitcase.

To make sure I say, "Did Gloria come to the Blue House yesterday?"

"Yes," my Forever Dad says. "Gloria came to the Blue House yesterday."

"Did she bring my Baby Doll?"

He gets a funny look on his face. "No, she didn't bring your Baby Doll. Ginny, I know you don't like us to even say it, but if you want a new doll, we'll get you one. Do you want to go to the toy store this afternoon?"

"No, thank you, I don't want to go to the toy store." I use my friendly voice even though it makes me really mad when people ask that question. "When is she coming back?"

"She isn't coming back. She scared your mom pretty badly and made quite a scene. She even ran over our mailbox."

I don't know what *quite a scene* is but I know that when Gloria is angry she yells a lot and fights. She breaks things and hits.

I look at the mailbox. It is lying on the ground with its side all bent and its door open. Like a mouth, not moving.

"Ginny?"

I come up out of my brain. "What?" I say.

"I said she isn't coming back. The police came to tell her she isn't allowed to visit."

But I know that Gloria never does what the police tell her. She is very sneaky. I know she wants to come back and I know I have to help her. I have to find out if I'm *too late*. Even though I'm scared. Even though Gloria gets really *violent* and is completely *unreliable* which is what one of the social workers said. I have to know what happened to my Baby Doll.

I hear the bus coming from around the corner.

"We can talk about this some more after school," my Forever Dad says. "Would that be good?"

I see the bus so I start counting.

"Ginny?"

"I see the bus," I say.

"Yes, I see it, too," my Forever Dad says. "We'll talk some more after school, if you want."

The bus takes thirteen seconds before it pulls up to the side of the road. My Forever Dad gives me a squeeze on the shoulder. I don't *recoil* because it's okay for him to do that. Because once he asked me if he could give me a hug and I said no so he asked if a squeeze on the shoulder would be all right and I said yes it would be. My Forever Mom can give me a hug if she asks but my Forever Dad is a man so it has to be a shoulder squeeze.

My brain is moving too fast. The pictures in it are like hands flying up at my face.

"Ginny?" he says.

"Goodbye," I say. And then I get on the bus.

When I get to school Mrs. Lomos is there waiting on the sidewalk right next to the bus. Today her earrings look like silver pears. "Good morning, Ginny," she says when I step down off the bottom step.

"Good morning," I say because that's what you say when someone says *Good morning* to you. Sometimes I also like to say *How are you today?* after I say *Good morning* but I am thinking about when I can ask Larry to get on the internet again so I can tell Gloria where to meet me. Because she didn't come to school like she was supposed to. I need to help her *get it right*. I'm guessing the library is a good place for me to get on the internet because sometimes there aren't any teachers there.

"I want you to meet Mrs. Wake," says Mrs. Lomos.

I look up from my hands to see a lady standing next to Mrs. Lomos. She is an old lady with glasses and a white sweater. She isn't wearing a Michael Jackson shirt. I love Michael Jackson because he isn't like other men. He isn't big and loud. He isn't scary. He's the nicest person in the world and when I hear his music I feel like I'm standing in a circle wearing small white shoes and when I feel that way I want to jump high and kick my feet back and spin when I land and put my shoulders up high and say, "Oooh!"

But I have a hard time talking about how I feel. Patrice says it's part of my *disability*.

"Mrs. Wake is going to walk with you to all your classes," says Mrs. Lomos.

"Is she going to go with me to the library?" I ask.

Mrs. Lomos gets a funny look on her face. "I don't think your class is going to the library today, Ginny. What do you have to do in the library?"

"There are books in the library," I say even though there are computers there too.

"Yes, there are. Maybe Mrs. Wake can help you pick one out."

Mrs. Wake smiles at me. I do not smile back. "Hello, Ginny," she says. "I'm very pleased to meet you."

Period One is language arts again. Mrs. Wake sits next to me the whole time and tries to help me with questions about a man named Nathaniel Hawthorne. Then at the end of Period Two I go to Room Five with Larry and Kayla Zadambidge and Alison Hill. When I get to the table and sit down Mrs. Wake finally leaves to go to the bathroom so I say, "Okay, Larry. I need to get on the internet."

And he says, "Dude, there's a computer right there," and points and starts singing a song that says if I want it, here it is, I can just come get it. "But won't you get in trouble?" he says when he finishes.

I am about to tell him that *he* can get on the internet for me but then Ms. Dana walks in. She sits down at the table and starts reminding us how to use an agenda book. I decide not to tell Larry right now that I won't get in trouble if he goes on the internet instead of me. Later I'll tell him that I can just look over his shoulder while he looks at Facebook or *Manicoon.com*.

But Ms. Dana keeps talking and talking and then Mrs. Wake comes back so I keep my new secret plan in my brain and shut my mouth so no one will see it.

At 9:42 I go to homeroom for Break. Mrs. Wake comes with me.

At 9:55 I go to band practice. Mrs. Wake comes with me.

When I get to the band room she sits down near the door and I go to my music stand and take out my flute. Mr. Barnes the band teacher says that the Harvest Concert will be on Monday, October 18th. He says that we'll play two songs about autumn and one about Halloween and one about the harvest moon.

At eleven o'clock it's time for social studies. Mrs. Wake follows me down the hall past the cafeteria and the lockers. She follows me all the way to the social studies room and sits down next to me on my left.

I make sure my mouth is closed so no one can see what I'm thinking.

Ms. Merton the social studies teacher is writing notes on the board. She does that every day. We're supposed to copy down the notes in our notebook.

I look at Mrs. Wake. "I don't have my notebook," I say. And it's true because my science notebook isn't with me.

"Where is it?" she says.

"In Room Five."

Mrs. Wake looks at the board. Ms. Merton has already written three sentences. All the other students are copying them.

"Do you *have* to write the notes in your notebook?"

"Yes," I say.

"All right," she says. "I'll run back to Room Five to get it. For now, copy the notes on a blank piece of paper. We can staple it into your notebook when I get back. Can you tell me what color it is?"

I think hard again. "Green," I say. "It's on my shelf."

Mrs. Wake leaves. As soon as she's gone I raise my hand. Ms. Merton sees me and says, "Yes, Ginny?"

"Can I go to the bathroom?" I say.

"Go ahead and sign out," says Ms. Merton.

So I stand up and go to the doorway and sign out on the sign-out list. I start walking down the hallway toward the library. It is three rooms away. I am almost there when I hear my name. "Ginny?"

I turn around. It is Ms. Merton.

"The eighth-grade bathroom is the other way," she says. "We're not supposed to use the one near the library because that one is for teachers."

I want to say *Well dang!* Because I'm not going to be able to get on the computer to chat with Gloria. Teachers and Forever Parents have stopped me from using the internet for four whole years. For a while I gave up and tried running away and looking in the phone book but none of those things worked. I have to be a *smart cookie* and make *this* work. I'm so mad I want to hiss.

But I don't. Instead I walk back down the hallway. I pass Ms. Merton and then I pass Mrs. Wake coming out of Room Five.

"Ginny, where are you going?" she asks.

"Ms. Merton said I could go to the bathroom," I say.

"All right," she says. "Let's go fast so we can get back to social studies. Oh, and I found your notebook." She holds it up so I can see. "It seems to have only your science notes in it, though. Let's check your backpack to see if the other one is in there."

9:08 IN THE MORNING, SATURDAY, SEPTEMBER 11TH

On weekends I get up at nine in the morning. It takes me only two minutes or sometimes three to stretch and put on my glasses and my watch and have a drink of water before I come out to go to the bathroom. Then I walk into the kitchen. I am standing in front of the refrigerator listening. I hear nothing. In the refrigerator there are grapes and milk. There are a lot of other things too but grapes and milk are what I need. I need to have nine grapes to start my breakfast and a glass of human milk but it's a rule that *We do not open the refrigerator.* And *We ask for food when we're hungry.*

I stand there waiting. If my Forever Parents were here they would say I was *hovering* which is when I stand really, really close to something. And wait.

My Forever Mom walks in. Her hair is still wet and she is wearing makeup. She never wears makeup in the morning unless she's going somewhere. "Good morning, Ginny," she says. "Someone is coming to visit today."

Or if someone is coming to visit.

So I say, "I don't like surprises."

"Oh, it's not a surprise," she says. "It's Patrice."

Patrice understands mostly everything that I tell her. She even understands some things that I don't say. I like her a lot but she knows how to see into my brain. I have to be careful around her and keep my mouth closed when I'm not talking.

"When will she be here?" I say.

"In about an hour," my Forever Mom answers. "Around ten. She's making a special weekend trip to spend a little time with you."

Patrice has never been to the Blue House. I always went to her office but I would like to show her my room and all my Michael Jackson things and I want to tell her about Gloria and the tire tracks and the Tic Tacs. I will not tell her about my secret plan to go on Facebook or on *Manicoon.com* at school because she might tell my Forever Parents.

At ten Patrice's car pulls into the driveway. Patrice gets out. She has her purple fuzzy sweater and her hair is short again. I run out to her car. I give her a hug and neither of us *recoils*.

"And how is my adventurous friend?" she says.

She is talking about me. She calls me *my adventurous friend* because she saw me every time I ran away and after what happened with Gloria at the apartment and after I tried to escape from my other Forever Homes. She says I have a lot of adventures.

So I say, "I am fine, thanks."

I stand there looking at her.

Then Patrice says, "Why don't you walk me inside, and we can talk with your Forever Mom for a little? Then you can show me your room. And did I hear that you'll be going to see the tall ships tomorrow?"

I bring Patrice inside and she says hello to my Forever Mom. They talk about the baby in my Forever Mom's belly. Patrice says to me, "Ginny, are you going to help your mom take care of Baby Wendy when she arrives?"

I don't know what Baby Wendy will look like but I'm guessing it will wear little overalls. My Baby Doll didn't have overalls but I wanted to get some for it. Gloria said we *couldn't afford them.* Michael Jackson had a chimp named Bubbles who wore overalls just like a real baby. Because when Michael Jackson was little he wanted a chimp so bad that he asked his mother over and over and finally I'm guessing she said yes, okay, *fine,* Michael Jackson, you can get a chimp. Michael Jackson used to pick Bubbles up just like I used to pick up my Baby Doll. Only Bubbles got so strong that Michael Jackson didn't have to hold him under his bottom anymore. He tucked Bubbles into bed every night but Bubbles got too big so Michael Jackson had to give him away. Because Bubbles might *attack.* He gave him away to a zoo and now Bubbles lives in a big cage where he can't hurt anyone. I saw him on television.

"Ginny?"

"What?"

"Do you think you'd like to help your mom take care of Baby Wendy when she gets home from the hospital?"

"Yes," I say.

"That's great!" says Patrice. "You can help pick things up when your mom is holding her. And when the baby is bigger, the two of you can learn how to play together. She's going to want to be just like you, you know. She'll want to do all the things her big sister does. Won't it be fun to be a big sister?"

"Mostly," I say.

"Good," says Patrice. "Now, do you know why I'm here, Ginny?"

"Because you want to look at my room?" I say.

"Not quite. I'm here because I want to talk with you about some things. I understand that Gloria came here to the Blue House a few days ago."

And I say, "She came on Thursday, September 9th, while I was at school. She is completely *unreliable*."

I stop talking and make sure my mouth is shut tight. There's a lot in my brain that I don't want Patrice to see.

Patrice looks at me in a funny way. "That's an interesting way to put it," she says. "Did you see her?"

I shake my head no.

"I wonder how she managed to find you," Patrice says. "Do you know?"

I shake my head once more but then my mouth opens and I say, "She left tire tracks in the yard and wrecked our mailbox which means she was either really pissed or really loaded. Plus she made quite a scene. I didn't see her when I got off the bus but my Forever Dad said she didn't bring my Baby Doll."

Patrice laughs but it is a friendly laugh. Sometimes people laugh in a way that is mean. Mostly it's like teasing. I can't always tell which is which. "Wow," says Patrice. "It sounds like you've had an exciting time."

I nod my head yes but she didn't ask a question so I don't say anything.

My Forever Mom makes a breathing sound. "Why don't you bring Patrice to your room and show her around?" she says.

So I bring Patrice to my room and show her all my things. She looks at the pictures on my dresser and all the birthdates and holidays I wrote on my calendar. Then she says, "Did your Forever Parents tell you that Gloria isn't coming back to the Blue House?"

"Yes," I say. "They said the police told her she can't."

Patrice turns around and around in the middle of my room looking at all my things. I am in the doorway. "That's right," she says. "Gloria got in a lot of trouble when she came here. She tried to get in the house and really scared your Forever Mom. So your mom called your dad and the police, and when the

police arrived, they had to force Gloria to leave. Your Forever
Dad came right from school. And then the two of them called
Social Services, and the judge got involved, and—well, let's just
say Gloria isn't allowed to visit again. That's why I came to talk
with you. How do you feel about all this?"

I remember the judge. The judge is a lady who wears a big
black cape like the teachers wear in *Harry Potter*. The movies,
not the books. I like movies better than books because in movies the pictures move. I met the judge on June 21st at the adoption. It's a rule that you have to do what the judge says. The
judge said I couldn't go back to Gloria's apartment and that Gloria isn't allowed to come find me. But the judge doesn't know
how sneaky Gloria can be. Neither does Patrice.

"Ginny?"

"What?"

"I'm sorry. I should have asked a clearer question. How do
you feel about Gloria coming here the other day?"

Patrice talks about feelings all the time. She taught me how to
do it too. So I say, "I feel really bad. My Baby Doll is all alone."
Then I look at Patrice over my glasses to see if she understands.

"I know your Baby Doll was important to you," says Patrice.
"Do you remember what we said last time we met? We said that
you were a little like a baby doll when you were in the apartment, getting left by yourself all the time. But you're safe now.
Don't you feel safe?"

"Yes," I say but I don't care about being safe. I don't care if
Gloria hurts me or Donald gets his gun. I have to find out what
happened to my Baby Doll after the police took me away. I need
to know if anyone found it in the suitcase or if I'm too late.

"Good. And the best way to stay safe is to make sure you
never, ever get in the car with Gloria if you happen to see her.
No matter what she says. Can you make me that promise?"

I make sure my mouth is shut tight and then I nod my head yes.

"I know I've said it before, but you're lucky you got out of that apartment alive. But if she were to come here and then get you to get in the car with her, it would be considered kidnapping. Do you know what that means?"

I don't so I shake my head no.

"Kidnapping is when someone steals a kid. If you go with Gloria, Gloria will be stealing you. And stealing is against the law. Does that make sense?"

It does so I nod my head yes. Three times because I think getting kidnapped is a great idea. That way I can go straight back to the apartment and run into my room to check the suitcase.

"And I need to ask you about what happened with the baby doll from school."

"You mean the *plastic electronic* baby," I say.

"Yes, that's the one," says Patrice. "I understand that you hit it, and then you put it in a suitcase. Why would you do that?"

"Because it wouldn't stop crying."

"But there are other ways to calm a baby down, aren't there?"

"Oh yes," I say. "You can give it some milk or pick it up and rock it. And if there's no milk or food you can give it your finger to suck on. You can sing it 'The Eensy-Weensy Spider.' You can change its diaper or give it a bath. Or just let it rest on you."

Patrice is looking at me funny. "You sure seem to know a lot about babies," she says. "Where did you learn all those things?"

So I close my eyes and yell, "From taking care of my Baby Doll!"

Then I look at her to see if she understands.

"You don't have to shout," she says. "But remember, your Baby Doll wasn't a real baby. You had to have learned those things somewhere else. From television, maybe?"

I shake my head no. "My Baby Doll *was* a real baby," I say.

"Ginny, that's not true," says Patrice. "Gloria didn't have any other children. I've been over your case file a thousand times, and you were the only one in the apartment. Did you have a baby cousin, maybe? I remember your aunt used to come visit you sometimes."

"Crystal with a C," I say.

"Right, Crystal with a C. Did Crystal with a C have a baby?"

I shake my head no. I am too mad to say anything else with my mouth now.

"At any rate," says Patrice, "I need you to know that your parents and I have come up with a new rule. It's the most important rule we've ever given you. *When Baby Wendy is born, you're not allowed to touch her.* We have to make sure you learn the right way to act around babies first. It's a scary thing when someone hits a doll and puts it in a suitcase, even if the doll isn't real. Suitcases aren't good places for putting babies at all, right?"

I pick hard at my fingers. So hard a dark drop of blood comes out. I watch the drop get bigger and bigger until it breaks and drips down my thumb.

"Ginny?"

I look up and at the same time put my hands behind my back. Where neither of us can see them.

11:03 AT NIGHT,
SUNDAY, SEPTEMBER 12TH

I am in bed now breathing fast and trying to calm down. We
went to Portland today to see the tall ships. Plus the fireworks.
It's the last fun thing we'll do before my Forever Mom starts
getting ready to have the baby, she told me. I left my watch at
home because I got poison ivy on my hands and wrists yesterday. I thought it was okay to leave my watch at home because
there's usually a clock nearby to tell me what time it is but I
got distracted because the fireworks were loud and made lots
of smoke and everyone kept saying "Ooooh!" when they saw
them. It was like they were all ghosts. And the smoke was like
the ghost of the fireworks. Then I learned that you can keep
fireworks and smoke in your brain if you just close your eyes
afterward. The pictures stay there with you.

Which was what I was doing when we got back to the car.
That was why I didn't see what time it was right away. I sat in
my seat with my eyes closed and leaned my head against the
window and kept looking at the blue and green and red and
white sprays of fireworks in my brain. Only the music was different. At the fireworks there were big speakers playing music

with flutes and drums. In the car my Forever Parents had the radio on instead. Someone was singing about a girl whose name wasn't even Billie Jean or Dirty Diana. It was Caroline or something. So I opened my eyes and said, "Can't we get some flutes and drums? I'm trying to watch the fireworks."

And then my Forever Mom said, "Honey, the fireworks are over."

Which was when I saw it was 10:43. It was way past nine o'clock.

I started picking at my fingers. "Do you see what time it is?" I said.

"It's 10:44," said my Forever Mom.

I looked and she was right. The clock had changed. It wasn't 10:43 anymore. It was 10:44 so I said, "Well dang!"

I started biting the skin on my lips. "It's past my bedtime," I said and in my head I wrote,

Bedtime = 9:00 at Night

"That's okay," my Forever Dad said. "It's okay to stay up late once in a while, isn't it?"

"But it's past *nine o'clock*," I said.

"That's right," said my Forever Mom. It sounded like she wanted to say something else but then she didn't. She just sat there quietly in the front seat while someone on the radio sang about the numbers twenty-five and six-two-four. And now the numbers on the clock said 10:45. None of those numbers were like the numbers in my head which were still nine and zero and zero.

"I have to go straight to bed," I said.

"Do you want to stay up a little to watch some TV? *Just to decompress?*"

Decompressing is like *deescalating*. It means *let's take a little time*

to calm down. I shook my head no. "I have to go to bed *now,*" I said because nine o'clock is my bedtime and I have to have nine grapes with my human milk in the morning. Nine years old is how old I was when the police came. It's how old I was before Forever started.

"What about brushing your teeth?" said my Forever Dad. "Don't you want to brush your teeth first?"

It's a rule that *We always brush our teeth before going to bed.* And I like rules. "Okay, yes, fine," I said. "After I brush my teeth. And after I go to the bathroom and wash my hands. And after I get a drink of water to put on my dresser and put on jammies. Then I'll go *straight to bed.*"

"Which jammies will you wear tonight?" my Forever Mom asked. "The ones with the cats, or the ones with the sock monkeys?"

"The ones with the cats," I said. "The ones with the sock monkeys are for Mondays."

Then I thought about my Baby Doll and decided to sing it a lullaby. Even though it couldn't hear me. Because I could still see the fireworks in my brain which is where I see my Baby Doll. I started singing "I'll Be There" for it. My Forever Dad turned off the twenty-five or six-two-four and my Forever Mom put her hand over the clock. When it came to the part about looking over my shoulder I said, "Oooooh!" just like Michael Jackson which is not the same way a ghost says it but still. Then I looked over my shoulder and inside my eyes I saw Little Michael Jackson giving Bubbles a great big hug through the bars at the zoo.

"You're doing great, Forever Girl," my Forever Dad said. It's all right for them to call me that for now because it's still true. I like being their Forever Girl and I'll miss them both but it's already way, way, way past my nine. Past nine o'clock and nine years old. I don't want to go back to that scary place but I have to, have to, have to.

In science we are studying hurricanes. I am working with Alison Hill on our project. We have to make a poster and write a report about how hurricanes work. We have to type a list of facts too. But my job is to make the poster. Mrs. Wake is helping me put dots of glue on a big piece of white poster board so that I can attach cotton balls to it. I'm not allowed to use the glue because Ms. Dana told her what happened last year when I memorized the combination to the supply cabinet in Room Five.

But in a minute I'm going to need the glue. It's part of my secret plan.

"That's very good, Ginny," Mrs. Wake says. "Now let's put some on the bands of clouds on the outside of the hurricane. Those outer winds are the most destructive, so we need to make sure they stand out."

I put two more cotton balls on the poster board. Alison Hill is near the window at a long table typing the list of facts. Alison Hill is good at typing. She is faster than Larry and faster than me but she gets really mad sometimes when you try to make her go as fast as she can.

I put down the cotton ball I am holding. "Alison Hill, are you done yet?" I ask.

"Not yet, Ginny," she says.

I look at my watch. The time is 11:35. I put my pencil down on the table hard so that it makes a slap. Then I make a loud breathing sound.

Alison Hill keeps typing.

I pick up the scissors and start cutting out the curved arrows that Mrs. Wake drew for me. I make the breathing sound again. "I am almost ready for those facts," I say.

Alison Hill slams her hands down on the keyboard. "Ginny, leave me alone!"

"Ginny," says Mrs. Wake.

But her voice didn't go up so she wasn't asking a question.

"I bet the facts would be done if Larry was typing," I say.

Then Alison Hill throws her paper and pencil in the air and stands up. I look at her. She has her fingers curled up like claws. Mrs. Wake walks over to her and starts to *deescalate the situation*. They start talking loud and fast.

So I grab the glue and squeeze it all over Mrs. Wake's chair. I squeeze and I squeeze and I squeeze. Then I put the bottle on the ground and move it under the table with my foot where she can't see it.

When Mrs. Wake is finished helping Alison Hill calm down she comes back to help me some more. She sits down. "Let's let Alison get her work done," she says. "Don't talk to her right now. She needs to focus."

So I say, "I can't find the glue."

Mrs. Wake looks around. "It was here just a minute ago," she says. "Ginny, did you eat the glue? Ms. Dana said—"

Then she gets a funny look on her face and puts her hand under her bottom.

I make sure my mouth is closed.

"Did you do this?" she says. And stands up. She is wearing a nice gray skirt. She tries to look at her bottom but her neck isn't long enough so she puts her hand there instead. She looks at her hand. She looks at me. Her eyes get big and wet. "Ginny, I can't believe you!" she says. Then she runs out of the library.

I start moving toward the computer where Alison Hill is working. Then I remember that Alison Hill knows I'm not allowed to use the internet without an adult.

I stop and start picking at my fingers.

On the other side of the library I see a fifth grader get up from a computer. I walk to the place where he was sitting and sit down in his place. Then I type *Manicoon.com* into the white space at the top of the screen. And click Enter.

On the screen I see Maine coon cats. I see their long ears and bushy tails. Their faces look at me like Fire's and Coke Head's. Above them I see tabs that say Information and About Me and Contact Me. And I see the words A Message for My Daughter. Under the words A Message for My Daughter I read,

So I came to the address you gave me and those fuckers called the police. But they can't shut me down. I have rights too, I told them. No one can take away freedom of speech. Four years ago they took you away and I've been trying to find you ever since. Thank God for the internet. Don't tell anyone about this blog though. I can't come back to the house where you live because the judge issued a restraining order. G., I love you so much. I want you back so we can be a family again. Do you have any idea how hard it's been without you? I'll do anything to get you back. You should see the new cages I put in. We're moving lots of tail. I'm clean now too. Rehab and everything. Crystal says I should lie low and cool it. But I can't cool it. She helped out a lot after you left but I have to see you. So name the time and place and I'll be there. Leave a comment and as soon as I read it I'll delete it. Ha. That almost rhymes.

I don't know what *Leave a comment* means but then I see the word Comment under Gloria's letter. So I click it and I see a place to type. I write, You can come to the Harvest Concert on October 18th. Please get my Baby Doll from the suitcase under my bed. Don't leave it there alone.

Then I click the word Submit which I'm guessing is like Send and then the X to make the screen go away and I go back to the table to wait for Mrs. Wake.

Before I went outside to get on the bus I counted the five slices of bread that were left in the bread bag and my Forever Mom said the word *approximately* means *close to but not exactly*. And that the bread is *approximately* gone. So if today is September 14th then tonight when I go to bed it will be *approximately* the 15th. Then at midnight the 15th will be *exactly* here.

Approximately is a good word to use when you can't get to a watch or a clock. It's also good for thinking about your Baby Doll if you don't know *exactly* if anyone found it or *exactly* the time Gloria might bring it to the Harvest Concert.

But I can't think about what time she might come because the bus is pulling into the school parking lot and I see a parked car that looks *approximately* like the Green Car. My watch says it is *exactly* 6:59. The car I see is green like I remember but it doesn't have the thick piece of plastic Gloria taped to the back window when it broke. And standing in front of the car is someone who looks *approximately* like Gloria but not *exactly*. She is far away but she is really, really skinny and mostly she has the same kind of hair but she isn't wearing the shirt from the Facebook picture.

I stare and stare at her out the window until we stop in front of the school. Then I get off the bus. I want to walk around the bus to see if it is her but Mrs. Wake is right there on the sidewalk waiting for me. She brings me inside.

Plus yesterday I told Gloria that she should come to the Harvest Concert so it can't be her.

Mrs. Lomos called my Forever Parents yesterday and told them about the glue. I had to write a letter of apology to Mrs. Wake. I take it out of my backpack and hold it out to her. "Here," I say.

She takes it.

We go to homeroom and then to language arts. Now it is *exactly* 7:45. Mrs. Wake reads the letter when she sits down. All she says is "Thank you, Ginny." Her mouth is a thin line and she is not talking as much as she did yesterday. I'm guessing she is angry but she isn't yelling so I don't have to be careful. But still I don't argue when she tells me to take out my homework. We are working on the hurricane project both in science and in language arts.

My homework was to make a list of things to take with me in case there is a hurricane and I need to seek shelter. I made a list of *exactly* twenty-three things with a line between number five and number six. Everything above the line is what Mrs. Wake helped me with yesterday. Everything under it is what I did on my own.

1. A cell phone (to call family and friends)
2. A flashlight (to look at things in the dark)
3. Food (to eat)
4. A radio (to hear news about the hurricane)
5. Batteries (for the radio and the flashlight)

---

6. Some books about Michael Jackson (to read when I'm not listening to the radio)

7. *My iPod (to listen to when I'm not reading books or listening to the radio)*
8. *The headphones to my iPod (to plug into my iPod)*
9. *My iPod charger (to charge my iPod)*
10. *Some games like Uno, for example (to play)*
11. *My hairbrush (to brush my hair)*
12. *A scrunchie (to hold my hair up)*
13. *My toothbrush (to brush my teeth)*
14. *Some toothpaste (to put on my toothbrush)*
15. *Deodorant*
16. *New underwear (just in case)*
17. *Socks (if my feet get wet)*
18. *Flip-flops (if my feet get wet again)*
19. *A blanket (for everyone to sit on)*
20. *Drinks (for us to drink)*
21. *A cooler (to keep our drinks cool)*
22. *Bendy straws (for our drinks)*
23. *Popcorn (to have with our drinks)*

"Come with me, Ginny," says a voice.

I look up from my paper. It is Mrs. Lomos. I am surprised she is here. I am surprised by her earrings too. They are little white masks.

"Come to my office for a minute," she says. I tell her that I am checking over my homework before I pass it in. She says that I need to go with her *now*. So I do.

The time is *exactly* 7:52. I follow Mrs. Lomos into her tiny office. She asks me to sit down. She shuts the door and says, "Ginny, when was the last time you saw Gloria?"

"I saw her four years ago on April 18th when the police came to take me away," I say. "She cried and cried and said, 'I'm so sorr—'"

"Are you *sure* that was the last time you saw her?" says Mrs. Lomos.

"You interrupted me," I say.

"I'm sorry to have interrupted you," says Mrs. Lomos. "It's just that you've told me how Gloria cried and said, 'I'm so sorry, I'm so sorry,' a lot of different times already. But right now it's important that you think very hard and tell me if you've seen Gloria recently."

I'm not sure if Mrs. Lomos is asking a question so I don't say anything.

Then Mrs. Lomos says, "Let's try again. When was the last time you saw Gloria?"

So I say, "Do you mean *exactly* or *approximately*?"

Mrs. Lomos's face looks surprised. *"Exactly,"* she says.

But I'm still not *exactly* sure that it was Gloria who I saw in the parking lot so I say, "The last time I *exactly* saw her was on April 18th four years ago."

"Did you *approximately* see her after that?" she says.

"Yes," I say. "I *approximately* saw her this morning."

"How can you be sure it was her?"

"I said it was only *approxi*—"

"Ginny, what did you see?"

"I saw a person near a green car and her head was mostly the same but her shirt was different."

"Thank you," says Mrs. Lomos. "Now, I have to make a phone call. While I'm doing that, I'm going to give you a very important job. I want you to write down everything that you did this morning."

She hands me a pencil and a pad of white lined paper. The pencil is not my Snoopy pencil which is the only pencil I like to use.

"Everything?" I say.

"Everything," says Mrs. Lomos. "Start with what happened

when you woke up, and end with what we just finished talking about."

So I look at the tip of the pencil which is very, very sharp and I get ready to write. Then I start thinking about how Gloria came to the Blue House and what it might mean that I saw someone who looks *approximately* like her when I got to school.

I think and I think and I think.

And now I see that it is 8:06 and Mrs. Lomos is back in her office with me again. She says, "Hi again, Ginny. Your mother and father are coming to school so that we can all have a talk. A police officer will be with them. Now, I know you don't like police officers."

Sometimes I see police officers on television or in a picture and I am fine with that but when police officers are in places where I don't expect to see them I get surprised. Like when there's one around the corner or when one comes to school to be a guest speaker and no one told me. But I don't say any of that. I don't say anything because I want to know why my Forever Parents are coming here to talk with me and why a police officer is coming too and mostly I want to know if I *approximately* or *exactly* saw Gloria when the bus was pulling into the parking lot. Because if I *exactly* saw her then I need to get outside and jump in the Green Car quick. Before the police officer gets here.

Because four years ago when I was nine years old a police officer stood in front of Gloria while the other police officer carried me away. While one of the policemen was holding me the other one pushed Gloria back and then Gloria tried to get past him so he grabbed her arm and pushed her face against the wall and her cheek got flat and her eyes got round and white and she yelled my name and said, "I'm so sorry! I'm so sorry, Ginny!" over and over while I kicked and tried to fight and Gloria yelled, "That's my daughter! That's my daughter!" and then "Ginny, you belong with me!" and then the one who was holding me started carrying me toward the door so I went *ape-shit*.

Because they didn't know where I hid my Baby Doll and when I tried to tell them they didn't listen. They put me in the back of the police car and brought me straight to the hospital.

I stand up from the small, hard chair in Mrs. Lomos's tiny office. I put the pencil down and pick it up again. It is still very sharp. I haven't written anything. I open the door.

"Ginny?" says Mrs. Lomos from somewhere behind me.

I don't listen. My feet start moving and I hear the *swish-swish* of my pants rubbing together and now I am running to the library which has a window where you can see the parking lot where I *approximately* or *exactly* saw Gloria leaning against the Green Car.

I pass Mrs. Wake. She opens her mouth to say something but I keep going.

I throw open the library doors and run past the computers. To the window. I look outside.

And see her. She isn't holding my Baby Doll. I look hard to see if I can see into the Green Car. I jump to see if I can see into the backseat but I don't see a car seat or a baby carrier or anything.

A police officer stands in front of Gloria pointing at the Green Car. He shakes his head. Gloria's mouth opens and I know she is angry. Even though I can't hear her. The police officer points at the Green Car again. Then two more police cars come driving up fast but their lights aren't on. I hear their engines through the glass. Two more police officers get out of each police car. Now there are five.

Gloria spits.

One of the police officers steps really, really close to her. She puts her hands up and turns her head down and away and reaches for the door of the Green Car.

There is a radiator in front of the window. I climb on top

of it and put my arms up against the glass. Then I put my face close to it and hit the glass again and again with my hands and start to scream.

Gloria looks up. At the window. I lean back to hit the glass as hard as I can. Then I hit it again and again. And again and again. I can't make it break.

I jump off the radiator and grab a chair. I lift it up high above my head and run.

Someone grabs me. The chair comes out of my hands and I fall. It is the principal and Ms. Dana. I am going *ape-shit* because I need to tell Gloria not to go. I need to tell her to come help me *escape* but Ms. Dana pulls me down and puts me on the floor. She is on top of me so I can't get up. I kick and fight. I bite her in the arm. She yells and lets go.

"Ginny!" I hear someone say. "Ginny!"

It is Mrs. Lomos. I see her feet.

I stand. "It—" I say. "It was *exa*—" But the words don't come and then the principal grabs me from behind. I am falling but as I go down I look out the window and see the Green Car driving away. Now I'm on the floor again next to a book rack with *Julie of the Wolves* and *Island of the Blue Dolphins*. My eyes want to cry but they can't because my breath is catching and catching and I can't breathe. I see Ms. Dana and Mrs. Lomos and Mrs. Wake and the librarian and now it feels like I'm under water or a blanket and then everything is dark.

My Forever Parents are home. Both of them. They are in the living room talking with a police officer who is not wearing a uniform. Not the one who came to school. I know he is a police officer because my Forever Parents told me. I am standing up in my room and I will not sit down again until he leaves.

I am angry because Gloria came to school and I didn't get to go with her. I told her to come to the Harvest Concert but she came today instead. When I wasn't ready. I couldn't see if my Baby Doll was in the backseat. She is completely *unreliable*. I wish she was like Crystal with a C. Crystal with a C knows I don't like expressions. *I'll always tell you the truth, Ginny,* she used to say to me. *Even if it's hard to hear.* I believed her 100 percent and I try to always tell the truth 100 percent too. Or *also* which is mostly the same as *too* but spelled different.

At *exactly* 3:40 the police officer comes into my room with my Forever Parents.

I hiss.

My Forever Mom puts her hand up like she is going to touch my arm.

I snarl.

I am one of the Maine coons now. All my fur is up. If anyone touches me—

"Ginny," my Forever Mom says, "the police officer isn't going to hurt you. He's here to help."

Police officers are never *here to help* even though my Forever Mom doesn't lie. If they were *here to help* they would bring me right to Gloria's. The police officer talks and talks but I don't listen. Then he says, "Do you understand?" And smiles.

His name is Officer Joel but his name doesn't matter because all police officers are *exactly* the same.

The police officer says that if I see Gloria again I should tell my Forever Parents or a teacher immediately. *Immediately* means *now, no matter what.* He says that I need to stay here at the Blue House with my Forever Family because *they* are my family now. When I tell him that I need to see if my Baby Doll is okay he says that Gloria is not a safe person. He says it isn't safe to go back to the apartment because she used to leave me alone too much and she hurt me. And all the strange men and the drugs. And didn't I remember what happened to the cat? The police officer says the same thing could have happened to me. "We wouldn't want something like that to happen to a little kid, would we?"

So I scream, "Then why won't you let me go get my Baby Doll?"

He shakes his head and keeps talking. He talks about unsanitary conditions and abuse and the cat. Snowball. He is wrong about what happened to it but I am so upset that all I can do now is say the word *wrong, wrong, wrong* over and over in my brain and put my hands over my ears because he doesn't understand. He knows only *approximately* what happened.

And I know *exactly.*

I am in Patrice's office. I didn't go to school. Patrice's office has three soft chairs in it. One has flowers all over it. She has a skinny black-and-white cat named Agamemnon who likes to *make bread* on your lap. *Making bread* is an expression because Agamemnon doesn't know how to bake. It doesn't hurt when Agamemnon makes bread because his claws were removed when he was little. He doesn't remember the operation, Patrice says. But right now I don't see Agamemnon. I look for him every time I come here because I really like cats. I want to get a cat but my Forever Parents won't let me. They say it isn't *appropriate*. *Not appropriate* means that something doesn't belong. Even though I think it really does. Especially after Snowball.

Patrice is in the kitchen. "Ginny, do you want to help me put together a snack?" she says. I stop looking for Agamemnon and go to help her. Patrice says that food and drinks help people relax. Today's snack is Hershey's Kisses and milk. I pour a whole bag of them into a bowl and bring it out into the room with the chairs. Then I sit down and start eating.

"So what's all this drama I'm hearing about?" says Patrice.

I don't know what *drama* is so I say, "I don't understand the question." Patrice taught me that. I'm supposed to say *I don't understand* when there's something I want to know or when I don't understand. Patrice says asking for help is part of *self-advocating.*

"*Drama* means a lot of feelings and loud actions," says Patrice. "When someone says there was some drama, it means there were some crazy things going on."

"I didn't see any crazy things," I say and put another Hershey's Kiss in my mouth. And then I look up because it's a rule that *You should make eye contact when you talk with someone.*

"I'm sorry," says Patrice. "I shouldn't put it that way. It's not drama at all, really. It's just that a lot is going on all at once. Can you tell me about what happened yesterday with Gloria? Your parents tell me she came to school."

I crinkle the silver wrapper between my fingers into a ball. "That's right," I say. "Gloria came to my school. I saw her in the parking lot yesterday when I got off the bus. She had the Green Car."

"When you first saw her, what did you think?"

"I wasn't sure if it was her."

"Why weren't you sure?"

"Because she had a different head."

"If you *had* been sure it was her, what would you have done differently?"

I don't answer because I don't want Patrice to know what I would have done. I close my mouth tight and start counting.

Then Patrice says, "No one knows how she managed to find where you live, but she wasn't supposed to come see you. It's not allowed, Ginny. It's just not safe. She's still completely *impulsive.* She hasn't changed at all. Well, maybe I shouldn't go *that* far, but she still flies off the handle."

"Did she peel out?" I ask. Because Gloria gets really, really mad when someone says she isn't allowed to do something.

"I'm not sure," says Patrice.

"Did she make quite a scene?"

"From what I was told, yes, she did. She tried to get into the building. The doors were locked and she wouldn't go away. She asked if she could see you, but since no one at school knew who she was, they called the police. Then she used a rock to try to break through the door. The police walked her back to her car, and that's when you climbed up to the window."

I sit and I think. I am glad Patrice is telling me what happened. Patrice always tells me the truth. She calls it *telling it straight* because a lot of people keep things secret from me.

"Ginny?" says Patrice.

"What?"

I am picking at my fingers again.

"It's extremely important that you never go with Gloria. If you do, you could get hurt. Your Forever Parents already have a restraining order against her so she can't come to the Blue House, and now they're going to have one that says she can't come to school. Do you know what a restraining order is?"

I shake my head no.

"It's like a rule, only bigger. It's like a law. A law for one person. I suppose we could say that it's *against the law* for Gloria to see you now. It's just not safe. I really don't understand why you want to go back to see her again. It bothers your Forever Parents, too. You almost died when you were there. Can you help us understand?"

"I want to see if my Baby Doll is okay," I say.

"Oh my goodness, Ginny, I *know* you've been through a lot—more than anyone should ever have to go through—but we've been over this so many times!" says Patrice. "Remember, we decided that the reason you want to take care of a Baby

Doll is because *you* were like a little baby when you were in
the apartment. And we don't want to see what happened to
the plastic electronic baby doll happen to you again. Do you
see what I'm saying? Gloria hurt you pretty badly, Ginny. Do
you remember what you looked like when the police took you
out of the apartment? Do you remember how thin you were?
And all the injuries? You were lucky to be alive. I know she's
your Birth Mom, but Gloria just isn't capable of taking care of
young children."

She keeps talking and asking me questions about all the bad
things Gloria did and every time I tell her yes, I know, I get
it, Gloria isn't a safe person which is why I need to go back to
get my Baby Doll. But Patrice just keeps shaking her head and
saying no, Ginny, I'm sorry, your Baby Doll isn't a real baby, I
checked the records.

So finally I make my hands into tight, tight balls and squeeze
my eyes shut and yell, "It's not in the records. It's in the suitcase."

She stops. "Ginny, I know you think that no one listens to
you, but we checked the suitcase. The police went back to look
after they brought you to the hospital. There was nothing inside."

"There was nothing inside?" I say.

Patrice shakes her head. "Nothing. There was a suitcase under
the bed, but it was empty. And the social workers visited you
quite a few times before you were taken out of the apartment.
Don't you think they would have known if there was a baby?"

I blink. If the suitcase was empty then I told Gloria to look in
the wrong place when I wrote to her on September 13th. But
I don't know where the *right place* is. I don't know where to tell
her to find my Baby Doll.

"Ginny?"

Someone must have taken it out of the suitcase after the police
took me out of the apartment. But who?

"Ginny?"

"When did they go back to look?"

"As soon as they left you at the hospital."

It was a short drive to the hospital in the police car. I didn't have a watch yet so I don't know how long but it couldn't have been a long time.

Which means I might not have been too late. Or I *was* too late and someone—

"Ginny?" Patrice says again. "Do you need a beverage?"

I look at her but I don't see her face. I don't see anything because my brain is working hard to figure out what happened after the police took me to the hospital.

Who took my Baby Doll out of the suitcase?
        I am on the bus thinking about things I don't like to
think about. Deep in my brain. Most of the time I keep them
locked away in the dark but now I have to bring them out because the police checked the suitcase when I was at the hospital
and they didn't find anything in it.

I think about Donald. Could it be him?

Donald had pants but mostly he didn't wear them at night
when he came out of Gloria's room to see me. It was always easy
to tell if the man in Gloria's room was Donald because Miller
was there. Miller was the cat's name and he belonged to Donald. Miller used to run in front of the cages and meow at all the
Maine coons.

Miller really liked me. Maybe it was because we both got our
names the same way. He didn't like to go away with Donald
when Donald left in the mornings. I used to watch him pick
Miller up like Miller was a baby and put him in the cat carrier.
Then he would bring Miller out to the car and drive away but
he always brought Miller back with him when he came to sleep

in Gloria's room which was where they went to play a game called *Hide the Cannoli*. I spent a lot of time looking for the cannoli when no one was home but I never found it. I'm guessing it was in a secret drawer or maybe they took it with them when they went away.

But one time I didn't want Miller to go so I picked him up and put him in a suitcase with a lot of blankets and pillows to keep him quiet. He scratched my arm and hand while I was holding him down but then I put a sweatshirt over his head and got the lid closed.

Then I zipped the suitcase and put it under my bed. Donald looked for him but couldn't find him and finally he said, "I'll just leave the damn cat here. You don't mind, do you?" And Gloria said, "No problem. Your two little cats will be right here waiting for you." Then he slapped her on the bottom and kissed her and went away.

And Gloria found some money and ordered pizza while we watched a vampire movie. The pizza was bacon and onion. It is my favorite. We had our fancy drinks. Soda in a can with a bendy straw for me and gin and tonic for Gloria. That's why she named me Ginny. Because gin and tonic is her favorite.

So I got to keep Miller. Only I didn't take him out because I didn't want Gloria to know I had him and I didn't want Donald to take him away again. Donald was away for five days and when he came back no one could find the cat. He must have gotten out somehow, they said. Donald was mad and he yelled and yelled at Gloria but then they went out to see Gloria's dealer and it was quiet. So I put my Baby Doll down on the bed and with the arm that didn't hurt I pulled the suitcase out and opened it and Miller was dead. Dead means you're asleep but you aren't going to wake up. And you smell really, really bad. I took my Baby Doll out into the living room and we stayed there until it was dark. Then Gloria came home by herself later and opened

the door to my room because of the smell. She saw Miller and
said, "Holy shit, Ginny! You killed Miller!"

And I said, "I did not kill Miller. I just tried to let him out
of the suitcase."

"What did you do, suffocate him? Or did he starve?"

Gloria touched him with her foot but he didn't move.

"We have to do something. If Donald finds out about this,
he'll kill you. You know, *make you dead*. I'm not kidding."

Then I got very scared because Donald has guns. And once
he threw Gloria all the way down the hallway and kept kicking
her. He likes hurting people and mostly I'm guessing he likes
making them dead too.

That was when Gloria took the suitcase outside and turned
it upside down so that Miller fell on the porch. Then she took
out her gun and said, "I love you, kiddo," and gave me her Diet
Cherry Coke. She shot Miller in the face so that he had no head
anymore. He was just a furry body with legs and a dark black
spot where the head used to be.

After Gloria shot him she said, "Now Donald will never know
it was you who killed Miller."

"Who will he know it was?" I asked.

"Ha!" said Gloria. "He'll know it was me. There's not a lot
of time to get rid of the evidence. It'll stink if I put it in the
garbage. If I can find something to dig with, maybe I can bury
it. Just give me a hug and let me look at my beautiful girl before my eyes are so swollen I won't be able to see you anymore.
Donald will be here any minute."

But Donald didn't come. Instead the police came. The neighbors must have heard the gun and called the cops, Gloria told
me before she went upstairs to hide. I heard them coming. I saw
the blue lights. Someone was knocking. Loud. Gloria ran fast. I
grabbed the suitcase and dragged it inside. Even though it hurt
my arm really bad. Then I picked up my Baby Doll from the

bed and put it in the suitcase. I put all my pillows and blankets around it even though the suitcase still smelled really bad. I saw its green eyes get big like round circles and blink when I put my quilt over them. Then I pushed the suitcase back under my bed and put more blankets around it and some clothes too. Then I climbed into the cabinet under the sink in the kitchen. And the police broke open the door to the apartment.

That was the day the first Forever started.

But I remember the day *exactly*. I know I put my Baby Doll in the suitcase. If the police didn't find it where can it be?

The bus stops. I come up fast out of my brain and take a deep breath through my nose. We are at school. I have to find a way to make Mrs. Wake leave me alone again so I can get back on a computer. I have to ask Gloria what happened.

"Hey, babe," says a voice.

I look up. It is Larry. He is standing up in the aisle with his backpack on. We are on the bus.

"It's time to go. But ladies first," he says with a big smile and sweeps his hand out. Then his face turns red and he looks at the ground. I stand up and walk in front of him and hurry out the door.

My Forever Parents are outside right now walking around the yard. My Forever Mom walks all the time now because she wants the baby inside her to *descend*. That means it is almost ready to come out.

I am in my room holding my quilt and crying. Because I am fourteen years old. Right this minute. Right now. And I'm not supposed to be. I'm supposed to be nine years old and keeping my Baby Doll safe. I'm not supposed to be here. I'm supposed to be nine years old.

My Forever Dad knocks on my door and opens it.

"Ginny, why don't you come outside with us? I thought you'd like to play catch."

"I don't want to," I say.

"All right," he says. "Then how about basketball? We could shoot some hoops."

"I want to stay in my room," I say.

"Ginny, it's your birthday. I know a lot has been going on and you're confused, but this should be a happy time. We're going to have presents and cake after supper."

He keeps trying to get me to come outside but I won't go. I need to be alone inside my brain right now. Even though it's my birthday. Even though there will be presents and cake after supper. At 10:36 he finally leaves.

Manicoon.com. Manicoon.com. I say the website over and over with my mouth. Quiet in a whisper. It is the only thing that matters. I tried to get on it yesterday but I couldn't get away from Mrs. Wake. I have to get on the computer one more time to ask Gloria where my Baby Doll went and to tell her to wait. And she has to wait for the Harvest Concert like I told her. She can't be *impulsive* and try to come sooner. She has to, has to, has to wait or she'll get caught and ruin everything.

We are in language arts writing poems about picking apples. Tomorrow we are going to the apple cider farm and the apple poems are helping us get ready. To help us write the poems we read one by Robert Frost. It has apple trees and a ladder in it. If I had a ladder right now I would climb out of this classroom. I have to *escape* from it so that I can go to the library and get on a computer.

Which means I have to find something new to glue Mrs. Wake to.

When you write a poem you have to talk about things that mean something else. The ladder in Robert Frost's poem means *heaven*, Mrs. Carter said. So in my poem I put a ladder that means *I am climbing out of my bedroom window to go with Gloria*. We have to draw a picture to go with our poem so I draw the Green Car and the Blue House and me on the ladder climbing out of my room. Next I will draw a picture of my Baby Doll in the Green Car but Mrs. Carter is standing next to my desk looking down at what I'm drawing. She says it isn't *appropriate*.

"No, I'm afraid it isn't," says Mrs. Wake when she sees the

picture. "And I think we should probably show this to Mrs. Lomos."

So Mrs. Wake brings me down to Mrs. Lomos's office. We pass the water fountain and the bathroom and the janitor's closet. I think about pushing her in there and locking the door. I run ahead and jiggle the door handle. It is locked.

"What are you doing?" Mrs. Wake asks.

"Jiggling the door handle," I say.

I think about locking her somewhere else but it would have to be somewhere really, really quiet. Otherwise someone might hear her banging to get out.

Mrs. Lomos says Mrs. Carter was right. It wasn't appropriate to draw pictures of Gloria and the Green Car. Or me escaping. When I ask why not she says because Gloria isn't safe and the picture means I want to go with her.

Which makes sense. So it isn't appropriate for me to draw what I really want because people might find out about it. I am surprised that Mrs. Lomos told me that but I'm glad because now I can do a better job at keeping it secret.

"We're going to keep you safe in spite of yourself, young lady," Mrs. Wake says when we are in the hallway going back to class. I don't know what that means so I ask her.

"It means we know what you've been up to," she answers. "We've finally got your number."

"I'm fourteen years old," I say.

"That's right," says Mrs. Wake. "Your birthday was two days ago, wasn't it?"

"Yes," I say.

I am at the kitchen table eating nine grapes for my afternoon snack.

"Ginny, we have to talk about the computers at school," my Forever Mom says. "We know about Gloria's Facebook page and her blog. She's been pretty quick to delete the comments you left for her, but we know the two of you have been in touch."

I put the first grape in my mouth and wait for her to keep going.

"The police can't make her shut the pages down, but we've been watching to see what she posts. The police have, too. So you can't talk with her that way anymore."

I don't know if she read any of my Comments. I don't know if Gloria had a chance to *read it and delete* the last one. I don't know if my Forever Mom knows that I told Gloria to come to the Harvest Concert.

"Ginny?"

"What?"

"Did you hear what I said?"

"Yes."

"Well, then, how do you feel about it?"

I think hard and make sure my mouth is shut. I want to be good and tell her but I can't.

"How did you feel about the apple cider farm?" she says. "And how about the fact that you're in a safe place and have plenty to eat? How do you feel about knowing that no one is going to hit you? And what about becoming a big sister and staying at the same school for two years in a row? Or staying at the same house?"

She isn't yelling but her voice is getting louder. Plus she asked five questions all at once. I don't say anything. I eat two more grapes and wait.

And then she yells.

"Why the hell are you doing this, Ginny? Why the hell are you telling Gloria to keep coming back? She beat the hell out of you! You had a fractured arm and were starving! You almost died! I'm supposed to have a baby in two weeks—we can't have this kind of insanity in the house with a newborn baby! Ginny, don't you see? This all has to end! We can't—"

She stops. I squeeze my eyes shut just in case. Then I hear her walk out of the kitchen. I hear the bathroom door close. She is crying.

Which means I'm not going to get hit.

I take a deep breath and finish my grapes. The last six.

"It works like this," says Patrice. "When a Forever Girl gets adopted, it's forever, unless she makes her new Forever Home a dangerous place. Do you understand?"

"Yes," I say.

"Within the past two weeks you beat up a plastic electronic baby and arranged to have Gloria try to kidnap you twice. You tried to throw a chair through a window, and you bit one of your teachers. Now, does that sound like a good environment for a baby sister?"

"No," I say.

"Do you know what could happen to you if you don't stop it?"

"If I don't stop *what*?" I say.

"If you don't stop trying to contact Gloria."

"No," I say.

"Then I'll tell you," says Patrice. "You could get yourself *un-adopted*. Ginny, your parents love you, but they aren't going to let you make the Blue House a dangerous place for Baby Wendy. So if you don't stop trying to get Gloria to come see you, you're going to have to leave the Blue House. Forever."

"Does that mean I'll have to go to another Forever House?"

"Actually, it means you'll probably end up in a facility for girls who aren't safe."

I think hard. Gloria won't know where I am if I go someplace else. Gloria won't be able to find me again. I'm guessing she doesn't know the address of the *facility for girls who aren't safe.* It took four whole years for me to get on a computer and tell her where the Blue House is.

Which means I have to be good. I have to *behave.* I can't try to *escape* or contact Gloria again. I have to wait until the Harvest Concert.

"Ginny, this isn't a time to be inward. How do you feel about what I just told you?"

I look at Patrice. "I want to stay at the Blue House," I say.

Patrice smiles. "That's the best thing I've heard you say in a long time. Now, let's talk about what we have to do to keep you there. You'll be seeing me three times a week for a long time, so we're going to work on this a lot."

It is the night of the Harvest Concert but it isn't night yet. The sun is going down but it is still day.

I have been very, very good at the Blue House and at school so that I wouldn't *get myself unadopted*. Even though the things in my brain keep trying to pull me into dark places. I have been picking at my hands a lot and keeping them in my lap so no one sees. I didn't try to get on the computer or to have Larry get on the internet for me. I told Patrice three times each week that I wanted to be a good big sister. And it's true. If I wasn't going to get kidnapped tonight at the Harvest Concert I would try very hard to help *take excellent care* of Baby Wendy when it's born.

In my backpack I have my flute, my quilt and a half gallon of milk. I'm all set to take care of my Baby Doll as soon as I find it.

Mrs. Wake is bringing me to the band room to warm up and practice with the rest of the band. The musicians have to be in the band room at five-thirty. The concert starts at seven.

We pass through the lobby and by the three glass doors that go to the front bus loop and the parking lot. I look outside. It is hard to see because it is so bright. The sun is shining right in my face. I wonder when the Green Car will come. I squint.

After the lobby we pass the office. Coming the other way I see some chorus kids. They are dressed in white shirts and black pants and they are carrying water bottles and black folders. Behind the chorus kids is a man with a blue coat. Someone's dad, I think. Then a lady wearing a red vest with a sweater under it. Someone's mom.

I turn around. Behind us I see two ladies talking and walking. Behind them I see another lady. She has her hair pulled back tight in a ponytail. She has a big brown unzipped jacket. She has a purple-and-brown flannel shirt. She is not heavy but she isn't skinny like Gloria. She stops next to the first lobby door and smiles and puts her finger on her lips.

It is Crystal with a C.

I don't know why Crystal with a C is here. It should be Gloria. But I am very, very happy. It's good that Crystal with a C is here instead of Gloria because Gloria is *unreliable* and *impulsive*. Plus she made quite a scene. Twice. And my Forever Mom said that everyone knew I was contacting her on the computer.

"Ginny?" says Mrs. Wake.

"What?" I say.

"Let's watch where we're going," says Mrs. Wake. "The band room is this way."

I look behind me one more time. The other two ladies are gone now. Crystal with a C is still near the first lobby door. I turn around to keep walking but I hear her footsteps. She is following us.

We pass the gym. There is a bathroom in there so I stop. "I have to go to the bathroom," I say.

Mrs. Wake looks into the doorway. It is dark in there except for a small light. Mrs. Wake looks inside. "It looks like the girls' locker room is open," she says. "Go ahead in, but then come right back out. I'll wait right here for you."

Before I go in I look back. Crystal with a C is at the last lobby door. She smiles. She points at me. Then she points to the door. I see her take out a cigarette and walk outside.

So I walk into the gym. The doorway to the girls' locker room is right inside. I walk in and pass all the lockers and benches and come out on the other side of the gym. I see the exit sign above the door. It goes out to the fields. I push it open.

And run.

I run across the back of the school. It still isn't dark yet but it's getting hard to see. I run past the janitor's car and the Dumpster. I run past the back door to the cafeteria. The loading dock. Then I get to the corner of the school where the teachers park. I slow down and look. No one is here either. I hurry past the empty parking spaces and now I am at the front of the school. I look down the long sidewalk to the lobby. I look out at the parking lot again. I don't see Crystal with a C.

So I look both ways very carefully and then I cross the bus loop. I stand between two empty cars looking. I walk down the rows of cars and I look and I look until I see a shape near a gray car. It is a person. With a red dot next to its mouth.

"Hey, Ginny," she says. "Ready to go on a little trip?"

I nod my head yes. And smile. Because Crystal with a C is the one who's going to kidnap me and she's the one who tells the truth. She opens the door to the car for me and I get in.

Crystal with a C gets into the driver's seat fast. She starts the car. She has a metal ball in the side of her nose that wasn't there before. And purple pointy glasses. Also new.

I smile big with my teeth and make my shoulders go up to my ears.

"Wow, that's a nice smile!" she says all at once. "I'd love to give you a hug, kiddo, but we need to get out of here quick as we can. Okay?" The tires make a tiny squeal and she pulls out of the parking lot. Crystal with a C *winces* which is what you do when you hear something loud or someone is going to hit. She looks in the mirror and then back to the road.

"Did you find my Baby Doll?" I ask. "Gloria said she did but—"

Crystal with a C glances in the mirror. I see her eyes there.

"I had a feeling you were going to ask that. You haven't changed a bit," she says. "Yes, we found your Baby Doll. I did, actually. Gloria called me from the police station, so I went over to the apartment right away. She didn't know where you put the baby, but I put two and two together and found the suitcase."

"Was it a—" I start to say but I can't finish the sentence. "Is it a—"

She looks at me. "Is it *alive?*" she says. "Is that what you're trying to say? Holy shit, of course it was alive! What did you think, that you killed your baby sister?"

I want to answer her question. I want to say *Yes, thank you, thank you for finally telling me* but my throat hurts and I can't move my mouth anymore but then it opens all by itself and my chest moves up and down fast. No sound comes out but hot, hot tears fall on my face and pants. I cry and cry and shake while Crystal with a C looks at me and looks back at the road and says something and looks back at me but I can't hear anything at all.

Then I stop. And breathe. I am better.

"—all right?" I hear Crystal with a C say.

I don't know what she asked but I nod my head yes anyway.

Crystal with a C makes a breathing sound. "Ginny, I just can't believe it. It's been five years. Five frigging years. I know your mom is a real piece of work and that you needed to be away from her, but it's just awful to imagine what you've been through, not knowing what happened to your sister. But right now I need to get us out of town, okay? You've got to let me drive for a while. We have ten minutes at the most, I'm guessing, before someone calls the police. I've got to take some back roads. We can't take the highway because the police will put up a blockade."

"What's a blockade?"

"It's a roadblock. You know, a place where the police park their cars across the road and stop everyone from driving. They'll be looking for you. They'll have an Amber Alert and everything."

"Is my Baby Doll with Gloria?"

"Yep, she's with your mom."

Crystal with a C pats my arm and makes a happy face. Her shoulders go up to her ears and come down again. Then she looks back at the road. "She was in pretty bad shape when I found her. I guess you were right to be worried. I was really scared for a while because she'd been in there so long. At least an hour, easily. I thought she was...*sleeping* at first, but she was just unconscious. She came right back when I gave her mouth-to-mouth."

Then Crystal with a C is quiet.

"Where did she come back from?" I say.

"Back from— Shit, I don't know. She's fine, okay? She's really fine. But if I hadn't gotten there when I did, things might have turned out differently."

"She's fine," I say. To help me remember.

"Right. So, to make a long story short, I brought her home and got her all cleaned up and fed. She was way too skinny. Not as bad as you, though. Do you remember when the judge described how you looked? In the decision papers? I'm not sure if you read them. Actually, you were way too young, so you couldn't have. He said you looked like you came out of a concentration camp, you were so thin and beat-up. I feel bad to this day. I was out of the picture for a while that first year when Gloria was taking care of the two of you. But what that judge said—he really nailed it."

Crystal with a C is talking too fast. I nod my head yes even though I don't know why.

"Anyway, she was suffering from malnutrition. The doctor I brought her to said she was surprised she made it so long. You kept her alive, Ginny. You saved your sister's life."

"By putting her in the suitcase?" I say.

"No! *God*, no! By keeping her fed and protecting her from your mother. I love my big sister, but she's not a good mom. And she's so fucking impulsive! I mean, she's come a long way, especially after the parenting classes, but she still doesn't have her act completely together. You'll see."

I don't know what *doesn't have her act completely together* means so I say, "Is my Baby Doll *safe* with Gloria?"

Crystal with a C laughs. "Safe enough. I still don't like to let more than a day go by without spending a few hours with both of them. Gloria sort of depends on me to do her thinking for her. I'm the one who got her to go to rehab and made her go to those classes. Plus, I had her move in with me until she got back on her feet."

"Does she give it plenty of food?"

Crystal with a C makes a breathing sound. "Yes, she gives it plenty of food."

"Does she remember to give it a bath?"

"A ba—"

"Does she remember to change its diaper?" I say and then I stop and start picking at my fingers. But I am so anxious that I have to keep talking. "Does she know what to do when it throws up? Does she put socks on its hands so it won't scratch its face?"

"Ginny, how the hell old do you think your Baby Doll is?"

"Almost one year old," I say. "Its birthday is November 16th."

"Whoa," says Crystal with a C. And then "Whoa" again. "Are you serious? Of course you're serious. You couldn't crack a joke if your life depended on it. But, girl, there's a lot we have to talk about. Not right now, though. I don't think you're ready for it yet. And I have to drive and think. I forgot the way your brain works."

"The brain is in the head," I say.

"No shit," says Crystal with a C.

I sit up straight and look around. I am alone in the car. The sun isn't up yet but I can see there are trees with yellow leaves outside the windows. Crystal with a C is gone.

I open the door and get out. The wind is blowing and I am wearing my jacket but I am still cold. Behind the car is a small white house with a chimney with white smoke coming out of it. I hear music inside. I pull my backpack high up on my shoulders and go to it.

Crystal with a C is in the house. I see her walk past the doorway as I climb up the stairs to the front porch. I go to the screen door and stand there waiting.

Crystal with a C walks past the door again. She sees me and puts her hand on her chest. "Ginny!" she says. "I didn't even see you. How long have you been standing there?"

"Since 5:28," I say. My watch says it is five-thirty.

"Well, come in, will you?" she says. "We can't have you standing out in the open. We're pretty far from the main road, but someone could still come up the driveway. You were fast asleep when we got here, and I didn't want to wake you. You used to wake up kind of wild. You didn't like to be touched. Not sure if that's changed or not."

I rub my arms and open the door and go in. Inside I smell bacon and toast and smoke from a woodstove. I am hungry.

Crystal with a C is in the kitchen now. I follow her. She is wearing a brown-and-orange shirt with squiggly white lines on it. She puts down a plate of food on the table. "I was going to make some for you after you woke up, but I guess you beat me to it," she says. She points to the food.

I sit and pick up a fork and start eating.

"So we need to talk about a few things," she says. "You're all over the news already. There's an Amber Alert, just like I said. I haven't been in touch with Gloria yet. It's just not safe. The police can see anything you put online, and they have access to cell phone records, too. So we're going to stay off the map for a while. Just a few weeks until we can head up to Canada."

"Is my Baby Doll in Canada?" I say.

"Baby Doll," says Crystal with a C. "Why don't you use her name?"

"Because you said *she'll always be my little baby, no matter what,*" I say. "So is it up in Canada?"

"You really took me at my word, didn't you?" she says.

"Yes," I say.

"Fair enough. But to answer your question, no, not yet. I'll find a way to get a message to Gloria when things have settled and tell them to come meet us. The two of us were born up there, you know. We both have dual citizenship. So do you. I even have your passport—I snagged it from Gloria when she finally brought you back to Maine. But your Baby Doll was born in my apartment. Gloria didn't want to go to the hospital because she was scared they would have taken her. She was pretty well-known by the police, at that point. Gloria, I mean."

I don't remember when my Baby Doll was born. I know its birthday but I don't remember the day. "Where was I when my Baby Doll was born in your apartment?" I say.

"You were home, waiting." She picks up a coffee mug from the counter and drinks from it. "Your mom was never great at being a mom, but she loves you. Loves you like crazy. I mean, crazy, crazy crazy. You know that, don't you?"

I'm not sure if I know that so I make sure my mouth is shut and nod.

"She's been looking for you for years. Online, on the phone, every which way. She cares more about getting you back than she does about her own safety. So when you found her on Facebook, she jumped in the car and came to get you. Then she went to your school. I tried to stop her, but she wouldn't listen. These sorts of things need to be taken slowly, but Gloria doesn't live that way. Finally I had to sit her down—this is after the police threatened to make her spend a night in jail—and say, 'Look, if you don't stop this, you're going to end up in prison. Then you won't see either of your girls.' That's when she told me about her plan to go up to Canada."

She puts her coffee down. "You're how old now?" she says.

"Fourteen years old," I say.

"And your Baby Doll is still *one*?"

I nod my head yes.

"So you aged five years, and your Baby Doll didn't age at all. You're pretty good at math, aren't you? The math doesn't add up."

"It's because *she'll always be my little baby* just like you said," I say. And then, "When does Gloria want us to go up to Canada?"

Crystal with a C shakes her head and makes a breathing sound. "I'm just going to let the first part of that go for now. As for Gloria, she doesn't even know that I'm doing this. If she did, she'd get involved, and then she'd end up in jail. But Canada is a great place for us to go. We've got a lot of family there. And it really is pretty easy to disappear up in Quebec. But, no, Gloria isn't expecting to meet us. She thinks I'm in my own apartment right now."

"When are we leaving?" I say.

"When things settle down. We could probably make a run for the border right now, but Gloria is going to be watched and questioned for a long time. I don't want the day we cross the border to be anywhere near the time you disappeared."

"Then who will take care of my Baby Doll?" I say.

"What do you mean?"

"You aren't spending at least a few hours with both of them every day and Gloria doesn't have her act together."

Crystal with a C makes a breathing sound again. "My big sis is going to have to manage on her own for a while. I think they'll be okay. With all the attention, Gloria's not going to step too far out of line. She can act pretty reasonably, when she's not strung out on drugs or with a man. Well, reasonably enough. Now, I'm sorry, but I have to get going. I have to go to work and act like nothing unusual is going on. Ha! But it's a long drive from here. I bought this place ten years ago. It's sort of my home away from home. There's food in the fridge—you know how to cook, don't you?"

She asks if she can give me a hug and I say okay. Then she gives me one and she leaves.

EXACTLY 6:23 IN THE MORNING, TUESDAY, OCTOBER 19TH

I stand waiting until I hear Crystal with a C's car pull out of the driveway. Then I start to hear some of the empty sounds I used to hear when I was alone in the apartment. The refrigerator and the ringing sound that comes from all the walls and rooms. I almost hear the sound of my Baby Doll breathing quiet, quiet on my shoulder. But then I hear the wind in the leaves outside and so I let my fingers go out straight again.

I go to the front porch and put my toes on a crack at the edge of the doorway. Outside I don't see neighbors or a street. I don't see any buildings. I see only white trunks and yellow, yellow leaves.

I turn back into the house and go into the kitchen. I stand in front of the refrigerator and think about the rule *We do not open the refrigerator.* My Forever Mom and Forever Dad made that rule because they know I have *issues with food.* But they're not here right now. And I'm not at the Blue House. I'm in Crystal with a C's Little White House.

My hands shake. I open the refrigerator.

Inside I see one carton of twelve eggs and one carton of nine and some ketchup and twenty-two slices of bread in a bag and seven onions and an eight-ounce block of Grade A pasteurized cheddar cheese. Four sticks of butter in a box. Two unopened half gallons of milk. I see other things too but I pick up the cheese. And the ketchup because ketchup is *quick and easy.*

I start eating.

When the cheese is gone I take one of the half gallons of milk out of the refrigerator because I want a drink. The one that belongs to Crystal with a C. The other half gallon of milk is the one I brought from the Blue House. I don't remember putting it away. Crystal with a C must have moved it. But I wonder if my Forever Parents are angry that I took it. I wonder if my Forever Mom needs the milk for my new Forever Sister who isn't born yet. Baby Wendy. Last week my Forever Mom said they were going to the hospital *any day now.*

Any day now.

I am glad that Crystal with a C found my Baby Doll in the suitcase. I am glad she took care of it and went over there every day but I'm also anxious about Gloria taking care of it herself. I know she won't give it food or keep it clean. I know she sometimes has strange men come sleep over. Plus there's Donald. I believe everything Crystal with a C says and I trust her 100 percent but there are some things she just doesn't know because she wasn't there all the time. Some things I remember deep in my brain and won't ever, ever talk about.

Which means I have to go find Gloria's apartment right now. I can't wait.

I walk into the living room. I need to find a computer so that I can look for Gloria's address because I don't know where I am or where she is or how to get there.

I look at the woodstove which has a fire in it. I look at the couch and at the chair. There's no TV. I look around for a computer but I don't see one. I walk down the hallway and find the bathroom. I pee. I find a bedroom with Crystal with a C's things in the dresser. Then I find another bedroom with a bed and a desk. The desk has a light on it and nothing in the drawers. The bed has sheets and a wool blanket and a pillow.

I look in all the closets and the cabinets. There is no computer in this house. There is nothing that can tell me what town I'm in or where Gloria is. I don't know her address.

So I will go find a library.

The library is where you go when you want to get on a computer to find something out. Or when you want to send a message to Gloria. I'm guessing Gloria might not be able to send me a message on *Manicoon.com* because the police are watching it but she might have her address on the page. I remember that there was a button that said Contact Me.

I take the half gallon of milk I brought from the Blue House out of the refrigerator for my Baby Doll. It really likes milk. Milk is what all babies need. I put the half gallon back in my backpack with my flute and my quilt. Then I zip my jacket and go to the bathroom again and put my backpack on and walk out the door.

The driveway leads down through the woods. Tall grass grows on the side of it. It brushes my pants as I walk. The wind is loud all around me and the air is cold. At the end of the driveway I come to a road. It goes left and right. There are trees across the street and trees on this side of the street and no other cars and no buildings.

I stand and think. A car goes by. A red car that comes from the right and goes to the left. I don't know if it's going to or from town. I'm guessing if I was in the car I would be going to school. And school is in town. So I start walking that way.

Right away I see a man coming toward me.

I start picking at my fingers.

The man comes walking up over a hill. He is dressed in clothes that are all green and brown with crisscrossed lines all over. He has big brown boots and a hat. He is carrying something over his shoulder. It is a gun.

I want to run and hide. I don't like men especially if they are policemen and this man is *like* a policeman even though I don't think he is one because he isn't wearing the right uniform. He is wearing what a hunter wears. The brown and green lines tell me he is good at hiding and sneaking.

"'Morning," says the man in a happy voice as he comes closer.

He stops right in front of me. I am glad he didn't ask me anything but then he says, "Are you on your way to catch the bus? The school bus came by about two or three minutes ago."

I want to say *Well dang!* but instead I say, "No."

He looks at me. "Someone coming to pick you up, then?"

I shake my head. Maybe if I stop giving answers with my mouth he'll stop asking questions with his.

"Well, then, what are you doing out here all by yourself on a school day?"

I can't tell him where I'm going. If I do I'll get caught.

"I am going for a walk," I say. Because it's true. I was walking.

"A walk? Are you walking to school?"

"No," I say.

"You're just walking, then," he says.

"I am just walking," I say.

"Okay," he says. And then, "Say, you don't happen to be wearing a Michael Jackson shirt under that jacket, do you?" He puts his finger out toward me.

I *recoil.*

When I look back at him he is putting his two hands out like he's asking me to be quiet. "Sorry," he says. "It's just that I heard on the radio that they're looking for a girl about your age wearing a Michael Jackson shirt and carrying a flute. Well, watch out for moose on your walk, all right? I went out for deer this morning, but moose are still crossing the roads. They're still out and about. The bulls are crazy this time of year. Okay?"

"Okay," I say. Then I step around him very, very carefully in case he tries to touch me again. I keep walking but I don't hear him walking away. I know he's still looking at me.

So I start counting.

At five I hear footsteps on the road so I look behind me quick. He is walking backward and still watching. I stare at him. He waves and turns and starts walking the regular way.

But now I am anxious because the man might call the police. I stop and count to twenty and then turn all the way around. The man is gone. I start going back the way I came to the driveway.

I'm guessing that if I go to town and find the library right now I will get caught. I will try again tomorrow.

Then I get scared because someone else could see me right now. Maybe another car will go by or I'll see someone else on the road. I step into the woods and walk through the trees and tall grass until I get back to the Little White House at the top of the driveway.

EXACTLY 7:09 AT NIGHT, TUESDAY, OCTOBER 19TH

It is dark outside. I see lights coming toward the house. Tires on the driveway. A car door shuts and someone comes up the steps.

I move fast into the living room.

Then Crystal with a C opens the door and walks right in. "Hey, Ginny," she says. She walks right past me into the kitchen and puts two plastic bags down on the counter. "How did it go today? Everything at work was fine. No one even mentioned the whole Amber Alert thing, except some new contractor in the break room." I hear her open the refrigerator. *"Whoa."*

I am still in the living room next to the screen door.

"Ginny, the eggs are still here, but where's the rest of the food?"

So I say, "I ate it."

"You ate it?"

I nod my head yes.

Crystal with a C walks into the living room. "Ginny, did you really eat all the food in the refrigerator? Except the eggs?"

I nod my head yes again even though I hid the bread and the

milk in a closet. She walks to the garbage can and looks inside it. She picks up the empty ketchup bottle and the little papers that went around the butter. And the empty cheese wrapper. "You seriously ate all this?"

"Yes."

"Did you cook something?"

"No."

She looks through the garbage some more. She picks out the empty brownie box. "This, too?"

I nod my head yes. It is good in milk.

"Without baking it? Did you get sick? Did you throw up, I mean?"

But that was three questions in a row.

Crystal with a C makes a breathing sound. "I don't know if I should get you a laxative or worry about diarrhea. Look, tomorrow you have to eat what I tell you. I'll even write it down. You can't eat everything that's in the refrigerator or you'll make your tummy really upset. You could get constipated. Do you understand?"

I don't know what *constipated* means so I say, "No."

"Just eat what I put on the list, okay?"

"I like lists," I say.

"Good. Now, why don't you put these new groceries away for me while I get dressed? Then we'll make supper together. I'll show you how to make scrambled eggs."

She drops the brownie box back in the garbage can.

"Wait," I say.

She looks at me.

"What town do Gloria and my Baby Doll live in?" I say.

"They're still in Harrington Falls. Now go get those groceries put away. I need to get changed out of these clothes."

I am standing with my toes on the crack at the edge of the
doorway trying to figure how to get out of the Little White
House without getting wet. Because it rained all day and my
raincoat is back at the Blue House. And I don't like to be wet. I
like to be dry all the time unless I'm taking a bath or a shower
or I'm in a pool. Not having a raincoat is making me very, very
anxious. I am trapped.

Crystal with a C doesn't have a raincoat either. I checked.

At seven o'clock it is still raining so I take my shower because
Crystal with a C said that's what I should do from now on if
she's not home yet. When I turn the water off and step out of
the tub I find something hard and black on my leg. I can't get it
off and I can't see what it is because I'm not wearing my glasses.
Then I put them on but it's too steamy to see. I hear noises on
the other side of the door. I'm guessing it's Crystal with a C so I
walk out of the bathroom and into the kitchen and see her setting the table. "There's something on my leg," I say.

And she says, "Ginny, get a towel!"

So I go back into the bathroom and get a towel and put it

around me. Then I come back out and say again, "There's something on my leg."

"Let me see it," she says. She stands up and looks. Then she says, "I need to get some tweezers. Come with me into the bathroom, all right?"

We go into the bathroom. She finds some tweezers in the medicine cabinet and pulls the hard thing off. It hurts when she pulls it so I say, "Ow!" Then she shows it to me. She says it is a tick.

The tick is a small black bug. I know because it has legs.

"All right," she says. "Let me check to see if you have any more. There are a ton of them out here."

She takes the towel off and looks at my legs and arms and back. She checks my belly and my sides. She finds three more ticks and takes them all off. One is on my back where a belt goes. One is near my knee. And one is on my ankle.

Then I say, "Why were they holding on to me?"

And she says, "They weren't holding on. They were biting. Ticks bite into people's skin."

"Why do they do that?"

"To drink their blood."

Then I get really, really scared.

So I say, "Like a vampire?"

And she says, "Yes, sort of."

The pictures in my head start moving faster. I remember the vampire movies Gloria used to watch on TV. When a vampire bites someone the person turns into a vampire. So I say, "Am I going to turn into a tick?"

"Of course not," she says. "But how on earth did you get covered in ticks? Ginny, have you been outside?"

That was two questions at once so I don't say anything.

"Ginny, I asked you if you've been outside."

"It is raining," I say.

"Yes, I know it is raining, and I know you don't like to get wet unless you're in the shower, but that's not the answer to my question. Did you go outside?"

"Yes."

"Where did you go?"

"Down the driveway."

"Today?"

"No."

"When?"

"Yesterday."

"Ginny, you can't do that. If someone sees you, you'll get caught, and then you won't be able to go with me to Canada. You won't be able to see your Baby Doll."

So I say, "But I have to make sure it's safe. Gloria can't take care of it."

"Holy shit! Yes, she can! It's only for a little while! Your Baby Doll isn't even—"

Then she stops. "Look, I'm not a psychologist. I don't know what you can process and what you can't. But there's something you're just not seeing yet, and I'm seriously afraid to explain it. I don't want you to blow a gasket or anything. So please, please, believe me that your Baby Doll is safe with Gloria for now. Maybe not forever, but for now. Just stay put, will you? It's only for a few weeks!"

It isn't raining anymore.

Before I was adopted I tried to run away three times from my different Forever Homes but the police always found me and brought me back. I ran away from Carla and Mike when I was still nine years old and then two times from Samantha and Bill when I was eleven. But this time is different because I'm not running away from Crystal with a C. She kidnapped me so she can't call the police. Even if she wants to. She'll get in trouble if she does.

I know it's mostly an expression but sometimes I am a *smart cookie*.

Crystal with a C left for work five minutes ago. I am wearing my jacket and standing at the crack in front of the front door. I already put the unopened milk and the bread in my back-pack with my flute and my quilt. So I go outside. It is a sunny day even though the trees and grass are still wet from the rain. And it is cold.

Now I know that Gloria and my Baby Doll live in Har-rington Falls. Even though I don't know where that is I can find it. I can stop at the library or ask a lady for directions when I find a sidewalk.

At the bottom of the driveway I look both ways. I look for hunters. I look for police. I see only the empty road with no cars or people or moose which are crazy this time of year.

I turn left and start walking. I'm guessing if I go to town no one will be looking for me because it's been two whole days since I met the man with the gun who sometimes forgets how to walk the right way. The sand on the side of the road kicks up against the back of my legs and gets in my shoes but I have to be okay with that because I have a long way to go to Harrington Falls. And I know that if I walk in the woods I'll get ticks that suck my blood.

I hear a noise behind me. An engine. I turn and see a gray car coming. In the window I see that it is Crystal with a C.

She drives next to me and stops. Her window is down. I keep going because I don't want to talk. The car pulls in front of me and stops. "Ginny, stop!" Crystal with a C yells. She gets out of the car.

So I stop to hear what she will say.

"Where the hell are you going?"

"I'm going to Harrington Falls," I say.

"We already talked about this. You have to go back to the house. If you don't, you'll get caught."

"I will not get caught," I say.

"Ginny, you're as subtle as an elephant in a traffic jam. You can't take care of yourself at all. And this proves it. You need to be watched constantly. But, honey, I have to go to work! I have to go to work, or people will start to wonder where the hell I am."

I look at my fingers.

"And now you're trying to hike across the whole state and you don't even know which way to go. And you have no clue how to deal with people. When it comes to dealing with people, you stick out like a sore thumb. See what I mean?"

I don't say anything.

"Ginny, get in the car."

"No."

"What do you think is going to happen if you find your way all the way to Harrington Falls? It's a two-hour drive! Do you know how long it would take you to walk that far? Even if you get there safely, the police will find you. They talk with Gloria every day. Don't you get it? They're actively looking for you! If you go there, they'll take you back to the Blue House. And I'll go to fucking jail! Now get in the damn car before some-one sees us!"

I hear a sound. Another car. I look up and see a black car coming from where I think town might be. It goes by and doesn't stop.

"See?" says Crystal with a C. "This isn't safe, Ginny. We have to go back to the house this second, or this whole thing will fall apart in a very big way. I'll even stay home with you, all right? I'll call in sick to work. Ginny, please!"

I make sure my mouth is closed and then I think. It's true that if I get to Harrington Falls and find Gloria's apartment the police will find me. I didn't think of that before. Plus they al-ready know about my hiding place under the sink. They'll find me and take me away again. Crystal with a C is right.

But my Baby Doll is still alone with Gloria.

So I say, "But my Baby Doll isn't safe."

"Yes, she is. I *swear* she is. She's much, much safer than she ever was before. I just can't tell you why because you'll flip! Remem-ber what happened when you asked if there was a Santa Claus? Gloria kept saying there was, and then I told you the truth. Do you remember what you did?"

I remember *exactly*. I got mad at Gloria and duct-taped all her drugs to the Maine coon cats and let them out of their cages. Then I flushed all her socks down the toilet.

I nod my head yes.

"So you've got to trust me," says Crystal with a C. "Because I promise, Ginny—I promise that your Baby Doll will be safe until we all get up to Canada. I just can't tell you why. You're not ready to hear it."

Gloria used to lie when she said *I promise* but Crystal with a C is different. I know she is trying to help me for real. And I know I can trust her.

"Ginny, please! You have to trust me that she's safe!"

I walk around the car and get in.

"Thank you," says Crystal with a C when I shut the door. Her hands are shaking and her face is wet. "Holy shit, thank you. Thank you!" Then she turns the car around and drives back up the driveway.

EXACTLY 11:33 IN THE MORNING, THURSDAY, OCTOBER 21ST

"Ginny, did you use all the milk?" says Crystal with a C. From the living room I hear the refrigerator shut. The milk is still in my backpack. I forgot to take it out when we got back to the Little White House.

Crystal with a C walks into the living room. I am sitting on the couch looking at the fire. "Look," she says, "I don't want to leave you by yourself. Shit. I mean, I *really* don't want to leave you by yourself, but we need milk for the batter I'm going to make. And I know you like to drink milk in the morning. So I have to run to the store. It's right down the road. If you get hungry, make yourself a snack. A *small* snack, okay? Don't go eating all the cheese and ketchup again."

I nod my head yes.

"I'll only be gone for twenty minutes," she says. "And, Ginny, stay in the house, all right? Don't go outside for any reason. Remember what we said before—your Baby Doll is safe, and if you try to go back to Harrington Falls, the police will find you."

She looks at me. I keep looking at the woodstove because she didn't ask a question.

"Ginny, did you hear me?"

I nod my head yes.

"I do wish you'd be a little more…talkative," she says.

When she leaves I stand up. I am going to make myself a snack.

Crystal with a C said that when you make scrambled eggs you crack them in a bowl and mix them up and pour them in a frying pan and cook them for five minutes. She showed me how to crack the eggs. That part is already done. I even picked the shells out. So I start to mix them.

I pour the eggs into the frying pan. My watch says it is 11:42. I take the dish towel off my shoulder which is where Crystal with a C puts it when she cooks. I put it on the counter next to the stove. Then I turn the stove on.

I go into the living room and sit down to wait.

At 11:44 I smell smoke.

I walk back into the kitchen. The dish towel is on fire.

At school we learned that if there's a fire you should call 911 and *stop, drop and roll!* But there isn't a phone here at the Little White House and the kitchen is really tiny.

The fire is getting bigger. It crackles. It reaches up to the shelf above the counter. I want someone to stop it but no one is here.

Then the smoke alarm goes off. It is loud and scary and I don't like loud noises so I put my hands over my ears and *recoil*. The noise doesn't go away so after *exactly* seven seconds I open my eyes and put my arms down and run to the sink.

Now the fire is on the counter too. I fill a glass with water and throw it at the flames. The fire goes down a little. Black smoke is everywhere. I throw more water on it and after three glasses the fire is mostly out but now the dish towel has a big black hole in it. It smokes when I pick it up. It smells bad. There are some red parts on the towel that are still glowing so I throw it away in the garbage. I don't want Crystal with a C to see it. Plus it's ruined anyway. My eggs have water in them now so I throw them away too. I scrape them into the garbage and put the frying pan down on the counter. The counter has a big black mark on it where the dish towel used to be. I put a bowl of apples on top of it.

But the smoke alarm is still going off and it's hard to see and I am coughing so I go outside and stand in the driveway. I look toward the road and start counting.

When I get to 537 Crystal with a C comes home. She gets out of the car and looks at me and then looks at the Little White House. I look too. Because I wasn't looking before. A lot of black smoke is coming through the screen door.

Crystal with a C runs inside.

When she comes out she has the garbage can with her. Smoke is pouring out of it. She dumps all the garbage on the ground. I see fire. She jumps up and down on the flames and on all the garbage. The fire goes out.

Then Crystal with a C hits the top of the car with her hands. "Ginny!" she screams. She is crying. She cries and cries and then she says, "The police are in town talking with everybody they see. They're showing your picture to everyone. Someone saw you, goddamn it! You've been seen! And now I come home to this?"

I don't say anything.

"Get in the car," she says. "Just get in the car! I'll go get your backpack. We have to leave!"

We are driving.

The backseat is filled with all of Crystal with a C's clothes. She threw them in fast before we left the Little White House. I am holding my backpack on my lap. When I asked where we were going she said she didn't know yet. She said we just need to be moving.

Crystal with a C cried three times while she was driving. Once at 11:53, once at 12:28 and again at 1:14. I do not know why she cried. When I ask her she says it's because she doesn't know what to do. We can't go to Canada yet, she says, and we can't go to her other apartment. And we can't stay in the Little White House anymore because the police will find us.

We are driving on the highway again. It is the same highway we were on when we left school three days ago. I know because of the signs. The sign we just passed said *Greensborough, Exit 33, 1 Mile.* So I say, "Why are we here again?"

And Crystal with a C says, "Because we have to go back the other direction. The police know we went west, so we have to go east. And that means backtracking. You know what backtracking is, don't you?"

I don't but the word makes sense. *Backtracking.* So I nod my head yes.

"We're going to have to take a little detour, too," she says.

"Because of the *blockade*?" I say.

"Yes, because of the blockade," she says. "We're going to have to go straight through town. So I'm going to need you to get down. Just scrunch yourself down below the window. Right now. Get on the floor and make yourself as small as possible so no one can see you. And I'll put a jacket over your head. That way the police won't know you're there when we go past them. I need you to hide, Ginny."

"I'm a good hider," I say. Then I get down on the floor and Crystal with a C puts a coat over my head. I can't see where we are anymore but that's okay because I know Crystal with a C will *come through for me.*

We turn and we slow down and turn again and drive for a little while. It's too dark so I can't see my watch. Then we turn three more times. Right, left, left. And the car stops.

I hear Crystal with a C's voice. "Ginny, stay right where you are. I'm going to get out of the car for a minute. Be ready."

The driver's-side door opens and closes. Seven seconds pass. Then the car door on *my* side of the car opens. "Okay, Ginny, get out!" says Crystal with a C in a loud whisper. "We have to move to a different car! Get out fast. Keep your head down low!"

I throw the coat back and pull my backpack with me and get out of the car. I crouch low and tuck my head down. I blink in the bright light. It is 3:55 and I am scared, scared, scared.

"Stay close against the car! Don't let anyone see you!" says Crystal with a C.

So I do. I am against the car in a tight, tight ball. Crystal with a C shuts my door. She runs past me. Behind the car. I peek to see where she's going.

But across from me on the other side of the sidewalk I see a big yellow house I know.

I pick my head up all the way. Across the street is Cumberland Farms and the gas station attached to it. I see the post office too. We are in the middle of Greensborough right near my school. Down the street I see the road that goes down to the bus loop.

I hear a click. The sound of the car door locking.

Crystal with a C is standing on the other side of the car. "Ginny, I love you," she says. Her face is different. "I tried. I swear I tried, but you're just too much. A real handful. Now go straight to the school and tell your teachers you're okay. But, please, don't mention me to anyone, all right? Don't mention the house or the fire or the color of the car or anything. Just tell everyone that you took a walk and got confused. You were perfectly fine these past three days, right?"

I am confused. "How will I get to Canada?"

Crystal with a C makes a breathing sound. "You're not going to Canada. Not today, anyway. Just go back to school, Ginny. Go back and pretend that none of this ever happened. Pretend you don't remember!"

But pretending would be the same as lying if I said it with my mouth. I want to explain that *I just can't do that* but then Crystal with a C gets back in the car and the engine turns on. The car pulls away. I want to run after it because Crystal with a C is the only person who can help me get back to my Baby Doll. There are other cars coming now and I know it isn't safe to run into a busy street but I am going to chase it anyway. I have to. I take one step forward. Then I hear a siren.

Blue lights come up the road fast. They come so fast I think they will rip the road in two pieces. Then there are more blue lights and a police car slides sideways in front of Crystal with a

C's car. The noise is louder than the smoke alarm. I see police cars with policemen getting out of them and people running and more police cars and policemen running at me. I turn to run but someone grabs me so I *recoil* and cover my face and squeeze and squeeze and squeeze.

My new Forever Sister was born on October 19th which was the day after the Harvest Concert. I saw it for *approximately* one minute yesterday. My new Forever Sister has blue eyes and small hands and feet. It mostly sleeps and cries. I stood watching it for *exactly* thirteen seconds in the living room while my Forever Mom held it. Then she said, "Welcome back, Ginny. Do you think you could back up a bit?" And then she said, "We're glad you're back from the hospital."

Because that's where I went before I came back to the Blue House. The police brought me to the hospital and after the doctors looked at me my Forever Dad came to bring me here. The doctors were all women. They wanted to see if I was injured because they all knew that Crystal with a C kidnapped me. I couldn't *pretend that none of this ever happened*. Plus the police took Crystal with a C away. So I'm guessing they figured it all out.

My new Forever Sister is named Baby Wendy. It's very little so it needs a lot of milk. You get milk from the refrigerator even though I know it comes from cows. But my Forever Mom says she is *breast-feeding* it instead. She is upstairs in the bedroom doing it right now.

I am in the living room picking at my fingers. My Forever Dad is making lunch. He doesn't understand. Finally I walk into the kitchen and grab my breasts to show him. "There's no milk in these," I say.

He drops a bowl of potatoes and puts his hands on his forehead. "No— Yes— Ginny, just slow down," he says.

"I gave my Baby Doll milk from a towel. Every day."

"From a towel?"

"You dip the towel in the milk and then let the baby suck. You get the milk *from a carton* in the refrigerator. Not from these."

He looks the other way. "It sounds like Gloria didn't breast-feed you," he says. He starts picking up the potatoes. "You couldn't remember something like that, though. You were too young. Did you really use a towel when you wanted some milk? Didn't you have any cups in the apartment?"

But that was two questions so I don't say anything.

He keeps talking. "Some moms feed their babies with milk from their breasts," he says, "and some moms feed their babies with cow's milk. It's called *formula*, actually. But it's a matter of personal choice."

He doesn't understand. "My new Forever Sister needs milk," I say.

"Right," he says.

"It has to drink a lot of real milk," I say.

"Right again," he says. "But let's not call your sister 'it,' okay? And remember, she *is* drinking real milk. Upstairs right now with your mom."

"No," I say. "*That* isn't real milk. Real milk comes from the refrigerator."

He opens the refrigerator and takes the milk out. Then he pours a glass and puts it on the counter.

"There," he says. "That's real milk. Real *cow's* milk."

"Exactly," I say because sometimes *exactly* means *right*. I pick up the milk and walk to the stairs.

"Ginny, what are you doing?"

"I'm bringing the milk upstairs."

"No," he says. "Don't do that. Put it back on the counter. Baby Wendy drinks breast milk."

I put the glass of milk down.

"Let's try one more time," he says. "The milk that you drink comes from cows, but babies can drink milk from their mothers, if their mothers decide to breast-feed. See?"

When people say *See?* they mean *Do you understand?* but my Forever Dad doesn't understand at all. "I know where milk for humans comes from," I say. I pick up the glass of milk and point to it. "This is human milk. You know, *hu*-man."

"You can pronounce it however you want, but it still comes from a cow," he says.

"So then why won't my Forever Mom give it to the baby? Why won't she give it milk that's real?"

"She *is* giving it milk that's real."

I look at him over my glasses and shake my breasts at him again. "But there's no milk in these," I say. I have had breasts for *approximately* one year and I know that milk doesn't come out of them. Nothing does.

"Ginny, put your— Watch— Just listen," he says. "I know you've been through a lot. I'm sorry if this is all confusing, but you're just going to have to trust me. Wendy is getting plenty of real milk. You can talk with Patrice about it when we go to see her after lunch. It's really nice that she agreed to set up an appointment with you today—after all, it's the weekend. But I bet she'll want to talk some more about going back to school on Thursday, too. Do you still think you're ready?"

He is *changing the subject* so I have to focus. I can't get distracted.

My new Forever Sister needs real human milk but it isn't getting any and I know that Gloria will forget to feed my Baby Doll because Crystal with a C is in jail and no one will go to check on them. In my brain for a second I see my Baby Doll's tiny eyes and face. Its eyes used to blink when I picked it up.

I come up out of my brain. The glass of milk is still in front of me on the counter. In my brain again I can see myself dipping a towel or my shirt in it and then putting the wet part in my Baby Doll's mouth.

"Ginny?"

"What?" I say.

"Please, don't worry about Wendy. She's getting everything she needs. I'm really sorry about how intense things are around the baby right now. Your mom is being extra cautious, staying upstairs all the time. It would help a lot if you didn't hover so much when she comes downstairs. Just…just give her some space, will you? You'll see. We'll all get back to normal soon. You'll go back to school next Thursday, and then everything will slowly go back to the way it used to be. Everyone is safe. You're home, the baby is healthy and your mom is doing well. Everything is going to be fine. Crystal is in jail now, and your baby sister has plenty to drink."

"Crystal *with a C*," I say. Then I go to my room.

EXACTLY 2:08 IN THE AFTERNOON,
SATURDAY, OCTOBER 23RD

"It's been two days since you've been back at the Blue House, and now you have a baby sister," says Patrice. "A lot has changed."

That wasn't a question so I don't say anything. I just sit in the flower chair and look at Patrice.

"Your Forever Parents tell me you've been pretty quiet at home. What's been going on in that brain of yours? Ginny, I want you to try to connect. I want to know how you feel. I want you to tell me how you feel about being back. Now, I know that Crystal didn't hurt you, but—"

"Crystal *with a C*," I say.

"All right, Crystal with a C didn't hurt you. The doctors at the hospital said you were perfectly fine, but I wonder if Crystal with a C said some things when you were at her house that you're still thinking about. Things that you remember. Could you tell me what those things are?"

"She said my Baby Doll is fine with Gloria for a few weeks but she likes to spend at least a few hours with them every day.

But now Crystal with a C is in jail. So I need to go back to the apartment."

She writes something down. "I wish she hadn't humored you about your Baby Doll," she says. "Remember, there was no baby in that apartment with you. The police would have found it. They even went back to look again when you told them it was in the suitcase. Now, how do you feel about what happened to Crystal with a C?"

"Angry," I say.

"That's good. It's okay to feel angry when you miss someone. It's okay to be mad and miss Gloria, too. Did you know that when you were gone, your Forever Parents missed you very much?"

"Yes," I say. Because they told me.

"Everyone missed you, Ginny. The whole town. The whole state, even. Everyone was looking for you and saying prayers and worrying. They wanted to find you and keep you safe."

That is the problem. Everyone wants to keep me safe but *safe for me* means *not safe for my Baby Doll*. Like this:

(Safe) for Ginny = (−Safe) for Baby Doll

But if I escape and go to Harrington Falls the police will find me. I need to come up with a new secret plan.

"We've seen each other every day since you've been back," Patrice says, "and we'll see each other all next week, as well. At home your parents say that you've been hovering too close to Baby Wendy, and of course that makes them worry. It freaks them out a little bit. They say it's creepy. Your mom, especially. They say you keep trying to bring the baby different things to eat and drink. They say you're trying to sneak up to the nursery all the time. Can you talk a little about that?"

"They aren't feeding it," I say.

Patrice looks at me funny. "What makes you say they aren't feeding it?"

"Because they don't give it milk."

"Your Forever Dad mentioned to me on the phone that this might be confusing for you. You know your Forever Mom is breast-feeding Baby Wendy, right?"

I nod my head yes.

"Then why do you think she isn't feeding it—I mean *her?*"

"Because milk doesn't come from breasts."

"Of course milk comes from breasts. That's what breast-feeding is. No one ever told you how breast-feeding works?"

I shake my head no.

Patrice smiles. "Then I think you'll be happy to hear what I'm about to tell you. Before I explain it, though, I need to ask if you remember the most important rule."

"When Baby Wendy is born you're not allowed to touch her," I say.

"That's right. And Baby Wendy is born. She's here. So you have to make sure you never, ever try to feed the baby yourself. Trust your parents a little, will you? They know what they're doing. Your Forever Mom is doing a great job of feeding Baby Wendy. Now, let's talk about *exactly* how she does it."

EXACTLY 6:44 IN THE MORNING,
MONDAY, OCTOBER 25TH

I don't hear any noise on the other side of the door. My head and face are close, close, close to it. Because I am listening.

I know that my Forever Sister is in there with my Forever Mom. I know that my Forever Mom is *taking excellent care of it* because my Forever Dad and Patrice told me so. But even though I believe them I need to make sure. I need to see.

I close my eyes and listen harder. Now my ears are ringing. My ear is so close to the door that it sounds like listening to the inside of a seashell.

"Ginny?"

I come up fast out of my brain. It is my Forever Dad. At the bottom of the stairs.

"Come down here. Right now. If your mom finds you—"

The door opens right next to my face.

I jump back and almost run into the laundry basket. My Forever Mom is in the doorway.

"Ginny, go downstairs," she says. Then to my Forever Dad she says, "It's all right. I can handle this." She looks at me again. Her eyes get skinny and her mouth turns into a short, short line.

"Ginny, you've *got* to stop sneaking around like this. No more hovering outside my door. This is the second time today. Wendy is fine. Now go downstairs like your dad said."

"Come on, Forever Girl," my Forever Dad says. "I've got the car all warmed up, and it's time to go."

Halloween is in three days. On Sunday. I am in Room Five
eating lunch with Larry and Kayla Zadambidge and Alison Hill because the teachers want me to have *a smooth transition* back to school. Plus my Forever Mom came downstairs for *approximately* three minutes this morning and said there was *a media circus* when I was kidnapped and all the kids at school will try to ask me questions. When I said I've never been to the circus and would like to go see it she said I didn't have to because I was already the main attraction. When I said I didn't understand she said a media circus is when a bunch of reporters come to your house looking for information about you and there are stories about you on television and the radio. She said that a media circus is understandable when there's a kidnapping but when you're coming home with a newborn baby and reporters are sticking cameras in your face and knocking on your door all the time it can make you pretty edgy. Especially when the kid who was kidnapped set the whole thing up and doesn't show any remorse.

After that she went upstairs and shut the door. My Forever Dad brought me to school.

Only the kids who go to Room Five are allowed to eat lunch with me this week. Plus Ms. Carol. Ms. Carol is a new teacher who follows me like Mrs. Wake used to. She is not an old lady. She has long hair and glasses that make her eyes look too big. When I asked Mrs. Lomos where Mrs. Wake was Mrs. Lomos said, "The principal decided it was best for her to move on."

"What are you going to be for Halloween?" says Larry to Alison Hill.

"I don't know yet," says Alison Hill. She is drawing a face on an orange pumpkin.

"Halloween is in three days, Alison Hill," I say. "You'd better decide soon."

"What are you going to be, Ginny?" Larry asks me.

I say, "I'm going to be a witch. Gloria always dressed me up like a witch and she was a witch too. We were witches together. We used to throw spells at each other in the kitchen and do spins on the floor in our socks so our costumes would twirl. Then we flew on our brooms in the living room and up and down the hall."

"There's no such thing as witches," says Kayla Zadambidge. "I'm going to be a queen."

Kayla Zadambidge has long hair. She is pretty and will make a great queen. So I say, "You will make an ugly, ugly queen, Kayla Zadambidge. Alison Hill, you should be Janet Jackson."

"Ginny!" says Ms. Dana.

Alison Hill makes a funny face. "Who's Janet Jackson?"

I put down the pieces of the candy corn that I am putting together. They are orange and yellow and white. I use a mean voice. "What the hell is wrong with you, Alison Hill? Janet Jackson is one of Michael Jackson's sisters."

Ms. Dana looks up from her desk. "Ginny, language!" she says.

Larry starts singing about the light fandango and cartwheels. Alison Hill says, "Maybe I should be a werewolf."

"Werewolves are scary," I say.

"How about a vampire?" says Alison Hill.

"No," I say. "Vampires are scary too. Plus they suck blood."

"How about someone from Star Wars?" says Larry.

"You could be Queen Amidala!" says Alison Hill.

"Or you could be R2-D2! That little dude is *the bomb!*" Larry says.

Then I look at Larry and say, "No, Larry, R2-D2 is a robot. Don't you get it? He's a fucking robot." I am angry, angry, angry.

"Ginny, let's go," says Ms. Dana. She stands up and points to the door. Ms. Carol's eyes get really big for a second behind her glasses and then go back to their regular size.

"What's with the language, babe?" says Larry.

"Ginny, come talk with me in the hallway," says Ms. Dana.

I stand up. I don't answer Larry's question because I am still mad. Because I don't have a new secret plan yet. I need to figure out how to get back to Harrington Falls without the police finding me. Or how to get a ride up to Canada and then have Gloria come meet me there. Or how to get Crystal with a C out of jail so she can kidnap me again. I'm sitting here at school while my Baby Doll is in the apartment with Gloria and no one, no one is around to keep it safe.

"Do you know who helped track you down when you were with Crystal with a C?" says Patrice.

"The man with the gun," I say.

"No. There was someone else. It was extremely lucky that the hunter spotted you, and he did help a lot by calling. But there was another person, too."

Patrice wipes her mouth with a napkin. We are eating brownies.

"It's a confusing time when someone is kidnapped," she says. "There were a lot of people across the country who thought they saw you in different places. When people look hard for a missing person, they make a lot of mistakes. So the police look for patterns. They look for numbers of sightings that are clustered in certain areas, and then they go to those areas."

"Who was the other person?" I ask.

"That's the interesting thing. The person who helped track you down didn't actually see you himself. But he used to know Crystal with a C, and he remembered that she had a vacation cabin. The hunter called from the town where the cabin was, and the police went there to investigate."

"Who was he?"

"Your dad."

"My Forever Dad knew where the cabin was?"

"No. Your Birth Dad."

"I don't have a Birth Dad."

"Yes, you do. Everyone does."

I don't say anything. I don't know who my Birth Dad is even though everyone has one. Maybe it's because I'm not *everyone*.

"Ginny, your Birth Dad helped us find you. Your parents didn't want to even mention him at first, but now— Anyway, Gloria left him when you were born. Literally at the hospital. She kept in touch with him over the years by phone and email, but she wouldn't let him see you. During the investigation he met your Forever Parents, and now he says he wants to get to know you."

I think. And think some more. "Why?" I say.

"Because he's your dad. Until last week, he didn't know where you lived."

I think. I think and think.

"Ginny, how do you feel about all this?"

"I don't know," I say.

"That's fair," says Patrice. "It's happening kind of fast. But I want you to know that your Forever Parents think it's pretty exciting. They think it's a great idea for you to meet your Birth Dad. As soon as you're ready."

"As soon as I'm ready?" I say.

"Yes, as soon as you're ready."

"When will that be?"

Patrice laughs. "Knowing you, I'd say in about two seconds."

We are in the parking lot at school and I am putting on my ghost costume. It is a sheet with holes in it so my eyes can see out. I was going to wear my new witch costume but then I changed my mind. Because I don't want to be me anymore. I want to be able to be invisible instead. I want to be (-Ginny) because my Baby Doll is all alone with Gloria and I'm mostly not smart enough to figure out how to go get it.

But I don't say that to anybody. I'm keeping it a secret in my brain.

When I changed my mind about the costume my Forever Mom said, "Honestly, Ginny, if we'd decided this last week, we could have bought two new sets of sheets for the price of that witch costume. And you could still be wearing the exact same thing you're wearing now."

But that wasn't a question.

I stand next to the car and wait for my Forever Mom to help straighten my costume. She straightens it at the bottom and moves the top so that my eyes can see through the holes we cut together. "There," she says.

"Ooooooh!" I say in a high voice. Because that is what a ghost says.

"Very good," my Forever Mom says. "You make an excellent ghost."

I say, "Ooooooh!" again because I am still wearing the costume. Plus I like making scary sounds. They make me feel strong.

"All right," says my Forever Mom. "It's time to go in." This is the first time she has gone anywhere with me since my Forever Sister was born. My Forever Dad is home watching it.

There are lots and lots of cars in the parking lot but I stop counting after nine. When we get to the door my Forever Mom pulls it open. Inside we hear music. We follow the hallway to the gym where there are kids from the whole school and all of them are dressed up and moving fast. There are orange and black decorations everywhere. A lot of the little kids have butterfly and pumpkin costumes. Some are dressed up as trains and cars. There are bigger kids dressed as M&M's and werewolves and zombies.

I start to pick at my fingers.

There are witches and princesses. Someone is even dressed like a cow. And all of them are making noise. So much noise I can't stand it. The music is way too loud. A lot of the kids are yelling and trying to scare each other. I see vampires and gypsies. I see a giant bug and a cat. I even see a kid dressed up as a baby. It is like all the things that are in my brain came out.

So I take my costume off. I pull the sheet down off my head and stand there holding it.

"Ginny, why did you do that?" says my Forever Mom.

And I say, "We need to leave now."

And she says, "Why?"

"Because it's too loud."

"Ginny," my Forever Mom says, "we just got here. I'm trying to spend time with you without the baby." She looks back and forth fast and lifts her foot and puts it down again. "Don't you want to walk around and find your friends?" she says. "What about Larry and Kayla? What about Alison? I bet Ms. Dana is here, too."

I think she asked me a question but I can't remember what it was so I don't say anything. A small boy in a green mask runs past me. His shoulder touches my costume. "Ow!" I yell and step back. Someone else knocks into me. I *recoil* and almost bump into a boy who is dressed like a football player. He says, "Hey!" and makes an angry face. I *recoil* again.

My Forever Mom's lip rises. "Fine," she says. Through her teeth. "No one can say I didn't try. Now let's go."

She shoves her hand out. I used to like holding her hand but I don't take it. Because I'm not who I used to be anymore and I don't think my Forever Mom likes the person I turned into. I don't think I like the person I turned into either.

We walk back out of the gym and through the hallway and back outside. The air is cold but it feels good on my face. Halloween is not the same as it used to be when I was with Gloria. Nothing is the same as it used to be. I am not Ginny anymore.

I am not Ginny.

I am *(-Ginny)*.

And that scares me, scares me, scares me. Because I don't know that girl.

My Forever Dad makes a breathing sound. "Ginny, please, stop checking your watch. I'm trying to talk with you."

We are at the kitchen table. My Forever Sister is crying. It does that a lot. The sound makes me want to run upstairs and pick it up because I know *exactly* what to do to help it. But I don't because I remember the most important rule.

"There are two things we need to talk about," he says.

I am happy. He is using numbers and numbers make me glad.

"First, you have to stay away from your mother's room. From our room, I mean. She's in there all the time now with the baby because she needs some privacy. You can't go in there anymore for any reason, and you can't stand right outside the door listening. And when your mom comes downstairs with the baby, you have to stop telling her how to take care of it. No more advice on what to feed it or what it needs. And the most important thing is that you have to stop hovering so much. Give your mom some space, okay? She won't put the baby down because she knows you'll bend down over it and stare. It scares her, Ginny. It scares me, too. I know that's hard to hear, but it's the truth."

"What is the second thing we need to talk about?" I ask. Because he finished with the first.

"The second thing is that I have the first letter," he says. He puts a folded piece of paper on the table. His face looks a lot redder than it used to look and he takes more pills in the morning now. At night too. And sometimes he lies down on the couch to rest after he finishes talking to me and closes his eyes. And breathes deep and slow. "From your Birth Dad. Are you ready to read it?"

I nod my head yes.

"Getting to know your Birth Dad will be easier this way," he says. "If the two of you exchange letters for a while, you'll have more to talk about when you finally meet."

"When will we finally meet?"

"We're not sure yet. We're going to give it a while and see how things go before we set a date."

Upstairs the crying stops. I take a deep breath and uncurl my fingers. "Can I read the letter now?" I say.

"Sure."

So I unfold the paper and read.

Dear Ginny,

I'm really glad to have the chance to talk with you. It sure has been a long time. By now you know that I'm your father. I met Gloria when a buddy of mine wanted a cat. He looked into Maine coons and set up a time to go see some. At your mom's house. My buddy didn't get a cat but I got a date. Your mom was the smartest girl I ever met. We dated for a while and then she said she was going to have a baby. I wanted to marry her. We even had plans for a wedding but she left with you a few days after you were born. I left to go to work and when I came back that night to the hospital she was gone. Apparently she went to Canada. I found her later back in Maine but she said she didn't want to see me. I think another man was involved and maybe drugs too. Anyway it was over between us so I stayed away. Dads don't really have any rights. I stayed in touch with her over the phone and email but that was the most she would allow. Then after a few years she changed her number. She stopped answering my emails and cut me out of the picture completely.

Then I heard about the kidnapping so I went to the police and told them everything I could remember. I said I didn't think Gloria could pull off something like that because she's not so great at keeping cool and they asked who could so I said her sister Crystal. Then I remembered the summer house she bought and the rest is history.

But I learned that day that you weren't with Gloria anymore and that you were adopted. Your new folks seem pretty nice. They're open to us getting to know one another. I hope you're open to that too.

Some things about me. I drive truck. I haul big rigs up and down the coast. I'm not home a lot but I have a nice place and a girlfriend who takes care of things when I'm away. We even have a dog. A beagle named Sammy. We don't have any kids of our own though.

So what do you say? Will you write me a letter? I hope you will.

Your Old Dad,

Rick

So I say, "Wait—why did he write that?" And point to the very last word.

"You mean *Rick*?"

I nod my head yes.

"That's his name," my Forever Dad says.

"His name is *Rick*?"

"It starts with the letter *R*," he says. "You know, like *red*."

"Humph," I say and I start picking at the skin around my fingernails.

Rick is a small name. It sounds like *lick* or *tick* or *dick* which is a bad word. *Rick* is a fast name. It makes your mouth feel like too much cherry candy or like you have something small and bright made out of red plastic in there.

"How are you feeling?" he asks.

"I feel hungry," I say. "And I feel like I should have a beverage. I should watch a video on my DVD player in my room and *have a little drink*. When is Rick coming over?"

"He isn't coming over," my Forever Dad says. "But he wants to know if you'll write to him. Do you want to write him a letter?"

"Mostly," I say. "But not today. It's not on my list."

"You could put it on your list if you wanted," he says. "I could help you write it."

I shake my head no. "Maybe tomorrow," I say. "Can I watch my video now?"

"Don't you want to talk about the letter?"

"No."

Because I don't. I already read it and I know what it says. It says that my dad *drives truck* and he wants to get to know me. I'm guessing the truck has plenty of room for all my things. I need time to go in my brain to think.

"I need to watch a video now," I say. I stand up.

"All right, then," my Forever Dad says. "You can watch your video. We'll talk about this some other time."

"And I need a beverage."

"Then I'll get you a beverage."

I am in bed thinking. My quilt is spread out over my belly and legs. I am lying on my back.

In my head I need to say what happens to me right after it happens. I need to say it all back to myself because it helps me understand. That's why I talk inside my brain. It's like a diary except I'm not so good at writing. I used to say it all out loud when I was in the apartment but Donald said it drove him bat-shit crazy. Then he said I should keep my mouth closed and not walk around with it open because it makes me look like a cave girl. No one can hear what I say inside my head because that's where my brain is. It helps me do things when no one is looking. Like when I used to look for mayonnaise and ketchup packets and food in the garbage when Gloria and Donald or one of her other man-friends were upstairs.

But now I have to get ready to write a letter to Rick. I can't just say the words in my head and leave them there. I have to write them. On paper. Writing is hard work but I need to do it because I have to get Rick to give me a ride up to Canada. I bet he has *dual citizenship* just like Gloria and Crystal with a C. And me. But I have to get him to tell Gloria to meet us there. That is my new secret plan.

So I will talk the letter in my head tonight and then I will ask my Forever Dad to help me type it tomorrow. The letter will go *exactly* like this:

Dear Rick,
I do not love the name Rick. No offense. I'm just saying. Maybe we could call you Richard or Kevin or even Bobby. We can't call you Michael Jackson because Michael Jackson is my favorite singer-dancer in the whole world. I have a picture of him on my wall in my room plus the calendar. He's my biggest fan.

I am writing you a letter because I put it on my list. I want you to come take me in your truck and bring me to Canada. Tell Gloria to come there with my Baby Doll and meet us. We can all live there together unless you want to go back to live with your girlfriend and Sammy instead. I'm OK with that. If you can't come right now then please go to Harrington Falls to see if my Baby Doll is OK. Gloria needs help taking care of it. Don't let her go away for a few days like she always does. Help her like Crystal with a C used to help her. Show her how to change its diaper and how to give it plenty of food. Bring some milk with you because there won't be any in the refrigerator. And even though it's too little to understand please tell my Baby Doll that I'm sorry about the suitcase. I tried to keep it safe but I got scared when the police came.

Something you should know about me is that I get mad when people tell me they'll do something and then they don't do it. You should underline that part and then save this note in your pocket and not forget. Write back

soon so I'll know if you're going to help me or not. Plus we have to figure out a way to get my Forever Parents to let me go with you. I don't think kidnapping will work this time.
Yours Truly,
Ginny Moon

I say the letter over and over until it says *exactly* what I want it to say. Tomorrow I will ask my Forever Dad to help me write it all down.

EXACTLY 4:17,
WEDNESDAY, NOVEMBER 3RD

When I got to school this morning I looked out the window of the bus to the place where I saw the Green Car on September 14th. I wanted to see it but it was not there. I remember driving in the Green Car near the window that was broken. The plastic used to move back and forth and sometimes Gloria would stop to put more duct tape on it. Sometimes we used to sleep in the car when we went somewhere. Gloria said it was like camping but a lot more fun because when you go camping you have to sleep on the ground. *We don't want to sleep on the ground, do we?* she used to say. I didn't answer because I didn't talk yet. I learned to talk when I was five.

That was a long time ago.

And now a man named Rick says he is my Birth Dad. I would like to get to know him but first I need to get him to bring me to Canada.

I come up out of my brain. I am standing on the bottom step waiting for my Forever Mom to turn around in the kitchen. I don't want to say anything because I don't want to make her mad. My Forever Sister is sleeping which is why my Forever Mom is downstairs. She comes down here sometimes when she thinks I'm not home or when I'm in my room with the door closed. I haven't seen her in three days.

"Are you staring at me, Ginny?" she says. Without turning.

I start to answer but then I stop. I am starting to forget how to talk with her. I only know how to talk with my Forever Dad now.

"Ginny, I asked if you're staring at me."

"I'm waiting for you to turn around," I say.

"And are you staring while you wait?"

Staring means you look with your eyes for a long time and don't move. Some people say it's *tedious*.

"Yes," I say. I put my head down. "I am sorry."

My Forever Mom turns around. She picks up a pan and puts it on the stove. "All right, what's up?" she says.

She does not mean the ceiling or the sky so I try hard not to look in those places. "I wrote a letter to Rick," I say. "I used my best handwriting."

When I say *Rick* it sounds quiet and dumb like there is a piece of poop on the floor and everyone is looking at it. Poop always looks quiet and dumb. Sometimes I feel that way too.

"I know," my Forever Mom says. "Your dad told me. Do you want me to hear it?"

"Yes, I do," I say and then I read it.

Dear Rick,

My name is Ginny and I am 14 years old. I love Michael Jackson. He died on June 25, 2009. He has all the best moves. I also like to listen to Diana Ross. Do you know what she did? A duet with Michael Jackson.

But I am glad we can write letters. I never knew I had a Birth Dad even though everyone has one. Can you come visit?
Sincerely,
Ginny Moon

Because I found out that I can't say what I really want to say in the letter when my Forever Dad helped me type it today. Today we spent *exactly* twenty-three minutes talking and typing. It started out the way I had it in my head last night but then I figured out that I had to change it. I will say what I need to say to Rick when he comes to visit. I will say it quietly in his ear. It will be *our little secret* which is something I heard in a movie.

My Forever Mom says, "You really think you're ready to meet him already?"

I nod my head yes.

"That's awfully trusting of you. Don't you want to see what sort of person he is? Through his letters, I mean."

I don't know what it means to see *what sort of person he is* or *through his letters* so I don't say anything.

"Don't you want to see if you can trust him?" she says.

"How do I know if I can trust him?"

She laughs. I am surprised but I really like the way it sounds. "I suppose you're right," she says. "For now, let's just send the letter. Leave it there on the counter, and we'll type it up and send it to him in an email. There's still no way we're letting you anywhere near a computer. So we'll type it all up and send it and then wait to see what Rick says when he emails back. If it all looks good, we'll go ahead and schedule a visit. Probably at the park. You know, meeting your Birth Dad might just turn out to be a very good thing for all of us. Who knows what the future will bring?"

I can think of a lot of people who might know but I don't say any of their names. Then my Forever Mom shuts the stove off and picks up the pan she was using and scoops some scrambled eggs onto a plate. I remember how Crystal with a C let me eat her eggs. But my Forever Mom doesn't put the plate down on the table for me. Instead she takes a fork out of the drawer and takes a bite. She chews and swallows. "How do you feel now that you've written the letter?" she says.

"I feel like I should eat something," I say.

She wipes her mouth with a napkin. "I mean, how do you feel *about what you wrote*? Are you happy with it? Is there anything else you might want to add before we send the letter to Rick?"

"I might want to add some hisses," I say even though *hissing* is not the same as *saying something*. "Like I do at school." It's what the Maine coons used to do when they met someone new. It makes me feel strong. I do a lot of things that the Maine coons do.

"Wait—you hiss at people at school?"

"Yes," I say.

"When do you hiss at people?"

"At lunch and when people laugh at me or say mean things. Sometimes I growl too but hissing is easier."

"Why haven't you told us this before? How often do you hiss at people?"

And that is two questions together and my Forever Mom is talking fast and her voice is getting louder. I start picking at my fingers.

"Ginny, hissing at people is not a good thing," she says. "You aren't allowed to do it anymore, ever. It's against the rules."

I look away and say, "Well dang!"

"What do you mean, '*Well dang!*'?"

I put my hands up in the air like Crystal with a C did and let them fall back down again. "I like hissing at people! It makes them laugh! Then they hiss back and a teacher hears them and makes them leave me alone!"

"Ginny, they laugh because they're making fun of you. It's weird to hiss at people. Only cats do that."

"No—*I* do that too!" I say and it's true, 100 percent. I learned how to do it a long time ago.

"I mean only cats are *supposed* to do that. Forever Girls aren't supposed to hiss. Ever. You can't act like a wild animal."

"Well dang!" I say again. I wipe my eyes. "I'm going to my room! No more Chinese Checkers! Just stay upstairs!"

In homeroom my teacher Mrs. Henkel asks me how my day is so I say, "My Birth Dad wrote me another letter last night so I wrote one back to him."

The whole class looks at me and is completely silent. I have never heard them be this quiet before. Then Mrs. Henkel says, "Ginny, don't you mean *your Forever Dad?*"

And I say, "No, I mean Rick. He's the man who Gloria left at the hospital. He *drives truck.*"

"You mean he drives *a* truck."

I shake my head. "No, Sarah, I don't. Don't you think I know what he said? He's *my* Birth Dad, not yours."

"Don't call Mrs. Henkel by her first name," Ms. Carol whispers. She blinks her too-big eyes.

The kids in the class are still completely quiet. I like them better that way.

"Have you been talking with your father?" she asks.

"Yes, I have," I say.

"Does Mrs. Lomos know about this?"

"Yes," I say again and I see Ms. Carol nodding. To Mrs. Henkel.

At *exactly* 10:08 during social studies I go to the bathroom. Ms. Carol comes too. When I come back to class Michelle Whipple says, "Ginny, do you *drive truck*?"

And I say, "No, I do not *drive truck*. My Birth Dad *drives truck*. I can't *drive truck* because I'm still a kid."

Michelle Whipple laughs so I hiss at her even though I'm not supposed to. Then she says, "What, are you going to scratch me or something?"

"No, I am not going to scratch you. What do you think I am, a cat?"

"You sure sound like one!" says Michelle Whipple. Then she laughs again and looks at me. I see her eyes looking at me while she smiles. I want to blast her with my eyes like Cyclops or stick her with claws like Wolverine or make fire go on her but I don't have superpowers or matches so instead I *attack*.

I don't want Michelle Whipple to ever see me again so I am going to take her eyes out. I grab her hair and pull it hard and try to hold her still because if she is moving I can't get my fingers close enough to her face. I knock a chair down and push a desk out of the way. I grunt and show my teeth and screech just like Bubbles. Michelle Whipple whips her head back and forth and screams and tries to hit my hands away with hers but I am attacking like a chimp and in a few seconds I will have one of her eyes in my hand.

Ms. Carol grabs me before I can get it out. She pulls me away from Michelle Whipple and holds me down so that I can't move. I am still very angry but I am not angry at Ms. Carol so I stop. But Michelle Whipple is screaming, "You crazy bitch! Crazy bitch!" over and over and so I yell back at her, "You just stop that, Michelle Whipple! You are hurting my ears! This is *tedious*!"

EXACTLY 3:31,
FRIDAY, NOVEMBER 5TH

I was suspended from school so I stayed home today. Now I am talking with Patrice.

"Your Forever Parents tell me you got into a fight at school. Can you tell me what happened?"

"Michelle Whipple made me angry," I say.

"Oh?"

"She said I sound like a cat."

"*Were* you sounding like a cat?" says Patrice. "I remember you used to make cat noises a few years ago when you were with Carla and Mike."

Carla and Mike were my first two Forever Parents. I ran away from them when I was nine years old. I told them I was going outside to play and on my way out the door I took Carla's purse because it had money in it plus a debit card. I walked around town looking for a map that would help me get back to Gloria's apartment but I got confused by all the cars plus I didn't know which town she lived in. The police found me and took me to the hospital and then they brought me back to Carla and Mike. Now I know that Gloria lives in

Harrington Falls but I can't go there because the police will find me. Like Crystal with a C said. So I need to ask Rick to be part of my secret plan instead.

"Ginny?"

"What?"

"Did you say you were making cat noises?"

I nod my head yes.

"It sounds like we're falling into some of our old patterns. We'll have to talk more about that later. For now, tell me what's going on with Baby Wendy. Are you seeing her more often?"

I shake my head no. "I want to see it but it's always upstairs with my Forever Mom."

"Do you miss your Forever Mom?"

I nod my head yes.

"She's worried, Ginny. Your mom is worried that you're going to hurt the baby."

I pick at my fingers. I remember the plastic electronic baby. The things I did to it. With my mouth I say, "I am not going to hurt the baby."

"I know that. And what you did in the first place, giving out your address to Gloria, getting yourself kidnapped. The reporters gave your parents a really hard time when you were away. They'd just brought a baby home and were learning how to be new parents, but the police and the news vans—"

Patrice stops talking. I take a bite of a chocolate chip cookie. I take two more bites fast and push the rest in my mouth.

"Look," says Patrice, "when you argue with your Forever Mom all the time and get in fights at school and then keep trying to sneak upstairs to feed Baby Wendy— And let's not forget the upcoming court case. They have to be witnesses. But it's all too much. A lot of it is completely understandable, considering what you've been through. But for her, it's just too much. Do you see that?"

I don't so I don't say anything.

Patrice looks down. She looks up at me and looks down again. "We're hoping that you really like Rick," she says. "We're really, really hoping. Did you bring the letter he sent to you this morning? Did your parents print it out and give it to you?"

That was two questions but still I nod my head yes.

"Can we read it together?"

I take it out. It is in my back pocket folded in eight rectangles. I open it and give it to Patrice. She reads it out loud.

Dear Ginny,
Yes, I think it would be good if we met sometime soon. Maybe if it all works out you can come visit for a few days and hang out with your old dad. See what he's like and give everyone a break for a while. I don't live too far away. I'm on the road right now and won't be back until the week after next. It's a long haul. Then I have a break for a few days before heading out again that Sunday. Maybe we can find a time before that to meet at the park, like your new dad said.
   Say, do you like to watch football? I bet you don't but if you do I wonder what your favorite team is. I know you like Michael Jackson a lot. Do you play any sports at school?
Your Old Dad,
Rick

"He doesn't live too far away," I say.

"That's right," says Patrice.

"I could go see him and give everyone a break when he gets back."

"I know this is all pretty exciting," says Patrice, "but you'll have to meet Rick a few times before you go to his house."

I look down at the ground. I am thinking.

"Ginny, do you know what the word *respite* means?" Patrice asks.

I shake my head no.

"It means *taking a little break*. I know it's awfully soon, but like I said— Anyway, your parents are hoping that after you get to know Rick a little better, you can go have a *respite* with him. That way they can spend some time alone together with Wendy, and you can get to know your Birth Dad. He's so, so happy to have finally found you. And after that—well, we'll see. What do you think?"

I nod my head yes three times. "Yes," I say. "I think it's a great idea." But Rick won't be home for *approximately* two weeks. I don't know if my Baby Doll will be safe with Gloria until then.

"Honestly, I think it's a little soon myself, but it's much better than the other alternative your mom and dad are thinking about. So you'll be going to meet Rick on Saturday the 20th."

I sit up straight. "Where will I go to meet him?"

"To the park, like he said. The arrangements were made right around lunchtime. You'll go there with both of your Forever Parents on Saturday the 20th, and your Grammy will come out to watch Wendy."

"I start basketball next week," I say to Patrice.

"That's right," she says. "Special Olympics starts back up this month. Maybe you could mention that to Rick in your next letter. Maybe you could invite him to come watch some of your games."

In my brain I picture Rick. My Birth Dad. He is sitting on the bleachers at school watching me make hook shots and jump shots and layups. Rick is not a big man. He will be a small man with skinny shoulders and long black hair and a small nose. He will smile all the time and wear white, white socks with black shoes. And big sunglasses.

He will be my biggest fan.

"And we should probably talk about the interview," says Patrice.

I come up out of my brain and make sure my mouth is shut tight and look up at the ceiling like I didn't hear. Because I don't want to go to the *interview*. Thinking about the *interview* makes me want to climb into a suitcase and zip myself in. Because at the *interview* I have to talk with a *detective* and tell him all the things Crystal with a C did and said. Instead of going to the trial. But I don't want to talk with a *detective* even if a bunch of social workers will be there. Because *detective* is another word for *police officer*.

"It's coming up soon," says Patrice. "But maybe we can talk about it on the phone in a day or two. Would that be all right?"

I come up fast out of my brain. "Yes, that would be all right," I say.

The secretaries in the office at school are smiling at my Forever Sister. It is on the counter asleep in its car seat. My Forever Mom is standing at the counter smiling while the secretaries make their lips look like round circles and say "Oh!" and "*So* cute!" and "B-*eau*-tiful!" It is like they remember only long vowel sounds.

I am sitting on the edge of a long bench right next to a garbage can. There are lots of crumpled papers inside and some shavings from a pencil sharpener. A cinnamon oatmeal granola bar wrapper and a brown apple core with *exactly* two bites left on the side that I can see.

"And how is your husband?" one of the secretaries says. The older one. I know she doesn't like me one bit. She's here every time I come into the office to talk with the principal. She always tells me to sit in the same place. The far, far end of the long wooden bench that is in front of the glass wall facing the hallway. It is like the spot at the end of the bench is only for me.

"I understand they had a hard time finding someone to fill in for him up at the high school. And they say he's got *just* enough sick days to cover the rest of the year. He's doing the right thing, of course. I mean, no one would ever question that. It's just that a whole school year is a long time. And what about you? Is your partner able to take all your patients? *So* glad *you* came in with the baby!"

She glances at me. Like I am a dog who chewed someone's shoes. I make a frowning face at her.

"He's doing just fine," says my Forever Mom. "Today he's at the doctor's—high blood pressure—which is why I'm here for Ginny's intake. And yes, Dr. Win is taking my patients for now. I don't know what I'd do without her."

Then the other secretary says, "I think someone's waking up!"

My Forever Sister's foot moves. The two secretaries take big breaths and hold them. Their eyes and mouths get big and freeze.

My Forever Sister goes back to sleep.

Then the secretaries start talking. "Is she eating rice cereal? And is she sleeping through the night? You know, I used to give my daughters rice cereal in a bottle right before—"

In my brain I remember my Baby Doll. It never had rice cereal or people to smile at it. Or a car seat or a mom who wrapped it up in nice blankets.

My leg starts kicking the leg of the bench with the back of my heel.

"Ginny, would you please stop that?" says my Forever Mom without looking because she is looking at my Forever Sister who is asleep like a doll or a dead cat or something. Like a plastic electronic baby that doesn't even move. They don't understand that when a baby sleeps it's time to leave it alone and go find food. Find something you can chew up so that it's soft enough to put in my Baby Doll's mouth and help it swallow. Go find something to eat so my own belly won't be so tight. And push my arms out straight and move my shoulders because I've been holding my Baby Doll so long to keep it happy that my whole body hurts, hurts, hurts.

"Ginny, stop!" says my Forever Mom.

I kick hard one last time and swing my leg at the garbage can. It makes a loud noise and knocks over. I am glad. My Forever Sister's tiny fists rise above the edge of the car seat. The secretaries and my Forever Mom all make breathing sounds and look at it. Then at me. With angry faces.

"Ginny," my Forever Mom says, "can you just, please, sit there and be patient? And pick up that garbage can. You almost woke Wendy up."

I get up and bend down and pick up the garbage can. I put the crumpled papers back in. I pick up the apple core. On the other side is a whole other bite I didn't see. I want to put the apple core behind my back and hide it but I won't because everyone is watching. Patrice told me how my Forever Mom breastfeeds Baby Wendy but I still feel like I have to find food for it and chew it up to help it eat.

I look at the apple core in my hand. I fight hard to make myself drop it back in the garbage.

"How do you like being a big sister for the first time, Ginny?" the younger secretary says.

It is a question she shouldn't have asked. Because I don't know how to answer it. To answer it I would have to be nine years old again on the other side of Forever. I would have to subtract myself from this side in order to get back.

"Ginny?"

"What?"

"Do you like being a big sister?"

I let out a big breath. I nod my head yes.

I am in the car going to Special Olympics with my Forever Dad. I am wearing my blue T-shirt and short sweatpants, the ones that show my sneakers and socks. The laces are pulled nice and tight. I am *ready for anything.*

When we get to the parking lot at school there are a lot of cars. It's dark and so it's hard to see. My Forever Dad reminds me not to open the door and jump right out. I need to wait for him to come and open it. It's not a good idea to run across a parking lot because you could get hit by a car or a minivan or maybe even a motorcycle. Motorcycles are *extremely dangerous* if you aren't wearing a helmet.

As I walk I think about Gloria. If she knew my practice was at six every Wednesday she might come to see it. She might even try to kidnap me. She is *impulsive* enough to try. And then she would get in trouble with the police. So I look around. I don't see the Green Car anywhere in the parking lot but I do see a police car. I stand close to my Forever Dad. He waves at the police officer in the car and the police officer waves back.

I put on a frowning face and cross my arms.

In the school we walk to the gym. When we get there I see Brenda Richardson and her mom and dad. Brenda Richardson is a new kid who goes to Room Five. I see Larry and Kayla Zadambidge and a lot of other kids. Some of them are kids from school but some are from other towns. I don't know their names. They have so many different heads and they are moving so fast that I can't count them. Larry sees me and waves one of his arm braces.

Ms. Dana is one of the coaches. She shows us how to line up with partners and pass the basketball back and forth. She shows us how to shoot layups and foul shots. She shows us how to put our arms up so that people on the other team can't pass the ball. There's a lot to learn but I'm good at learning so I like it.

The other coach is Coach Dan. He's mostly nice but he's also a man so I don't talk with him. I talk only with Ms. Dana.

Everyone at Special Olympics gives each other hugs when they make mistakes but I don't like hugs so I get high fives instead. I love Special Olympics. It is like Bubbles finding a lot of other chimps or Little Michael Jackson finding his brothers or Michelle Whipple finding a whole bunch of Michelle Whipples even though Michelle Whipple is *a real asshole* which is mostly an expression. Because a person can't be an asshole for real. But Special Olympics is the best. It is *the bomb* which is what Larry says and I can't wait to come back to Special Olympics next week on Wednesday at *exactly* six o'clock after supper.

Alison Hill throws the ball to me. It bounces far down the court. I have been practicing only a little while but now I need a drink.

I see my Forever Dad and walk to him. The time is *exactly* 6:13. He is sitting on the bleachers with the other Forever Parents talking with a man wearing a leather Patriots jacket and a leather Patriots hat. I ask my Forever Dad for my water bottle.

He hands it to me and I take a drink. "Are you having a good time out there?" he says.

"Yes, I am," I say when I finish drinking because if you talk while you drink the water will fall out of your mouth. Juice does that too. And milk. When milk falls out of your mouth you have to wipe it fast with a cloth to soak it up and suck on it. In my brain I see my Baby Doll lying on my quilt.

Then I remember. I remember what I'm supposed to be doing. I'm supposed to be back in the apartment taking care of my Baby Doll. Or up in Canada taking care of it. I am not supposed to be playing a game.

Someone yells my name. I don't know who it is and I don't care. Because I am sinking into my brain.

"Ms. Dana taught you a new kind of pass tonight," my Forever Dad says.

I don't see him. "I need to go back," I say.

"All right," he says.

I turn and take two steps.

"Ginny?"

I come up out of my brain and look around. I see the bleachers and the lights and the gym all around me. I am confused.

"Aren't you forgetting something?" my Forever Dad says.

I look at my hands. I am still holding my water bottle. I give it back to him. He laughs. The sound makes me smile a little.

Then I hear another voice. The man in the leather Patriots jacket is laughing with us but he is laughing more than I want him to. More than he's supposed to be. It is not a mean laugh but he is laughing way too much.

I look at him hard. He stops and looks away.

"Oh," my Forever Dad says. "I almost forgot. I was talking with Grammy and Granddad. They asked if you might want to spend a few hours at their house on Saturday while your mom and I go somewhere. What do you think of that?"

"I can't sleep over on Saturday, November 20th," I say. The man in the leather Patriots jacket looks up at the ceiling. "Or on Friday, November 19th. Because on Saturday I'm going to the park to meet Rick and on Friday I need to get ready."

"Good job remembering," my Forever Dad says. "But I meant this Saturday, the 13th. And how do you feel about going to meet Rick, since you mentioned it?"

"I think it's a great idea," I say.

"Good. Now, let's get you back out on the court! You sure do have some super-duper basketball moves."

I go back to the court and when I get there Ms. Dana hands me a ball and tells me to pass it to Alison Hill. I look back at the bleachers. My Forever Dad is talking to the man in the leather Patriots jacket again. I still don't know who he is but I feel different when I look at him. He makes me want to hiss.

I am at the Blue House even though I should be at school. I have to miss school today so I can go to the *interview*. With my Forever Dad. We are leaving right after breakfast.

I go into the bathroom to brush my teeth and pee and then I check the whiteboard. It is on the wall next to the kitchen on the way into the dining room. My Forever Dad put the whiteboard up when he stopped working at school for the rest of the year to take care of me. He said the whiteboard helps me *order my day* and *not be so anxious*. Every day he writes on it what we're going to do. Today the whiteboard says *Go to Wagon Hill* and then *Go to the interview* and then *Out for lunch* and then *Home again, home again, jiggety-jig.*

Which is from a nursery rhyme.

We are going to Wagon Hill to get some exercise. Exercise makes us feel better, he always says. "And today I need you feeling really great so that we can get through the interview."

I go to the table and sit down at my spot. Next to my milk are two pieces of toast and some vanilla yogurt and a bowl with nine grapes. "Where will we go at Wagon Hill?" I ask. I don't like going to Wagon Hill because we always go for walks there. There are lots and lots of different paths to walk on and they all join up together so the walk never ends until someone says *It's time to go home* but I never know when that will be.

"Oh, probably just for a little walk. Don't worry—we have to be back to the car by nine-thirty in order to be on time for the interview, so we'll aim to be back at the parking lot by then."

I like that my Forever Dad helps me know when we'll do things. He makes me feel calm and safe. Almost like Michael Jackson.

When we get to Wagon Hill we park the car and walk up out of the parking lot. There are big open fields everywhere with a river far away through the trees and an old wagon up at the top. There are paths that lead through the fields. In the summer the grass in the fields is so tall that the paths are like a maze. Someone cuts them out with a giant lawn mower.

"Do you want to walk to the river, or to see the wagon?" my Forever Dad says. He is wearing his green fall jacket and breathing heavy because we are walking.

So I say, "If we go to the river can we go swimming?"

"Ginny, it's a warm day for November," he says, "but it's still much too cold to go swimming."

So I say, "If we go to the wagon can we go for a ride in it?"

He says no again because the wagon is an antique and there aren't any horses.

So then I say, "Well how can I know where I want to go if there's nothing fun to do in either direction?"

"It's not about having fun today, Forever Girl," he says. "It's about getting some exercise." He stops and leans against a big rock. "Just hold on a minute."

I look at my watch. He makes a breathing sound.

"This is really *tedious*," I say.

My Forever Dad laughs. And stands up again. "No, it isn't,"

he says. "I like spending time with you, you know. We haven't really been able to do that since the summer. Let's go up to the wagon. It's a shorter distance."

It gets windier as we walk up the hill. I have my red windbreaker on and I am glad. Then we get to the wagon. It is painted bright green. There are three other people there. Their jackets are open enough so that I can see what they're wearing. None of them are wearing Michael Jackson shirts.

My Forever Dad sits down on a bench and leans forward with his arms on his knees. I ask if I can climb into the wagon. He says yes. So I climb up into the back. The floor of the wagon is made of six long boards. It looks like a place where Michael Jackson could perform so I start snapping the fingers of my right hand down next to my right leg. *One, two, three, four.* Then I bend my left knee and start moving my chin up and down.

I sing.

I sing "Billie Jean" in a low soft voice and when I get to the chorus I get louder and louder. The wind is blowing and my hair is blowing back. I look out over the fields and at the sky and sing just like Michael Jackson does. I say *"Ooh-hoo!"* and *"Ow!"* in all the right places.

Then I sing "Bad."

And "Beat It."

I do all the spins and stand on my tippy-toes. When I finish I see the three people who aren't wearing Michael Jackson shirts. They are standing below me on the ground looking up. Their mouths are open. They have funny looks on their faces but then one of them starts clapping and the other two join in.

I see my Forever Dad too. He is standing next to one of the wagon wheels. I don't remember seeing him move there. "That was great, Ginny, but it's time to get down. We have to go," he says.

I stomp my foot and make a frowning face. "I don't want to," I say. "I want to do another number."

"Ginny, it's time. Get down *now*," he says.

"I don't *want* to!" I say louder.

I am *escalating* the situation. Patrice says I do that because it makes me feel in control. I put my face in the wind and let my hair blow back again. I put my hand up in it just like Michael Jackson does and smooth it back.

The three people smile at my Forever Dad and turn away. It is like my audience is leaving so I stomp my foot loud against the boards of the floor. A lady looks back but then turns away again and keeps walking.

"Ginny, please," my Forever Dad says. He puts his hand on his chest and looks away and takes a deep breath. "I can't get upset about this. I'm not supposed to yell or get too excited. Just come down. Come down now. Get down and we'll take a walk. Then we can go to the interview and get some lunch. You can pick the place."

I climb down.

I like my Forever Dad a lot because he's nice. Not as nice as Michael Jackson. Plus he really can't dance. Or sing. But he's still pretty okay.

EXACTLY 10:37 AT NIGHT, TUESDAY, NOVEMBER 16TH

I am on my hands and knees on the carpet. My Baby Doll is somewhere crying but I can't find it. I don't know if it's in my room. I don't know if *I'm* in my room. I am awake but it's dark out and it's dark inside my brain. When I'm deep inside there it's all the same place. All the houses I've ever been in are still in my head and so when I wake up at night with my eyes open I can still fall into any of them by accident.

The crying is getting louder. I can't turn on the light because Gloria will see me. Or Donald. I have to find my Baby Doll and hide it before they come. I will put my quilt over it and put it in the closet. Or maybe out the window.

I find a bed. I can feel the mattress and the sheets. I check behind it and under the covers. My hand touches a heat register. I crawl around the whole room looking and looking. My Baby Doll is not anywhere but I can still hear it. I want to turn on the light but I'm scared, scared, scared.

Upstairs I hear footsteps and more crying. Is my Baby Doll upstairs? Because I don't think I can get up there to find it without getting caught. The footsteps are coming closer. I want to hide but I can't leave it alone where it is. Wherever it is. I can't climb out the window by myself because then Gloria or Donald will find it instead of me. So I crawl to the middle of the room and stand. I get ready to go *ape-shit* so that I'll be a bigger problem than the crying. I have to make them think about me. Only me and not my Baby Doll at all.

I take a deep breath. With my eyes still closed I start to scream. As loud as I can.

The door opens fast. I feel the light turn on. I keep screaming and squeezing my eyes shut. I have to be so loud that—

"Ginny! Wake up! You've got to wake up! You're safe!"

I open my eyes but I don't stop. I hear a different man's voice but I see Donald. I scream even louder so that Gloria will come down too.

"Ginny, wake up. Wake up! No one is going to hurt you!"

And then—

"Stop screaming!"

I hear a woman's voice now. She sounds scared. "Ginny, please! You're scaring the baby!"

So I stop and listen.

"The baby is trying to get back to sleep upstairs. That's all it is. That's all it is."

"My Baby Doll is cr—"

I am coming up out of my brain. I see my Forever Dad. He is standing right in front of me. "No," he says. "It's Baby Wendy. Baby Wendy is upstairs trying to get back to sleep."

Which means I am at the Blue House. I am with my Forever Parents. I am safe.

I feel my knees and legs. I fall. Someone catches me before I hit the carpet.

"Can you get back into bed?" my Forever Mom says.

I nod my head yes. My Forever Dad helps me climb back in. My Forever Mom makes a breathing sound and fixes my blankets. Her mouth is a straight, straight line. She stands up straight and crosses her arms. Then my Forever Dad brings a wet washcloth. And puts his hand on my shoulder. I do not *recoil* even though he is a man. I lie still and let him wipe my face. "It was just a dream," he says. "Do you want to come sit with us in the living room? Do you want some company?"

I shake my head no.

"All right," he says. "Do you want to go back to sleep, then?"

I nod my head yes.

"All right," he says again. "If you need anything, come get us. We'll be out in the living room for a while until the baby falls asleep. Okay?"

I close my eyes and nod my head yes. I feel the light turn off and they leave.

On the other side of the door I hear them talking in quiet voices. I open my ears big to hear. "Why the hell do you have to be so accommodating?" says my Forever Mom. "I don't know how we can do this anymore. When it was just us, it was okay, but things are different now. She isn't safe!"

"We made a commit—"

"Bullshit!" she says. "That's bullshit! We didn't—"

"Shh! And yes, she *is* safe! The circumstances—"

"Now you sound like Patrice! Things were different before the kidnapping! Before the baby *and* the kidnapping. Before all the— She was manageable! *This* was manageable! But don't you remember what she did to that doll? And then she gave that lunatic mother of hers our address, and she came here and threatened— And then all the reporters and police? And you had to bring her to that damn interview and deal with all those lawyers! And *then* you had to go to the trial! Think about your health! Your doctor said— What the hell would I do if— School counselor or not, you're barely holding yourself together! I know you've got all those sick days, but it's been too long for me. Now some of my patients are starting to leave! Look, we can't expose a baby to all this! I won't!"

Then their voices get quiet. I know they're walking away to talk somewhere else. I know that when my Forever Mom said *She isn't safe!* she wasn't talking about my Baby Doll. But my Baby Doll isn't safe either and I'm the only one who can do something about it.

My Forever Dad is sitting with the man in the leather Patriots jacket and hat. Mostly I'm guessing he likes blue and red. They are talking a lot. It is like they are BFFs.

There is a girl here who pulls her socks up all the time. She reaches down and pulls up the left one and then the right one and then makes two fists and says *Yes!* when it's her turn to do a drill or go in the game or practice a layup. She says her name is Katie *MacDougall*. Not Katie *McDonalds*. She is visiting with Larry from a different school, she says. Larry is her cousin. And Larry says he is *her* cousin too. I didn't ask her which one and I didn't ask her where she lives or when her birthday is or what her favorite color is but I'm guessing it's black and gray because that's what color her socks are. My Forever Parents say when I meet someone new I shouldn't ask where they live and when their birthday is and how many cats they have because that is *a little too forward.*

On the other end of the court Katie MacDougall is pulling her socks up again. I pull mine up too. Having my socks pulled up makes me feel even more *ready for anything* than tightening the laces on my sneakers. Larry comes over to me on his arm braces and takes his arms out so he can shoot hoops. Katie Mac-Dougall walks over to us. She has her mouth open a little and she is breathing loud. "Katie MacDougall," I say when she gets here, "I have known you since *approximately* 5:42."

"Yeah," she says.

"Will you tell me your birthday?"

"My birthday is September 20th," she says.

"September 20th," I say. "That's *exactly* two days after my birthday. No one told me I was older than you!"

"I really like your socks," Katie MacDougall says and pulls hers up some more.

I grab mine and pull them up as high as they can go. Which is higher than hers. "Yeah," I say. "They are the bomb."

I start passing the ball back and forth with Katie MacDougall. She throws the ball too hard and I miss it. It bounces past me and rolls to the bleachers. The man in the leather Patriots jacket catches it. He stands up and I see that my Forever Dad isn't with him anymore. My Forever Dad isn't anywhere.

The man is standing in front of me holding the ball. I am walking toward him. "Here you go, Ginny," he says. He holds the ball out. I take it.

"Thanks," I say. I don't know if he's a stranger or not because a stranger is someone you don't know and I have seen him here before.

"Great job out there tonight," he says. "You're really pretty good."

So I say thanks again even though *We do not talk to strangers.*

He keeps looking at me like we have been talking for a long time. "Your dad will be right back in a minute," he says.

And I say, "He must be in the bathroom."

The man in the leather Patriots jacket is supposed to sit down again or say, *Well, you better get back out there.* He is supposed to

act like a regular stranger. But he doesn't. He just stands there
looking at me and when I look at his eyes he looks at the ground.
Like he did the other day. I look where he is looking but I don't
see anything interesting or different there. I keep looking.

Then in the gym I hear Katie MacDougall talking about how
she wants to try to be one of the Harlem Globetrotters. I look to
the side and see my Forever Dad walking out of the bathroom
but I want to know what the man in the leather Patriots jacket
is looking at so I pick my head up and ask him.

"What are you looking at?" I say.

He swallows and doesn't look up. "Just a really pretty girl
who turned out okay," he says.

His eyes look wet. It's like he's going to cry which doesn't
make sense because he's a man. So I'm guessing he has something in them. I look down at the ground again. I see my sneakers and his work boots. When I look up again my Forever Dad
is standing there.

"Excuse me," he says. "What's going on?"

So I say, "This man has wet eyes."

The man in the leather Patriots jacket wipes them. "We were
just talking," he says.

"Not anymore you're not," my Forever Dad says. His voice
is angry. "This isn't what we agreed on."

"The ball rolled over here to the bleachers," says the man in
the leather Patriots jacket. "I caught it and gave it back to her."

My Forever Dad looks at me. I hold up the ball. In my hands
it feels as big as the whole world.

"She's not supposed to talk with strangers," says my Forever
Dad.

"I'm a stranger?"

"We're trying to help her build good habits. So until you're
introduced at the agreed-upon time, a stranger is *exactly* what
you are. Right, Ginny?"

I nod my head yes. "Exactly," I say.

The man in the leather Patriots jacket steps back one step. He puts his hands up. "Okay. Got it. My bad," he says. Then to me he says, "It was nice talking with you, Ginny." And walks away.

"Go ahead and play some more," my Forever Dad tells me. So I do. But when I pass the ball to Katie MacDougall I see my Forever Dad and the man in the leather Patriots jacket talking on the bleachers again. My Forever Dad is shaking his head and leaning with his chin out. He is talking loud and pointing but not yelling. I feel bad for the man in the leather Patriots jacket. It looks like he's getting in trouble.

I am glad I didn't hiss at him last week.

EXACTLY 10:55 IN THE MORNING,
SATURDAY, NOVEMBER 20TH

We are in the car going to the park to see Rick. My Forever
Parents will be with me the whole time so I won't be able
to just say all the things I want to say. Or ask him to drive me to
Canada to meet up with Gloria and my Baby Doll. I have to be
careful like I was in the letter. I will have to wait.

I pulled my socks up nine times when we left the house. I will
pull my socks up again once more for good luck when we get
there. It's not very cold out even though it's November but I'm
still wearing my winter coat and hat.

When we get to the park I wait for my Forever Parents to get
out of the car first. They always make me wait for them because
I like to get out fast. They open the door. I jump out and pull
my socks up one more time and then start looking for Rick. I
don't see him. I see only the parking lot and some trees with no
leaves and the monkey bars and the swings moving in the wind.

Then I see a man standing next to the seesaw. He is wearing a blue-and-red Patriots jacket and a blue-and-red Patriots
hat. My Forever Mom leans close to me and says, "There. Do
you see him?"

And I say, "That's the man from Special Olympics."

"Actually, that's your Birth Dad," says my Forever Dad. "That's Rick."

So I say, "I'm guessing he likes blue and red."

Rick walks over to us. He and my Forever Dad shake hands. Then he puts his hand out for me to shake. "Hey, Ginny," he says.

I shake his hand. I can't see his eyes because he's wearing dark sunglasses. But I see two of me reflected in them. One in each eye.

I don't say *Hello, Rick* or *Hi* or anything. I just shake his hand and stand there.

"It's been nice coming to see you at Special Olympics," he says.

That wasn't a question so I don't say anything. I don't want to talk because I'm trying to figure out why he didn't tell me who he was before.

"We wanted to get to know Rick before he met you," my Forever Dad says. "We wanted him to see how you get along with other people."

"I've heard a lot about you," Rick says. "And honestly, it was hard not being able to meet as quickly as I would have liked. I haven't seen you since you were a tiny baby. We only had one day together at the hospital. Going to see your practice was— It was really great."

I am still thinking so I don't say anything. I think and I think.

Rick keeps talking. "You understand, don't you?" he says. "I couldn't stay away. But your new folks wanted to be careful, after everything that happened. Can't say I blame them."

When he says *your new folks* he puts his head down a little.

Rick seems like a nice quiet man. I'm guessing he'll bring me right to Canada if I ask. He'll *do his very best* to try to help me.

I just have to find a way to make my Forever Parents go away so I can ask him.

"Where is your truck?" I say.

"I don't have one. I drive a little old Honda."

"In your letter you said you *drive truck*."

He smiles and he shakes his head. "I do," he says, "but the trucks aren't mine. I drive them for different companies. I'm even getting a special license so that I can haul some really important freight. Yep." When he says *Yep* he smiles with his mouth a little on the side and he tugs with both hands on his jacket.

"So where is your little old Honda?" I look at myself swaying back and forth in his glasses. I wonder which one is Ginny and which one is (-Ginny). I wonder which one is the real me.

He points to the parking lot. I see a gray car there.

"Gloria has a green car. The window was broken," I say. "But then it got fixed."

"You remember your mom's car? Heck, I remember that car, too."

"I saw it on September 14th in the parking lot at school."

"I think it's time to go on the swings," my Forever Dad says.

"You two can go on the swings," I say. "I'll stay here and talk with my Old Dad Rick."

My Forever Mom laughs. "Sorry, but we need to stick together."

I point at the swings. "You can stick together over there if you want," I say, "and we'll stick together right here."

"Ginny, we're not letting you out of our sight," my Forever Dad says. "Not after what happened before."

He means the kidnapping.

"You know, going on the swings sounds like a great idea," says Rick. "I'm in the mood for a good swing."

We walk to the swings. All of us together. I am mad because my Forever Parents *won't let me out of their sight*. I'm wondering if *they've got my number* too.

I get on one of the swings and start swinging. Rick gets on the one next to me. The chains are cold. My Forever Parents stand in front of us watching. I don't think I'm going to get to ask what I want to ask so I say, "Do you know if anyone is going to check on my Baby Doll?"

And he says, "Check on your Baby Doll? No, I don't know anything about that."

And I say, "I need to find it because it might be hungry. Do you think Gloria is *acting pretty reasonably*?"

Rick looks at my Forever Parents. They move their shoulders up and look back at him. Rick pushes back and starts to swing. "So, what should we talk about?" he says.

"You didn't answer my question."

"Heck, I don't know," he says. "It's just a doll, right? Isn't there anything else you want to talk about?"

"Yes," I say.

"What?" he says.

I look at my Forever Parents and put my head down. I know they can hear me so I can't ask what I really want to ask. Instead I ask the next best thing. "I want to know if you'll go to Gloria's apartment to make sure she's taking care of it."

Rick drags his work boots on the sand. He looks at my Forever Parents. They look back at him. "That's really the same topic, isn't it? Your folks told me you think about your old Baby Doll all the time," he says. "You must really miss it."

I nod my head. "Yes, I do," I say.

"Maybe we can go to get you a new one, then," he says. "I've never been able to get you a present, so maybe—"

"No," I say. "I do not want a new one. I want you to go make sure the old one is safe. Gloria can't take care of it."

"Okay, okay," says Rick.

Then my Forever Mom says, "No, Rick, don't say *okay*. She'll take you literally."

"What? Oh, got it," says Rick.

"Ginny, he means *okay, he won't go get you a new Baby Doll.* So don't worry. We wouldn't let anyone do that to you." Then to Rick she says, "This is what we were talking about. She won't let go of the idea. There's no use trying."

"I always thought it never hurts to try," says Rick in a quiet voice. He looks at me. "Do you have a favorite color?"

I try not to get distracted but I have to answer. "I like red," I say.

"I like red, too. Red and blue."

"Those are the Patriots' colors," I say.

He laughs. "I do love the Pats," he says.

"When can we have a *respite*?" I say. "When can we *give every-one a little break*?"

"It's too soon for that," my Forever Dad says right away. "Isn't that right, Rick?"

Rick is quiet for *exactly* three seconds. "Right," he says. "It's too soon. But maybe we could set up another time to visit." He turns his head and looks right at my Forever Dad. "Would *that* be all right?"

My Forever Dad's eyebrows get pointy like a *V.*

"Of course it would," my Forever Mom says. "After all, we want the two of you to spend a lot of time together. As much as possible."

"But no respite yet," says Rick.

"Right. No respite yet," my Forever Dad says.

At the table it is only me and Larry. Alison Hill and Brenda Richardson and Kayla Zadambidge are in line getting their lunches. Ms. Carol is standing next to the water fountain talking with another teacher. She is watching me but she isn't close enough to listen.

"How did things go with that Rick dude this weekend? Was he nice?" says Larry.

That was two questions but I know he means the same thing by both so I say, "He was the man from Special Olympics."

"You mean the one your other dad always talks to?"

I nod my head yes. Larry nods too.

"Whoa," he says. "Who knew?"

"No one knew," I say. "Only my Forever Dad."

Larry makes a funny face. "How come you call him your Forever Dad all the time? I mean, I know you were adopted, but couldn't you just call him your dad? I mean, it's not like you're going to go live with someone else."

I think. "I'm going to go have a *respite* with Rick," I say. "My Forever Parents need a little break."

"A break from their own kid? That's weird," says Larry. "Say, you're not thinking of going to go live with that Rick dude, are you? Because, babe, if you went away..."

He stops talking. Then in a shaky voice he starts singing a song about how God only knows what he'd be without me. Sometimes he stops singing and says *Dum-dum, Dum, Dum* starting low and marching up.

"You dig?" he says when he finishes the song.

He means *Do you understand?* So I say, "No, Larry, I do not dig."

"Don't you want to be my— Don't you want us to be boyfriend and girlfriend? Someday, I mean."

"No, Larry," I say again.

"Man, that stinks," he says. And throws one of his arm braces down. It clatters and bounces. His face is tight and there are tears coming out the corners of his eyes. Then he says, "I mean, us special kids—we need to stick together, you know? It's not like either one of us has a shot at getting with a regular girl. I mean, a regular person. So fine, I get it. You're not interested. We can just be friends. But I still don't want you to go anywhere. You'll always stay right here in Greensborough, right?"

I don't say anything. In my tray I use my fork to turn some spaghetti over. I have to answer the question unless I take too much time thinking of an answer and Larry says something else.

Which is *exactly* what happens.

"Anyway, I hope you'll stay. We'll be in high school next year. High school lasts four whole years. It's going to be a blast. You don't want to go to high school somewhere else, do you?"

"No," I say. Because I don't want to go to any high school at all. I want to go to Canada to take care of my Baby Doll. Or stay somewhere else with it. Anywhere. Five years is a long time and now that Crystal with a C is in jail I have to keep it safe from Gloria.

"Well, that's good. Sometimes I think you just can't stand it here. It's like you'll never be happy. There's some good stuff here for you, you know? Like me. I'll do anything for you. Don't you know that?"

"I know," I say. And I will remember it.

EXACTLY 11:41,
FRIDAY, NOVEMBER 26TH

Rick is in my room right now. With me and my Forever Parents. My Forever Mom is in the doorway and my Forever Dad is sitting on my bed. Thanksgiving was yesterday so today he came over to visit. He will stay for lunch. My Forever Parents said they wanted him to see how I am at home. They want him to see how I set my room up so he can get ready for our *respite*. They are with us right now but when they leave I'll ask him to bring me up to Canada and to tell Gloria to come meet me there.

"What sorts of things do you like for breakfast?" says Rick. He is looking at my Michael Jackson posters and my calendar. "You sure do like to keep track of birthdays."

"Mostly eggs and cereal and pancakes and French toast," I say. "And toast with butter and bacon and oatmeal. And nine grapes. With a glass of human milk."

He bends down to look at all the books in my bookcase. Then he looks at my pictures. All the frames are red. "Do you know how to cook? It's no problem if you don't."

I nod my head yes. "Crystal with a C taught me how to make scrambled eggs," I say.

Rick straightens up. "You always call her *Crystal with a C*," he says. "I wonder how the heck else people spell *Crystal*. With a *C-H*, maybe?"

I shake my head no. "With a *K*," I say.

"With a *K*? I don't think I've ever heard of someone spelling *Krystal* with a *K*."

"That's how we spell my Baby Doll's name," I say.

My Forever Mom's eyes get as big as Ms. Carol's.

"Ginny, did you just say your Baby Doll has a name?" my Forever Dad says.

I nod my head yes.

"And her name is Krystal with a K?"

I nod my head yes again.

"Who called it that?"

"Gloria."

"But you always call it *my Baby Doll*," my Forever Mom says.

"Krystal with a K is my Baby Doll," I hear myself say.

Krystal with a K. The words sound funny when I say them because I've never said them before. Because in my brain my Baby Doll *will always be my little baby* just like Crystal with a C said. Gloria is the one who lies and Crystal with a C is the one who tells the truth.

"Wait," my Forever Dad says. "Your Baby Doll has a real name. Who named it Krystal with a K?" One of his eyes squints and his mouth turns sideways.

"Gloria named it Krystal with a K to tell the difference from Crystal with a C," I say.

"Ginny, are you saying that...that your Baby Doll is actually a *real baby*?" says my Forever Mom.

Everything stops. Everything freezes. Because they *get it*. They finally, finally understand.

I nod my head yes and I try to say *yes* with my mouth but the word is stuck. I can't make it come out. My brain can't let it go because it never called my Baby Doll Krystal with a K even though that's its name. Then all at once the word pops out by itself and I hear my voice say, "Yes." And then "Yes!" again.

Because that's what I've been trying to tell people for five whole years.

"Holy shit," says my Forever Dad.

"There is a *real baby* and Gloria named it after your aunt? After Crystal *with a C*?" says my Forever Mom.

"Yes!" I say.

Rick is shaking his head back and forth and moving his hands in the air. "I don't know anything about any of this," he says, "but Gloria always looked up to Crystal. They were really close. Crystal looked out for her a lot when they were younger. I wouldn't be surprised at all if she named a baby after her."

I nod my head yes.

"So why did you call it *my Baby Doll*?"

I think. "Because it was my job to *take excellent care of it*," I say. "Plus I didn't know how to spell. Plus—"

"I need to make a phone call," my Forever Mom interrupts me. "I need to make a phone call right now. Rick, we're going to have to cut this visit short." She leaves the room fast.

"But I just got here," he says. "If we're going to make this work, you guys are—"

My Forever Dad's voice gets louder. "Rick," he says.

"All right, all right," says Rick. "Ginny, I'll send you an email tonight, okay?"

"Rick, please leave. We need you to go!" my Forever Mom yells.

Rick shakes his head. "You people," I hear him say. And then he gets his coat and leaves.

EXACTLY 4:17 IN THE AFTERNOON, MONDAY, NOVEMBER 29TH

"A lot has been going on in your life," says Patrice. "Again." She is sitting in the flower chair.

"Mmm-hmm," I say because my mouth is full of graham crackers.

"Do you like spending time with your Birth Dad? With Rick, I mean?"

"Mmm-hmm," I say again.

"That's good," says Patrice. "Before you know it, you'll be going to visit him at his house. The plan is to have you go there for a weekend after Christmas break. Everyone is hoping you're comfortable with him. They're hoping you might want to stay with him. Maybe even go live with him, if you like him enough. He seems to really like you, even if he doesn't get along perfectly with your Forever Parents."

I nod my head yes and take another bite of graham cracker.

"You know, I made a call to Social Services after your Forever Mom called me," says Patrice. "I asked them to go to the apartment to visit Gloria. She was the prime suspect when the kidnapping investigation was going on, so she was used to having police and other people come to ask her questions. But she wasn't expecting Social Services to come visit her again. They brought a policeman with them, too. Can you guess what they found when they went to the apartment door?"

"A Maine coon cat?" I say.

"No. Your little sister. They found your Baby Doll."

I stop chewing and listen.

Patrice makes a loud breathing sound and then she is quiet but I hear a loud ringing in my ears getting louder and louder. I can feel every single hair on my head like it is electric.

"The social workers knocked on the door, and when Gloria opened it, the police officer walked right in, and there she was. Your sister. And yes, there was quite a scene, but the bottom line is that we were wrong, Ginny. And I'm sorry. For five years now you've been telling us that your Baby Doll was a real baby, and you were right. Krystal with a K is completely undocumented, as it turns out. That's why no one knew. Gloria did an amazing job of keeping her hidden. She must have been really scared that the police were going to take her away."

I nod my head. "Gloria doesn't like the police," I say. "And she's a *smart cookie*."

"No one will deny that," says Patrice. "But we're starting to piece everything together now. It's almost as if there was a big puzzle right underneath our noses, and now that we see it, we can finally put it together. So again, I'm sorry. But I'm excited, too, because now I'm beginning to understand. I understand why you know so much about taking care of babies."

I want to tell Patrice that I'm happy. I want to tell her that I'm so, so glad but I'm falling deeper and deeper into my brain and I can say only what I see. What I remember.

"It was my job to take care of it," I say. "Gloria said I need to take excellent care of my Baby Doll and keep it quiet."

"She said that?" says Patrice.

But I don't hear anything else Patrice says. I hear only Gloria. *Take excellent care of your Baby Doll, Gin. Don't let anyone see or hear her. Donald is coming over tonight and I want it to be magical.* That was when I learned how to put my finger on my Baby Doll's lips so it could suck on it and be quiet. And when I learned to pick it up and say, *Ush, ush, ush.* To make it quiet. To put milk or mayonnaise on a spoon to feed it because after a while there wasn't a bottle but still I had to make it quiet.

Quiet is what scares me the most even though it keeps me safe. I see Gloria go out to meet her dealer. The door closes behind her.

"Gloria left you with Krystal with a K all the time," I hear Patrice say. "She used to go away for hours and hours to parties or to get drugs. You kept Krystal with a K hidden so the neighbors wouldn't see her. And the worst part is that when Gloria *was* there, she was too angry to take care of the baby herself or was just plain high."

"I did a good job of taking care of my Baby Doll," I say. "Can I please go back to take care of it again?"

Patrice looks at me funny. "You know, I was wondering how old Krystal with a K is now. Do you know? I mean, I don't even know when her birthday is."

"November 16th," I say.

"November 16th? I wonder how old that makes her. Let's see."

Patrice looks up at the ceiling and starts counting on her fingers. I know she is trying to do some math.

I swallow what's in my mouth and take a drink of milk. "My Baby Doll is *approximately* one year old."

Patrice doesn't move her mouth at all. It's like her smile is frozen. "Only one year old?" she says. "That means she's not old enough to go to school yet."

I nod my head yes. "You have to be five years old to go to kindergarten."

"And how many years has it been since you left Gloria's apartment?"

"Fo—" I start to say but then I stop because I remember that my birthday was September 18th. I used to say *four years* all the time when people asked me how long it's been since I was in Gloria's apartment but now it's *five*. Because another year passed. "*Five* years," I say.

"Exactly," says Patrice.

"Exactly," I say too but I don't know why I say it. I am too busy thinking.

"It was a big surprise when you told everyone her name this weekend," says Patrice. "No one knew she had a name."

"I called her *my Baby Doll*," I say.

"Right. Because she really was like your Baby Doll. You carried her around and took care of her all the time. But it's been— How long has it been again? Oh, I remember now. Five years. Five whole years—and that's why you want to go see her so badly. A lot could have happened in that time. You want to make sure she's safe."

"Right," I say. "I need to see if Gloria is changing its diaper and if it has food to eat. Plus if no one is there to make it quiet when Gloria has her man-friends come to—"

I stop talking and look down at my lap. It has a lot of crumbs on it. Then I say, "I need to make sure no one hurts her."

"I think we can help with that," says Patrice.

I look up.

"Social Services is going back to the apartment," she says. "They're going to send some people over to verify the facts and get some things straight. They're going to visit the jail to talk with Crystal with a C, as well."

"What does *verify the facts* mean?"

"It means some social workers are going to go to the apartment to figure out why there's no record of Krystal with a K's birth. Today, actually. We have our suspicions, but we need to hear what Gloria has to say. And they're going to make sure that little Krystal is safe."

"Little Krystal," I say.

"Five years is a long time for Gloria to take care of her, don't you think?"

I think. I think and I think some more. "Yes," I say. "Five years is a very long time."

"My Baby Doll's name is Krystal with a K and she was born on November 16th," I say. "It's my sister. It still lives with Gloria but *you have to trust me that she's safe*. Because *she's fine, okay?*"

I take a deep breath and open my eyes. I am at the lunch table in the cafeteria with all the kids from Room Five.

"But I don't live with Gloria anymore. I live with my Forever Parents at the Blue House. And last night Patrice called to tell me the social workers went to the apartment and found out Gloria had an *undocumented birth*. Because Gloria *gave birth to* my Baby Doll in Crystal with a C's apartment. It doesn't even have a *social security number* or *vaccinations* but they're going to get it some. I think I need a beverage."

I pull up my socks as high and tight as they can go. Ms. Carol is sitting next to me listening behind her glasses. "Slow yourself down there, Ginny," she says.

Brenda Richardson looks at me from across the lunch table. Her eyebrows are wrinkled and her mouth is open. "Wait," she says. "You have a sister?"

"That's right," I say. "Its name is Krystal with a K and it was born in November. It is my Baby Doll. You didn't forget its birthday, did you?"

"I thought your sister's name was Wendy," says Brenda Richardson.

"That's my Forever Sister," I say.

"But she's a baby, right?"

"Yes. Both of them are babies. *Real* babies with feet. And mouths that open all the way. But I'm talking about Krystal with a K."

"Where does it—I mean *she*—live?" asks Larry.

"With Gloria."

"And where does Gloria live?" asks Kayla Zadambidge.

"At the apartment where the Green Car is parked," I say. "It's in Harrington Falls."

"Is that in California?" Larry asks and then he jumps up and puts his arms out and starts singing a song about waxing up some surfboards.

"Ginny needs a beverage!" yells Kayla Zadambidge.

Someone gives me a chocolate milk with a straw already in it. "The police took me away from Gloria because she wasn't taking good care of me. But Krystal with a K stayed in the apartment because I hid it in the—"

I stop talking. In my brain I see everything that happened all over again. Then I remember that Crystal with a C found my Baby Doll.

Everyone looks confused.

"Maybe you should tell Mrs. Lomos," says Kayla Zadambidge.

"Mrs. Lomos already talked with me. She says it explains a lot that my Baby Doll is a real baby," I say. "It was born on November 16th, you know. Did all of you write that down?"

Larry and Kayla Zadambidge start looking through their bags

for pencils and papers. Brenda Richardson takes a bite of her cookie. "I have a sister, too," she says. "Her name is Peg."

"Did you carry it around when you were little and take care of it?" I say. "That's what I did with mine."

"Peg is older than me," says Brenda Richardson.

"I want to take excellent care of Krystal with a K," I say. "I want to wrap it up in my quilt again and give it lots of human milk. Not breast milk. That's different. It can sleep in my bed under my arm like before."

"Babe, I know you love your little sister, but I think you should stay here with all of us. You don't want to move away, do you?"

I pick up the chocolate milk again and take a drink. Then I put it down.

"I don't know why the social workers are letting it stay with Gloria," I say. "Gloria doesn't know how to take care of babies. Plus she gets mad and—"

I stop talking again.

"Is Gloria your mom?" asks Brenda Richardson.

My brain pushes me back up into the conversation. "Don't you know I already told you that?" I say. "Gloria is my Birth Mom. She's the only Birth Mom I'll ever have." I pick at my fingers. "And Rick is my Birth Dad. He wants me to come spend a weekend at his house after Christmas. He says it will be good to *give everyone a break*. Plus my Forever Mom doesn't like me anymore because she thinks I'm a crazy girl. Last night I heard her say to my Forever Dad that she can't wait until I'm gone. Then they can all *breathe again*."

I try to think but I don't know what to think anymore. Ms. Carol writes something down in a notebook.

"Ginny needs another beverage!" Kayla Zadambidge says again.

Larry puts his hand on my shoulder. I *recoil* but he just slips out of his arm braces and kneels down and sings to me about a little surfer watching on the shore. Alison Hill giggles. But I can't pay any attention to Larry. I sink back into my brain. The social workers don't understand that Gloria can't take care of my Baby Doll. They don't understand that she gets mad and hits. They don't understand that Crystal with a C *spent a few hours with them every day.*

Which means I have to make sure Patrice tells them not to leave Gloria alone with it. Gloria needs someone with her all the time or my Baby Doll will *suffer serious abuse and neglect* which is what happened to me.

Someone pushes me another carton of milk from across the table. This time it's white. I take the straw out of the chocolate milk and drink the whole thing.

My Forever Dad isn't home. He is supposed to be here when I get off the bus but I don't see his car in the driveway. He stopped working after the kidnapping so that he could take care of me. Maybe he is at another doctor's appointment. He goes to the doctor's all the time now.

I want to tell him that I need to talk with Patrice again. Just on the phone. I need to talk with Patrice now so that she will tell the social workers that Gloria gets mad and hits. I need to tell her that they can't leave her alone with my Baby Doll.

The bus pulls away behind me. I go inside. I put my backpack down in my room and go to the stairs. And listen.

I hear my Forever Mom's door close.

I don't want to go up there but I have to. My Forever Dad said it's *for the best* if I just leave my Forever Mom alone. But I have to ask someone to call Patrice. My Baby Doll isn't safe.

I walk up the stairs as quiet as I can. I stop in front of the door to the bedroom. I knock.

She doesn't say *Come on in* or *Wait just a minute* or anything. I don't hear any sound at all.

So I open the door.

She is on the bed holding Baby Wendy. Her eyes are thin slits. "Ginny, get out of here!" she growls.

"But I need to—"

"Now!"

I take a deep breath. I have to stay calm. "I need to—" I say again but this time she interrupts me.

With a yell.

"Ginny, get the hell out of here! Stay away from me and my baby!"

So I close my eyes and yell back, "I need to talk with Patrice!"

Then I hear Baby Wendy crying. Right there in front of me.

I step forward. I know how to help a crying baby.

My Forever Mom jumps up fast.

I back up.

But the crying is getting louder so I start saying, "Ush, ush, ush." I put out my hands to pick up the baby.

Something hits my face. It knocks me onto the floor.

The crying gets softer. It is far away. My head hurts and I hear footsteps. I hear the front door shut. I get up on my knees. My Forever Mom is gone and Baby Wendy is gone and I don't hear the crying anymore but then I hear the car. When I stand up and look out the window I see it backing up. It backs onto the street and zooms away.

EXACTLY 1:58 IN THE AFTERNOON, SATURDAY, DECEMBER 4TH

It snowed last night. We are at Wagon Hill and I am going sledding with my Forever Dad. I don't know what time it is *exactly* because I am wearing gloves and I can't see my watch. I'm wearing my big sunglasses over my regular glasses and when I get out of the car I say, "I know what you're thinking—I am the spitting image of Michael Jackson."

And he says, "You're right. That's exactly what I was thinking."

Wagon Hill is a lot of fun in the winter because it's a great place to go sledding. We went sledding here last winter too before my Forever Mom knew she was pregnant. It is the best sledding hill in the world. It is longer than the football field at the high school except it's slanted. You can go really fast on it. It is extremely distracting which is great because things were *a little intense* yesterday at the Blue House. That was what my Forever Dad said when he told me we were going sledding. Then I said I had to talk with Patrice and he said he would call her right away. And he did. He even let me talk with her on the phone and she said not to worry, the social workers were already visiting Gloria every day. Even on the weekends. So I was happy. Patrice said she will give me an update when I go to see her on Wednesday and that I should try not to *obsess* so much about it.

We already went down the hill once and it was great but when you get to the bottom of a hill you have to walk back to the top. There's no one to bring you back on a bus or to pull you. I ask my Forever Dad if he will pull me back to the top and he says no. There are other dads pulling their kids so I say, "Well why not?"

His breathing is loud. His face is red. "Because you weigh a hundred twenty-five pounds, and those little kids are only four or five years old," he says.

But I still see lots of kids getting pulled. "This isn't fair," I say. "Look at all those kids. They don't have to walk. This is *tedious*."

My Forever Dad keeps walking. The top of the hill is far away. Sometimes he stops to rest and breathe and I see lots of clouds coming out of his mouth. I'd rather be home watching a video or listening to Michael Jackson or reading a book for *exactly* thirty minutes. Or organizing my backpack for the *respite*. Walking up the hill is no fun at all. "Can't you just pick me up in the car or something?" I say. "I'm not having any fun."

He turns around. "Did we get hot chocolate on the way here?"

"Yes. From Dunkin' Donuts," I say. "It was too hot so we said we should probably leave it in the car to cool a little so that it doesn't burn my tongue."

"And haven't you been looking forward to going sledding since summer?"

"Yes."

"Then can you maybe try to be just a little bit grateful?"

I know that sometimes you have to pretend that you're grateful or you get hit. But my Forever Parents don't hit. They say that they *don't believe in it* which means I don't have to pretend. But on Wednesday which was three days ago my Forever Mom hit me when I tried to pick the baby up. So maybe she hits now but my Forever Dad still doesn't.

Plus *grateful* means you're happy about something or that you like it or that you maybe don't mind. But I mind walking up the hill. "This is so, so *tedious*," I say.

My Forever Dad puts his hands up and lets them fall against his legs. "Come on," he says. "We'll get to the top faster if we keep walking." I follow him.

"Isn't there something more fun we can do?" I say.

He turns around again. "Are you crazy?" he says. "We are here because you want to go sledding, and now you don't even want to go? Do you have any idea how much bullshit we go through for you? Do you have any idea how high my blood pressure is? Your mother won't come out of the bedroom and I'm missing a ton of time at work. This isn't routine, Ginny. This is pretty much unbearable. I'm trying to be as gracious and generous as I can, but I don't know how much longer we can keep it up."

Bullshit means poop that comes out of a cow but sometimes it's an expression. "You're joking me, right?" I say. I look at him over my glasses.

But my Forever Dad doesn't laugh or smile like he usually does. "We're going home," he says. "No more sledding today. I just can't do it."

"But I want to go down one more time!" I say. And I stomp my foot.

"The car is over there," he says pointing to the side of the hill. "We'll get there faster if we cut across the trails. Watch out for all the sleds, all right?"

He starts walking across the sled trails. A little girl comes down right in front of him in a blow-up sled shaped like a donut. He waits for her and then crosses. But I still don't want to go home so I stay where I am. He sees that I haven't moved and starts coming back toward me. Two more sleds zoom past.

When he gets over to me his breathing is really, really hard. "Ginny, you have to come back with me to the car. If you don't, you won't be allowed to watch any videos or listen to Michael Jackson for a whole week."

I cross my arms and start walking next to him. "This is not fun!" I say. I stomp across the snow. "I will not be treated this way! I want to go live with Rick!"

"Ginny!" my Forever Dad shouts. "Look out!"

But I am not listening because I have more to say. "I am going—" I say but then my Forever Dad grabs my arm and pulls me down onto the ground. Some little kids start yelling and laughing. Their voices are right in my ear and then they slide away. From where I am lying in the snow I see a big long wooden sled with four kids on it. It goes down the rest of the hill fast.

I sit up. Then I stand. Snow is on my pants and coat. "I am angry!" I say. Some people stop walking up the hill. They look at me.

My Forever Dad stands up too. "Ginny, that sled almost hit you! And you're complaining that I moved you out of the way? Let's just get to the car," he says and takes my arm.

I *recoil*. "You are not allowed to touch me," I tell him when I stand up straight again. "This is *my* body! Patrice said so! No one is allowed to touch my body unless I say it is okay! And I do not say it is okay!"

Because I don't like it at all when men touch me. They should all stay upstairs with Gloria in her bedroom and leave me alone.

He puts his hand on his chest and breathes some more. "If you don't start walking to the car, you can use that damn body of yours to walk home," he says. "And if I get to the car before you do, I'm going to drink your hot chocolate."

"Oh no you're not!" I say. I start walking fast. I go right past him and move out of the way when three more sleds come down the hill. I keep walking and walking and then I get to the place where all the cars are parked. I stand next to ours until my Forever Dad gets there. He unlocks the door and I climb inside. I put my seat belt on and grab my hot chocolate. It is warm, not hot, so I am happy.

EXACTLY 3:55 IN THE AFTERNOON, WEDNESDAY, DECEMBER 8TH

"So the date will be Friday, January 7th," says Patrice. I want to ask her for the *update* but she said a *real* date and dates are important. When I hear a date I have to put it in my brain and think about it. A lot.

Plus I am excited. January 7th is when I'll go to Rick's house. For a *respite*. He will have a bedroom all set up for me but I'm hoping I don't have to go see it. I'm hoping he brings me straight up to Canada instead. I will talk with him about it as soon as we get in the car. The social workers will visit Gloria every day to keep my Baby Doll safe and then Gloria will drive it up to Canada to meet us. Then I will take over and *take excellent care of it* again.

"He'll pick you up right from school," says Patrice. "All your things will be in the backseat, ready to go."

"Will my quilt be there?" I ask. Because if my secret plan works out I won't be coming back to the Blue House. I'm okay leaving everything else there but not my quilt because my Baby Doll likes my quilt and I'll need something to wrap it in at night.

"Of course," says Patrice. "Remember, you'll help your dad pack everything the night before."

"On Thursday night," I say.

Patrice nods. "On Thursday night. You'll only need enough clothes for two days, but you can certainly bring your quilt. Now, let's talk about your Forever Mom. I understand that something happened between the two of you this last week. Maura called to explain it."

"She hit me," I say.

"Why did she do that?"

"Because I was going to pick up the baby."

"Did she say *not* to pick up the baby?"

"No."

"What did she tell you, then?"

"She told me to *get the hell out of here*."

"It's wrong to hit people, Ginny. It's completely unacceptable and it's never, ever okay. And I know you know that. What your Forever Mom did was wrong, and I've already talked with your parents about it. But I still need you to do something for me. I need you to remember that we need to keep some space between ourselves and people who are yelling at us. They just aren't safe. It wasn't safe to walk toward your Forever Mom when she was angry. Can you remember that? I mean, can you keep a safe distance from your mom if she gets angry and yells again?"

"No," I say.

"Why not?"

"Because she might be holding a crying baby. I know how to help crying babies," I say.

"I believe you," says Patrice. "But a baby who's crying isn't necessarily in danger. Was Baby Wendy in danger when you tried to take her?"

"No," I say.

"What were you thinking about when you tried to pick her up?"

"I was thinking about my Baby Doll."

"That's what I thought," says Patrice. "So we should probably talk about how to tell the difference between what's real and what's in our minds." She stops and licks her lips. "Ginny, I want to ask how you feel about your Forever Mom. She's changed a lot since you came home and she had the baby. How do you feel about her?"

I think. I don't feel happy or sad about my Forever Mom. I just feel excited and anxious about going up to Canada.

Patrice keeps talking. "Ginny, part of my job is to help you *attach. Attachment* means *forming a strong relationship* between yourself and someone else. Now, I know you have trouble with emotions because of your autism, but some things have happened that have made it extremely difficult for you and your mom to attach in order to remain close. Your dad is doing a great job of taking care of you and spending time with you. He's trying hard to keep everyone together, but it's putting an incredible amount of stress on him. I hate to say it, but I don't know that attachment is even possible between you and your mom right now. You have to *want* attachment. I know *you're* willing, but if she isn't..."

She stops. I wait.

"It's all about Baby Wendy," Patrice finally says. "You have to show her that you're safe around the baby. That having you in the house is safe for the baby."

So I say, "I'm not allowed to touch it *whatsoever.* That's the most important rule."

Patrice looks away. "That's right," she says. Her eyes look wet. "Even when it cries. Even when you think it needs something to eat. Even when touching the baby is probably the one thing that would help the most at this point."

We are sitting in the conference room around a big table. Every single chair is filled.

"Part of the purpose of today's meeting is to let Ginny's teachers meet Rick," says Mrs. Lomos. "Rick?"

"I'm pleased to meet you all," says Rick. He stands up and his chair knocks into the bookcase behind him. He sways and takes his hat off fast with both hands and crumples it and sits down again.

"Hi, Rick," say all my teachers. All of them are there. Mrs. Winkleman and Ms. Dana and Mrs. Carter and Mrs. Henkel. Ms. Carol and Ms. Merton and Mr. Crew. Even Ms. Devon the principal. Plus my Forever Parents.

"We need everyone here to be aware that Rick is Ginny's Birth Dad, and that there might be times when he'll come to school to pick Ginny up," says Mrs. Lomos. "Right now Ginny takes the bus, but there'll be times when her Forever Parents will call to say that Rick is picking her up."

"He has our formal permission," says my Forever Mom. "All the paperwork is signed in the office. You're also welcome to talk with him about Ginny's grades and records, too. Rick is becoming an important part of Ginny's life."

"I'm going to his house for a *respite* on January 7th," I say.

Everyone smiles and nods except my Forever Dad. His eyes are down and there are wrinkles on his forehead.

"I'm sure you'll have a great time," says Mrs. Lomos.

"My Forever Mom says she needs a break," I say.

Everyone is *exactly* quiet. "Things have been pretty rough at home and school," Mrs. Lomos says very fast. She looks at all the faces. "All of us will bend over backward to keep our kids safe, but we all need a break sometimes. Ginny is no exception."

Rick moves in his chair and makes a noise with his mouth.

"Is there something you want to add?" says Mrs. Lomos.

"I just wish someone would talk about what a delightful young lady she is," says Rick. "Maybe say how funny and smart she can be. With all this talk about keeping people safe and taking rests, it's like we're trying to put her in a box. We're trying to keep her apart from everything. I'm no psychologist, but I think what she needs is to be closer to people."

I am confused and my Forever Mom knows it. She puts her hand out to touch my hand but then pulls it back under the table. "It's an expression, Ginny," she says. "No one is putting anyone in a box." Then to Rick she says, "Yes, Rick. Everyone agrees that she's a creative problem-solver. And extremely resourceful, too. We're so glad you can be a part of her life so you can see firsthand just what a delight she can be."

Rick looks down and away. Then back. "I just—" he starts to say but my Forever Mom interrupts him.

"Thank you, Rick," she says. "Thank you *so* much."

There will be a Winter Concert tonight and Rick and my Forever Dad are coming to see me play my flute in it. My Forever Mom will stay home with my Forever Sister. Rick is eating over before we leave. We'll eat early at *exactly* four-thirty. Then I'll change into *concert attire* and we'll go.

Rick is walking in the door right now.

"Patrice says the social workers went to the apartment," I tell him. "She says they're having an investigation. They'll be going to visit every day."

"I bet Gloria doesn't like that," says Rick. He takes his coat off. My Forever Dad takes it from him and hangs it up in the closet. We go to sit in the living room. I sit on the couch and my Forever Dad sits next to me. Rick sits in the chair by the window. My Forever Mom leans in the doorway. Her hair is longer than I remember it.

"The paper they wrote said *upon their arrival* my Baby Doll *exhibited no unusual signs of stress*," I say. Because Patrice read the paper to me on the phone last night.

"Well, that's good," says Rick.

"They're going to visit it every day," I say, "because Crystal with a C isn't there anymore. They're going to *keep an eye on things* for a while."

Rick takes a drink of his coffee. "Did you ever wonder if maybe Gloria changed?"

"Her shirt looks mostly different."

"Right, but I mean maybe *who she is* changed. Moms are people, too, you know. They change, just like everyone else. From what I understand, things were pretty difficult for Gloria when you were in the apartment with her. You're a pretty special kid, Ginny. Plus, there was the baby to deal with, and she was an addict."

In my brain I see that he is right. People change. I changed and no one knows it. I changed into (-Ginny).

"So you don't think she gets mad and hits anymore?" I say.

"I didn't say that," says Rick. "But if we're honest, we don't know that she still does. Like I said, moms change."

"My Forever Mom changed," I say.

On the other side of the couch my Forever Dad sits up. My Forever Mom stands up straight.

"Really?" says Rick.

I nod my head yes. "She—"

"Ginny," says my Forever Dad, "Rick's right. Gloria probably changed a lot since you were living in the apartment. But we have to let the social workers finish their investigation. No one realized that your aunt went over there every day to help her take care of your Baby Doll."

"Who knows?" says Rick. "If Gloria gets the help she needs, maybe she can come visit you."

Everyone looks at Rick.

"I don't think that's going to happen," says my Forever Mom.

"Why not?" Rick says.

"Yes, why not?" I say.

"Because I won't allow it," she says.

"We're talking about someone who was involved in a kidnapping," my Forever Dad says.

"Crystal is in jail," says Rick.

"Crystal *with a C*," I say.

"Right, but you don't think she acted alone, do you?" says my Forever Dad. "We don't know what the police discovered, but I don't believe for a second that the two weren't working together. The case is far from over, but come on, Gloria isn't someone we want around Ginny. She's way too volatile."

"Like I said before, people change," says Rick. "Didn't you folks ever go through a rough patch? I know I sure have. And now look at all of us."

I look but I don't see anything different. I hope no one looks at me.

"Gloria will never come to this house for a visit," my Forever Mom says. "Not over my dead body."

"All right, then," says Rick. "I see how it is. I'm a little more open than you, that's all. Maybe a little more forgiving."

"We just want everyone to be safe," says my Forever Dad.

"I know, I know," says Rick. "But sometimes it's safer to get people together than it is to keep them apart. I sure appreciate what you're doing here, though. With me and Ginny. Just being able to see and talk with her after all these years has sort of filled me up. And if everything works out…"

He stops talking and smiles at me. I don't know why but I smile back.

At *exactly* seven o'clock I took my shower at Grammy's house and then I put on my jammies even though I wasn't in my bedroom at the Blue House. Everyone knows that the true meaning of Christmas is *Jesus the Crisis Savior of the World* but what it's really about is presents. There were lots of people at Grammy's house and all of them had presents for me. I got a new Michael Jackson T-shirt and a book about Michael Jackson and some clothes and some coloring books. Plus a Michael Jackson puzzle and a Michael Jackson mug.

After opening the presents I ate fish and broccoli and sauerkraut and something called pierogi with meat and cheese in them and mashed potatoes and salad for supper and then after supper at *exactly* 9:07 we had little hot dogs on toothpicks and little *kielbasas* and I threw up in the sink. I wanted to go have some more but my Forever Mom said no, that was quite enough.

Now I am sitting in the car and we are on our way home. The clock in the car says 11:56. It is past my bedtime but all week we talked about how it's all right to stay up late on Christmas Eve

because Christmas Eve is a special occasion. My Forever Sister
is asleep in its car seat and my Forever Dad is driving.

At the Blue House we pull into the driveway. It is all snowy
because there was more snow this afternoon at *approximately* four
o'clock when we were at Grammy's but now there are new tire
tracks in it. From the car I can see that there is a big present on
the front porch next to the door.

We all get out. I have all my presents in a big bag with two
handles on it. I look at the big present on the porch. I'm guessing it's for me because I like presents. I would like to open it.
I see an envelope sticking out of the door. Then my Forever
Dad stops. "Ginny," he says, "get back in the car with your
mom and sister for a minute."

Everyone gets back in the car. My Forever Dad walks to the
porch and taps the present with his foot and opens the envelope
and takes out a piece of paper and reads it.

It is dark and starting to get cold sitting in the backseat.

After my Forever Dad finishes with the envelope he opens
the door to the house. He opens it fast. Then he goes inside
and turns on all the lights. Then he comes back to the car and
opens the car door and says, "Everything is fine. Let's go inside and I'll make some quick phone calls." He holds the door
for everyone and tells me not to touch the present, to just go
straight in and to wait.

I stop and look at the present. It has candy canes all over the
wrapping paper.

"What did the letter say?" I ask.

"I'm sorry, but I can't tell you. Just come inside as quickly as
you can. This is important, Ginny."

In the house I put my other presents from Grammy's house
in my bedroom and my Forever Mom says to go upstairs with
her while she gets my Forever Sister ready for bed. She tells me
to go into the bathroom to get washed up. Downstairs I hear

my Forever Dad on the phone. He says something about a letter and trespassing which is a word from the *Our Father* which is a prayer which is something you say at church. But I don't think he's talking to a priest. I brush my teeth and wash my face. I want to go back downstairs to get my hairbrush from my bedroom so I can look out the window but my Forever Mom says to just stay where I am until my Forever Dad is off the phone.

When I'm done flossing my teeth my Forever Dad is already upstairs in the bedroom. He talks with my Forever Mom and they say good-night to Baby Wendy. Then they tell me to go downstairs to get ready for bed.

"Now can I ask about the present on the porch?" I say.

"I'm sorry, no," says my Forever Dad. "We can talk about it in the morning when you wake up. Do you remember what time you should wake up tomorrow?"

"At nine o'clock," I say because nine is when I like to wake up. It helps me remember how old I'm supposed to be.

I go to bed. I'm ready for Santa to come but I still want to know what's in the big present on the porch. I'm guessing my Forever Dad knows because he read the letter. I wish he would tell me what it said.

So I'm guessing that the present is from Gloria because they try not to talk about her. I'm guessing Gloria brought me a present for Christmas and left it on the porch. Which means if we'd been home when she came here my Forever Parents would have called the police.

I start picking at my fingers.

In the living room I hear my Forever Parents talking but I can't tell what they're saying. I want to go out there to talk with them about the present and about Gloria but I know they'll just get mad. So I stay in bed. I will sleep until *exactly* nine in the morning like I'm supposed to and then I'll get up. There will be lots of presents to open but I won't care because it will be light and I'll be able to look out the window. I'll ask my Forever Dad again to tell me about the present. I'm hoping he'll just *tell it straight* like Patrice.

We are supposed to open presents when I wake up which will be at *exactly* nine but it is only 6:16 and my Forever Mom is in my room. She says I need to wake up early because we have to go to Grammy's house again. We are going to open my presents there instead.

"But it isn't nine yet," I say. I look at the clock and now it is only 6:17. My curtains are still closed and the lights are on in the room.

"That's because we've had a change of plans," my Forever Mom says. "So go ahead and go to the bathroom and get dressed. Use the upstairs bathroom, okay? We already have the car packed, so as soon as you're ready, we can go back to Grammy's."

Now I am brushing my hair in front of the mirror. It is still dark outside. I press my head against the cold black window. My breath fogs up the glass. The big present from Gloria is out there on the porch. Crystal with a C said that Gloria *loves me like crazy*. But she doesn't know how to take care of little kids or babies at all. She doesn't know how to take care of herself either or she wouldn't have brought the present here. Because it was really, really dangerous even though I want to know what's in the box. It's like Forever is a thing she has to break through and she's using the present to get through it. Like she's in there trying to break through the dark. The dark inside the present. Or like she's cracking her way out. She's trying hard, hard, hard. First she made a crack by the Blue House and then she tried to break through the doors at school and now she's trying to break out of the dark inside the present she left for me on the porch.

I lean back from the window and finish brushing my hair. In the mirror I see my glasses and what I'm wearing. My nice pajamas with the little owls on them. The scrunchie holding up my hair. I have a lot of nice things now. I didn't have nice things when I was in the apartment. And my body looks different. I'm still really skinny but not as much as I was before. I really hope my Baby Doll remembers me when we all get up to Canada. I hope it won't see that I'm (-Ginny).

I go downstairs. My Forever Mom is coming out of the other bathroom. From the living room I look out the window.

The porch light is on and I can see that the present is gone.

Where is it? I look and look but I don't see it anywhere.

"Time to go," says my Forever Dad. He is carrying a diaper bag. My Forever Mom is holding my Forever Sister in its car seat.

We go to the car. I look for the giant present but still don't see it. When we get into the car I see that the seat behind me is down and there are lots of bags there. They are filled with presents from Santa and from my Forever Parents. I am anxious because I want to know what Gloria sent me. I want to know what the letter said so I keep moving my knees back and forth and pulling up my socks and talking and being careful not to say the wrong thing. My Forever Sister is next to me in its car seat and the presents are behind me and my Forever Parents are putting on their seat belts. "I want to open my presents as soon as we get to Grammy's," I say. "I want to go inside and take my boots off and hang up my coat and then go right to the Christmas tree. I want to open the big present from Gloria first." It is freezing cold and I can see my breath in the car when I breathe.

"What makes you think the big present is from Gloria?" my Forever Dad says.

Then before I can answer my Forever Mom says, "The big present isn't coming with us."

I don't know if I should answer the question or tell my Forever Mom that I am angry. Because she interrupted me before I even started talking and *We do not interrupt*. But if I say that I'm angry we'll get into an argument and then I'll never figure out where the present is. So I say, "I want to go right to the tree and open all my presents. The ones from Santa and the ones from you."

"We aren't going to open presents as soon as we get there," my Forever Dad says. "It's really, really early and we're going to be guests at Grammy's. We have to remember that we're not going there just to open gifts. We're going there because Grammy and Granddad invited us back."

"Why did they ask us to come back so early?" I ask.

"Don't you think this is fun?" my Forever Mom says in a funny voice. "I know I just love getting up before the crack of dawn on Christmas Day after we've been up all night watching the windows because someone gave out all our personal information on Facebook and now the Queen of White Trash knows where we live. Especially when it's only ten degrees outside and we have a two-month-old baby. Don't you think?"

She asked a question but I know I don't have to answer it. She wants me to say something so she can yell at me. I sit quietly in my seat and push my hands together between my knees and imagine I am in a box.

We are still at Grammy and Granddad's house. We have been here all day. Officer Joel came to visit us here. I tried hard not to hiss at him. He talked with my Forever Parents for a long time in the kitchen while I stayed in the other room and played with my new toys. I got a Michael Jackson Pez dispenser and a Michael Jackson calendar and a Michael Jackson key chain and a book about Michael Jackson. That makes four more Michael Jackson things. And I have a new backpack with two pockets on the sides and a special secret pocket inside that closes with a zipper.

It will come in handy when it's time to go up to Canada with Rick.

When Officer Joel leaves my Forever Parents come back into the living room. My Forever Mom takes my Forever Sister back from Grammy and gives it a hug. Everyone always says it's so cute.

My Forever Dad sits down on the couch. He looks at me and I look at him and then I say, "Merry Christmas! Can I open the big present now?"

And he says, "Ginny, the big present isn't here, remember? Besides, it wasn't for us. Whoever left it at our house must have made a mistake."

I don't say anything back to him. He isn't *telling it straight*. He is lying. He never lied to me before. This is the first time. He is trying to keep me safe, I'm guessing, but now I know I can't believe what he says.

"Can we open some presents then?" I say.

"Yes, of course we can," he says back. And then he hands me a big box wrapped in blue wrapping paper with white snow-flakes and a white ribbon. I put a big smile on my face and open it anyway.

EXACTLY 11:05 IN THE MORNING, SUNDAY, DECEMBER 26TH

I was right. The big present was for me. It was from Gloria. I know because I was being very quiet and making no noise at all while my Forever Sister was sleeping and my Forever Mom was talking on the phone even though *We don't listen to other people's phone conversations.* I heard her stop talking and then I saw her look into my room but she didn't know I was in the living room and she put her hand near her mouth and she said, "It was a stuffed animal—a giant cat. Can you believe it? A giant freaking cat! After everything that happened—talk about having no sense!"

Then she stopped talking. Sometimes when you're on the phone you have to wait for the other person to say something. Then she said, "Of course not. Brian put it in the shed that same night and then drove it to the dump the next day. We didn't want to bring it to Goodwill because the mother might see it there. You never know. She shops at places like that."

And my Forever Mom is right. Gloria does shop at places like that. She once brought me to the Goodwill store to find new boots. And we found them for *exactly* $2.95. Gloria didn't have enough money with her to buy them so she made me ask an old lady and the old lady got the boots for me. I was so excited I put them on right there and gave the old lady a hug. And Gloria cried a little which made me confused because I liked the boots. Boots that were black with pink fringe at the top. That was when I was really little. It's hard to remember now.

But I want that giant freaking cat. Because it is a message from Gloria. Plus there's the letter. She is trying to tell me that she won't give up. I want to get her message and send her one back that says, *You have to be careful or you're going to get caught. Just wait for me to talk with Rick at the respite and then we can make our plan to run away up to Canada.*

I am angry because I can't tell my Forever Dad about all these things. I want to talk with him and tell him how I feel but I can't because he wants to keep me safe. I want to yell and complain and say *Well dang!* But I can't. Because if he knew what's in my brain then he would know that I was sneaking and listening to phone conversations which I'm not supposed to do. I'm going to have to do a lot of things now that I'm not supposed to do and they're going to make me really anxious but I have to do them anyway because my Baby Doll is probably getting *abused and neglected* like I was and I have to stop it.

EXACTLY 8:23 AT NIGHT, FRIDAY, DECEMBER 31ST—NEW YEAR'S EVE

I't is New Year's Eve. Grammy and Granddad and Uncle Will and Aunt Jillian and Uncle John and Aunt Megan are all here at the Blue House. And Rick. All of them are wearing funny hats and I am wearing one too. My hat is like an upside-down ice-cream cone. It is red with silver writing on it that says *Happy New Year.*

For dinner we all had Chinese food. Uncle Will brought two big bags that were brown like the ones in the grocery store and inside them were *exactly* six big plastic rectangle containers with covers and five white containers with little metal handles. I had chicken on a stick and beef on a stick and little red ribs and something that looked like brown spaghetti and some crab Rangoons and chicken fingers. Then my Forever Mom made me eat some broccoli and pea pods. I don't like vegetables, mostly. And after that I had to take a break, she said. Because "We don't want a repeat of Christmas Eve, do we?"

All the food containers and lots of extra napkins and plastic forks are still on the table. My Forever Dad keeps looking out the window every few minutes or so. It is like he's waiting for

Santa Claus or something so I say to him, "Don't you know that Santa already came? This is New Year's Eve."

He doesn't answer so I know he's looking for Gloria.

Now I'm sitting on the floor at the coffee table in my jammies with Aunt Megan and Aunt Jillian and Rick. Rick has a drink with lots of ice in it. We are playing a game called Yahtzee. I like it because when you roll the dice you get to look at the numbers on them and count them. The game comes with a special pad with places on it to write down your score. And sometimes you get to yell, "Yahtzee!" really loud and then one of my Forever Parents gets to say, "Shh!"

In the driveway I see lights which means someone is here.

I'm scared because if it's Gloria she might get caught. But she might have my Baby Doll with her so I jump up and look and I see a car there but I can't see who's in it because the headlights are shining in my eyes. I look away fast and shut my mouth and put my hand over it so no one can see inside.

Then I hear Aunt Jillian say, "Ginny, why are you covering your mouth?"

And Aunt Megan says, "Brian?"

But I am sitting down again with my mouth shut tight. I look away from the window and take my hand away. I see my Forever Mom holding her cell phone and my Forever Dad is standing at the window again and Rick and Uncle Will and Uncle John and Granddad are standing at another window and the bright, bright lights are shining into the house from outside. It is like Forever is shining at us. It is trying to burn through the walls with big laser beams.

"It's a car," says Uncle Will.

"What color is it?"

"How the hell should I know? It's pitch-dark, and there are lights shining in my face."

Uncle Will looks out the window again. "White, I think."

Then there's a knock at the door.

My Forever Dad opens it. It is a pizza man. I know because he is carrying a pizza. And I know *exactly* what kind it is because I can smell it. "Can I help you?" my Forever Dad says.

"I'm here to deliver a pizza," the pizza deliveryman says.

"I'm sorry, but we didn't order one."

"It's for Ginny," says the pizza deliveryman. "And it's already paid for."

"Excuse me?" says my Forever Dad.

"The pizza is for someone named Ginny," the pizza delivery-man says. He takes out a piece of paper and gives it to my Forever Dad. My Forever Dad looks at it and crumples it up and puts it in his pocket. "Even the tip is included," the pizza deliveryman says.

Then the pizza deliveryman gives the pizza to my Forever Dad and says, "Happy New Year," and walks away.

My Forever Dad shuts the door. Everyone is looking at him. The pizza is bacon and onion. It is my favorite. It smells *good*.

So I say, "Can I have it, please?"

And my Forever Mom says, "Ginny, your dad and I need to talk."

So I say, "I'm okay with that. I'll start eating the pizza while you talk."

"No," my Forever Dad says to me.

So I say, "Why not?" Even though his voice is an angry voice.

Then Rick says, "Yeah. Why not?" but no one listens to him.

My Forever Dad looks at my Forever Mom. My Forever Mom looks back at him. "Well, I don't know what the hell to do," she says.

"It's food," says my Forever Dad. "We can't just throw it away."

"We can't just accept it, either."

"Again, *why not?*" says Rick a lot louder.

This time everyone looks at him.

"Because Gloria isn't allowed to see Ginny," my Forever Dad says.

Rick puts his drink down. The glass makes a loud clink. "She isn't seeing her," he says. "She's just trying to do something nice for her daughter. What's wrong with that?"

"If you give that woman an inch…" says my Forever Mom.

"Then *what?*" says Rick. "She'll violate a restraining order and get herself arrested? Come on."

"She's completely unpredictable," my Forever Dad says.

"Un*reliable*," I say. "Can I have my pizza?"

"Look, I just think you folks are way too uptight about some things," says Rick.

"I think my friend Rick here has had a little too much to drink," says Granddad. He puts his arm around Rick's shoulders.

Rick sways. He smiles at Granddad. "Maybe. Maybe," he says. "But still—"

"Rick," says my Forever Dad.

"—you can't keep people separated. Eventually the situation will just explode in your face. You know, *ka-boom.*"

My Forever Mom looks like she's going to yell. Then my Forever Dad says, "Rick, please, let us handle this." Then he turns to my Forever Mom. "The damage is done. The pizza is in the house."

So I ask, "Can I please have it?" because it's a rule that you have to say *please* when you ask for something.

"Not now, Ginny," my Forever Mom says.

"But it has my name on it," I say and point to the box. Everyone looks. It says *G-I-N-N-Y* all in capital letters on the side. In black magic marker.

"Son of a bitch," my Forever Dad says and he puts the pizza down on the table. It makes a loud noise. "Go ahead. Eat it."

So I open the pizza. I am so excited my hands are shaking. I count the pieces out loud. "One, two, three, four—"

"There are eight pieces!" my Forever Mom says to me. "All pizzas *always* have *exactly* eight pieces in them. You don't have to count!"

But I have to make sure so I start counting again.

"Do it in your head!" she says so I finish in my brain. She is right. And I know the pizza is from Gloria. I'm guessing she thinks she is the smartest cookie ever. She is still trying to break through the walls of Forever. She is telling me again that she won't give up even though everyone says she isn't coming back. *You are wrong, wrong, wrong,* she is telling them, *and this bacon-and-onion pizza proves it.* But I know if she breaks through and kidnaps me she will get caught. The police will catch her and take her to jail.

I look at Rick. He is leaning against the bookcase and holding his glass again. I have to talk with him about going up to Canada. If Gloria keeps trying to break through Forever I can't wait for the *respite.* I have to talk with him tonight.

"This isn't a violation of the restraining order, is it?" my Forever Mom says.

"I don't think so."

"And what about this? We can't let her eat the whole thing. It's eight whole pieces of frigging pizza. She already gorged herself on Chinese."

I don't say anything because my mouth is full. Plus it sounds like they might take it away. I start eating faster.

"Ginny, slow down," my Forever Dad says. "No one is going to take your food. Only have one piece tonight. You can eat some more for breakfast tomorrow."

Pizza is not a breakfast food but I don't want them to say I can't have it for breakfast so I say, "And lunch?"

"And lunch."

"And supper?"

"Sure. Supper, too," he says.

"What the hell are we supposed to do?" my Forever Mom says. "Call the police and say we'd like to report a delivered pizza?"

"It's a form of harassment," says Uncle Will.

"That's probably debatable," says Granddad.

"Damn right, it's debatable," says Rick. "If it were me—"

"It's *not* you," says my Forever Dad.

"Right. But it *will* be someday. That's what the two of you said, isn't it? And I'll tell you what I'm going to do when it happens. I'm going to set up visitations."

I stop chewing. No one says anything.

"That's right," says Rick. "*Vi-si-fuck-ing-ta-tions.* Try spelling *that.*"

"Rick, you have to stop," says my Forever Dad. "We can't talk about these things in front of Ginny. If you can't abide by—"

"*Abide?* Where the hell do you think we are, a college classroom?"

"I'm just trying to say that Ginny needs a stable, uncomplicated environment, and what we're doing right now isn't exactly—"

"I don't like the way you treat her!" says Rick. "I don't like the way you treat me. I know you got into this because you couldn't have a kid of your own, but now you got one, and you're in over your heads. Way over your heads. And—"

"Ginny, time for bed," says Aunt Megan. She puts her hand out to me. When I take it she brings me into the hallway. I listen to Rick and my Forever Parents argue but in my brain I'm thinking. I have to talk with Rick but he sounds really angry and my Forever Mom is yelling at him. Maybe I can talk with him at Special Olympics instead. I'm hoping Gloria won't try to break through Forever again before then but she sent me a giant freaking cat and then a bacon-and-onion pizza. If she doesn't stop she's going to end up in jail with Crystal with a C.

And who will take care of my Baby Doll then? Will it have to go to jail too?

The yelling gets louder in the living room. "Could someone *please* drive this asshole home?" I hear my Forever Mom say. And then, "He's not welcome in my house anymore, but I still don't want it on my head if he dies in a fucking snowbank."

Upstairs I hear my Forever Sister start to cry.

I lick my lips. "I think I need—"

"What, a beverage?" says Aunt Megan. "I'll go get a glass of water for you while you're getting dressed. I think a nice glass of water is exactly what everyone needs right now."

I am going to Special Olympics with my Forever Dad. It is cold and dark.

When we get inside I see Rick right away. He is sitting by himself on the bleachers. We walk toward him and he stands up. I see Katie MacDougall and Brenda Richardson shooting hoops but I go right up to Rick and say, "Can we please talk about something?"

And Rick says, "I'm sorry, Ginny, but I'm here to say goodbye."

I am confused. *Goodbye* is something you say when you are leaving. When you see someone you know you're supposed to say *Hey* or *Hi, how are you?* instead. I don't know why he said he's *here to say goodbye.* I wait for him to explain.

"I need to go on a trip," Rick says. "I have a big delivery to make down south."

"Are you going to *drive truck?*"

Rick makes a breathing sound and smiles. "Yes, I'm going to drive truck. But I'm going to be away for a long, long time. So I wanted to give you something."

And I say, "Is it a present with a giant freaking cat inside?"

Rick looks surprised. He looks at my Forever Dad and then looks back at me. "Not exactly," he says. "It's this."

Then he hands me the present. It isn't wrapped in wrapping paper. It is wrapped in a white-and-green bag that says *Barnes & Noble* on it instead. I take the bag in my hands and look at it closely. I shake it. It doesn't make any sounds. I can't guess what it is. But I know that I need to look excited so I open my mouth a little bit and smile and make my eyes big round circles. "What is it?" I say.

There are special kids bouncing balls and running all over the gym. "You'll have to open it to find out," says Rick.

My Forever Dad looks away and his eyes look up at the ceiling.

I open the present. Inside is a set of the *Star Wars* movies, Parts Four and Five and Six. I do not know where Parts One and Two and Three are. I start to ask him if he's going to give me the first three movies too when he says, "I thought you should have the complete set."

I want to tell him that it isn't a complete set because the first three movies are missing but he keeps talking.

"Ginny," he says, "I have to go now. You can send me emails, though. I'll answer every single one. I promise."

Then he puts his hand out to shake hands and I look down and shake it and then he hugs me. I do not *recoil* but I don't hug him back. Because hugging back is like saying goodbye. Rick lets me go and moves back. "Shit, this is hard," he says. He wipes his eyes. He nods to my Forever Dad and turns around and walks out of the gym.

When he is gone I look at the place where he was standing just seven seconds ago. I want to see him there again but I know he isn't coming back. He's going on a trip down south to *drive truck*.

I want to ask him about the *respite*. I want to ask him if he's still going to pick me up from school on January 7th and bring me to his house.

"Dad?" I say in a soft voice. It is so quiet I almost don't hear the words.

"What?" says my Forever Dad.

But I am not talking to him. I am talking to the only person who could bring me to the other side of Forever. To the other side of the equal sign. He is gone.

The bus didn't come to get me at *approximately* 6:45 because there's no school today. There was a snowstorm so school was cancelled which means no one goes there, not even the principal. I don't know if the bells still ring when there's no school. I don't like it when school is cancelled. I don't like *un-structured time.* That's what Patrice calls it when there aren't any bells or schedules.

I want to go out to play in the snow but my Forever Dad can't take me yet. He has to finish cleaning up because my Forever Mom is upstairs with my Forever Sister. He cleans up all the time now. My Forever Mom will stay upstairs all day. It's like she lives there.

I am trying to pick out a movie. I'm allowed to watch only one a day because I would watch movies all the time if no one said not to. My Forever Dad wants me to *socialize* more. He wants me to talk with them so that I can *attach* even though the only person to attach to now is him. Patrice says I still have a hard time with *attachment.*

But right now I'm having a hard time picking out a movie.

It's hard to pick one out because I have so many. I watched *Baby: Secret of the Lost Legend* on Monday. I watched *The Princess Bride* on Tuesday. I watched *Madagascar* on Wednesday. I watched *Finding Nemo* on Thursday.

Then I remember that Rick is gone. He isn't going to pick me up today at school. Even if school wasn't cancelled he still wouldn't be there. My Forever Dad helped me understand. He said we don't have any plans right now to reschedule the *respite*. Which means I'm not going up to Canada this weekend and my Baby Doll is all alone with Gloria.

It is too much to think about all at once. I want to scream. But someone will hear me.

I pick at my fingers instead. Then I pick up my quilt from my bed and hold it near my mouth and nose. My brain needs a rest so I turn around fast and grab the first movie I see. *Return of the Jedi*. It was on my dresser next to my Snoopy pad and my Michael Jackson pocket calendar.

I hold the DVD case and close my eyes. I remember that Samantha and Bill had *Return of the Jedi* but I'm not in their house right now. When I was there I had a Forever Sister named Morgan who pushed me and pinched me a lot when no one was looking so I pooped on her rug and wrote *Please stop hurting me Morgan* on the wall in her room and put the rest in her heat register. Dealing with Morgan was really *tedious*. I was there for only three months before that happened. Then the police came to take me away.

I sit down on my bed and open up *Return of the Jedi* and take the DVD out. A small piece of paper falls on my bed. Its edges are ripped and it has three blue lines on it which means it's from a piece of notebook paper. I pick it up and look at it carefully. I don't see anything on it. I turn it over and on the other side there is some writing.

It is a phone number.

The number is *555-730-9952* and underneath it is the letter G. I look at it hard. I put it up close to my eyes. Then I understand. I am holding Gloria's phone number.

Which means Rick is still helping me even though I didn't get to talk with him about going up to Canada. Because now I can call Gloria myself. I can tell her that her secret plan *isn't half bad*. I can tell her that we can go up to Quebec where *it's pretty easy to disappear*. She just has to find someone else to come give me a ride so she won't get caught because that would ruin everything. And I have to tell her not to send any more presents or pizzas or anything else. And to just hold on a little longer and not hit my Baby Doll. All I need is a phone and a quiet place so I can tell her.

555-730-9952

In my brain I memorize the phone number.

I put the piece of paper in my mouth and chew and swallow. Now no one will ever find it. If I keep my mouth shut no one will know that the number is in my brain or that Rick helped me. He is the best dad I ever had.

When I wake up at nine in the morning I sit up and shut off the alarm clock and yawn like Chewbacca. I want to make a list of things to do. On it I will write *Find a place to call Gloria* but then I decide that writing it down would be a bad idea. Plus I don't have a phone yet. So I get up and put my glasses on and walk out into the hallway and go to the bathroom. I come out and go to the dining room table and take my pill and sit down to drink my milk. I look closely at the glass of milk and see that there aren't grapes next to it.

So I say, "There aren't any grapes."

And from another room my Forever Mom shouts, "Ginny, the grapes have to wait."

I wait *exactly* nine seconds but still no one brings me any grapes so I say, "There were grapes here yesterday." And then, "There are always grapes here. I'm supposed to have grapes every day to *keep me regular.*"

But my Forever Mom doesn't say anything back. So I look up from where my grapes are supposed to be to see where she is.

She is in the living room kneeling in front of my Forever Dad who is lying down. My Forever Mom is pushing on his chest and blowing in his mouth and putting her head on his chest like she is listening. Then pushing again and again and blowing some more and pulling her hair and pushing, pushing. My Forever Sister is sitting near the couch in its bouncy seat chewing its stuffed bunny.

So I say, "*Approximately* when will I get my grapes?"

My Forever Mom still doesn't answer. She picks up her cell phone. It falls out of her hands. She picks it up and presses some buttons. Then she stands. "Ginny, Grammy and Granddad are on their way here right now. They're going to watch you. An ambulance is coming to pick up your dad."

"Will Grammy get my grapes?" I say.

My Forever Mom turns and picks up my Forever Sister and gives it a hug. "I have to put your sister down," she says to me. "Just stay there at the table, all right, Ginny?" Then she walks upstairs.

Now it is 9:09. I am still sitting here with no grapes. I don't have nine grapes or even fourteen. I have zero. My Forever Sister is too small to get my grapes. My Forever Dad isn't getting up to get them. He is still lying on the floor not moving.

I start biting my fingernails. How long will I have to wait? I know where the grapes are but I'm not allowed to open the refrigerator without permission. It was different when I took the milk on the night of the Harvest Concert because I needed it for my Baby Doll. I don't like to break rules or tell lies. It's only okay to do if I'm trying to take care of my Baby Doll. It's only okay if I have to. So I say, "Gee, I really, really wish someone would help me."

No one answers.

I sit up big and tall so that I can see my Forever Dad's face.

His eyes are closed so I'm guessing his ears are closed too. "I'll just sit here and wait," I say to him. But still he doesn't answer.

Now there are flashing lights in the driveway but they are not the same flashing lights that a police car makes. I see an ambulance parked there. Two men run to the door. My Forever Mom comes into the living room without my Forever Sister. She doesn't say anything to me. She runs to the door and opens it and the two men come in. They are carrying black bags with handles. They kneel down in front of my Forever Dad and now I can't see him at all. I see only the backs of the two men.

Then I see Granddad standing in front of me. He says, "Ginny, go into your room and get dressed. We'll get your breakfast ready after that. Your mom and dad have to go to the hospital for a little while."

I get up and push my chair in and go into my room. When I'm finished getting dressed I come out and sit down in my chair again. No one told me yesterday that Grammy and Granddad were coming to visit. I am surprised and confused.

Grammy comes into the dining room holding my Forever Sister. She hands it to Granddad and Granddad brings it into the living room. He sits down on the couch and starts looking at a book with it. Then Grammy comes out of the kitchen with a roll of paper towels. "I want to pick the snow up off the rug," she says.

I see the snow. "Where did the snow come from?" I say.

"From the paramedics' boots," she says. "Ginny, everything is going to be all right. We'll just do what you normally do in the morning, and we'll wait for a call from your mom."

"Where is she?" I say. Because I don't see her. I don't see my Forever Dad either.

"She is on her way to the hospital with your dad in the ambulance."

I look at the floor. My Forever Dad isn't where he used to be.

"Can I have my grapes now?" I say. "I need to have *exactly* nine." Because if I have my grapes it will be like nothing is happening. It will be like everything is *exactly* the way it's supposed to be.

"Would you like a hug?" says Patrice.

"No," I say.

"Let's just sit down, then."

I sit in the flower chair and look around. I am thinking about how I'm going to find a phone to call Gloria. Adults keep their cell phones with them all the time so it's really hard to borrow one without asking. Plus at school kids aren't allowed to have cell phones. But kids still have them sometimes in their lockers or their backpacks. Maybe school is the best place to look.

"It was nice of your Grammy to bring you here," says Patrice. "It's great that your grandparents live so close by."

I don't say anything.

"Do you like having them stay with you?"

"No."

"Ginny, your dad will be in the hospital for at least a week," she says. "Do you know why?"

"He had a heart attack," I say.

"Yes. He's had high blood pressure for years, but there's been a lot of stress at home lately. The doctors say he needs a different lifestyle. It's not your fault. He just needs things to be simpler. It would have been great if you could have gone to live with Rick, but things didn't work out the way everyone planned. I'm glad he's going to stay in touch through email, though." Then she says, "I'm sorry that things fell through. Rick and your Forever Parents just don't agree. He wanted to raise you in a very different way than they did, in a way that was too…open. But there's a very special place in Connecticut that your Forever Parents are looking at. I'd like you to look at it, too."

Patrice takes out some papers with pictures on them. I see a brick building and little white cabins near a lake and lots of little girls in a big group. They are all wearing pink T-shirts and smiles.

Patrice puts the papers in my hand. "Am I going to this place?" I say.

"We're not sure yet," says Patrice. "But your parents are going to look at it as soon as your dad gets back. They'd like you to go have a look, too."

Go have a look is mostly an expression. It means *going there.* "When are we going?"

"Probably a week after your dad comes home. It was only a mild heart attack, so the doctors are expecting an easy recovery. He'll be home in about a week."

"A week after he comes home," I say. One week is plenty of time to find a cell phone and a quiet place to call Gloria.

"You know," says Patrice, "your mom sent me the letter you wrote to Rick yesterday. It looks as though you're still calling Krystal with a K your Baby Doll."

I hear her but I'm not listening. "It's my job to take excellent care of it," I say.

"Yes, I know," says Patrice. "Gosh, it's been a long time since you were able to do that. How long has it been?"

"Five years," I say.

"Right. I remember now. A lot has happened since then. You've gotten so much bigger! Do you know how many inches you've grown?"

I don't so I shake my head no.

"Ten inches. That's almost a whole foot! I wonder how much your Baby Doll has grown. After all, Baby Wendy is already a little bigger than she was when she came home from the hospital. She was twenty-two inches long when she came home. Your mom tells me she's already twenty-four."

"My Baby Doll is very small," I say.

"Of course she is. But will she always be small?"

I start coming up out of my brain. Patrice is looking at me. My eyes look back but I don't really see her. I see only my Baby Doll wrapped in my quilt. I see its tiny eyes and nose. It smiles when I lean close and waves its arms up and down. *So excited! So excited!*

"Yes," I say. "Always."

We are standing in the kitchen. Looking at each other. There is a white plastic bag behind her on the counter. I don't know what's in it.

"I need to spend a lot of time at the hospital," my Forever Mom says, "but most of that time will be during the day while you're at school. Grammy and Granddad will come over a lot to help out. I need you to—"

She stops talking and takes a breath. Her mouth makes a straight line. "I just need you to get through this. Without any *incidents*."

"What's an *incident*?"

"It's something you do that's unexpected," she says. "Something that causes trouble. You know, like—"

She stops in the middle of her sentence. "Actually, if you don't mind, I don't want to give you any examples. I don't want to put any bright ideas in your head."

I don't know what *bright ideas* means but I'm guessing it's mostly an expression.

"I know you've been spending a lot of time with your dad

lately. I know you've gotten used to him, and he's gotten used to you. And that's great. It really is. But you need to be patient with me, Ginny. I have to be the one taking care of you now. For a little while, anyway."

"Until he comes back?"

She looks away and then looks back. "Right. Until he comes back. After that we'll see. Patrice will help us work through it. Let's just go over the rules for this week, okay?"

I nod my head yes.

"The most important rule is one you already know. Do you remember it?"

"There is no reason for me to touch Baby Wendy whatsoever," I say.

"Right. Good. Now, the next rule is that *you have to make a list each day and follow it.* Because it's important for us to keep busy, isn't it?"

I nod my head yes.

"Good. And when you make your list, you should show it to me, and I'll add some extra things to it for you. There's a lot of work to do around the house, now that your dad isn't home to help out anymore. The extra things I'll add to it will be a few more chores, like emptying the garbage or clearing the table. Maybe helping me bring groceries in after I come home from shopping, or sweeping off the cars when it snows. Nothing too hard or complicated. Do you understand?"

"Yes," I say.

"Great. And the next rule is *when Baby Wendy's crying gets to be too much for you, you'll go out and take a walk.* Just get your hat and boots and go outside."

"And my coat."

"And your coat. And your gloves, too, of course. The point is when Wendy cries, you should go outside and get some fresh air. I can't have you freaking out and screaming in your room like you do, or climbing out the window. Things like that are just too much, okay? So if you hear Wendy cry, and it's light enough out, you should just go outside until she stops. And if it's in the middle of the night…"

She turns around and takes something out of the bag. It is white and has buttons on it and looks like a radio.

"And if it's in the middle of the night," she says again, "you'll have this on, so just turn it up louder. It's a noise maker. Patrice recommended it to me. It makes the sound of rain or the ocean so that you can't hear what's going on outside your room. I bet you can figure out how to work it."

She puts it on the counter next to me. I pick it up.

"The noise maker will help you sleep at night, too," she says. "It's very soothing. And another rule is *no hiding food*. You have plenty to eat here at the Blue House, so there's no need to store up food and squirrel it away in drawers or in your closet. Right?"

"Right."

"And the last rule is *if you know I'm upstairs, you need to stay downstairs*. Wendy needs to eat every three hours or so, so I have to go up there a lot to feed her. When I go up there, you'll need to be a big girl and take care of yourself down here, okay?"

"Okay."

She swallows. "And I also want to say that I'm very sorry I hit you that time when you walked in on us. It's just that I thought you were going to try to take the baby. I get pretty territorial about Baby Wendy. Moms get that way with their first kids. She's so tiny. I have to keep her safe."

But that isn't true so I say, "But, Maura, Baby Wendy is not your first kid."

She puts her hand on her lips. "What did you just say?"

"*I* am your first kid," I say.

"Right. Of course you are—but did you call me *Maura*?"

I nod my head yes.

"Why?" she says. "You haven't called either of us by our first names since the day you came to live here."

I don't know the reason why. The name just came out of my mouth so I don't say anything.

Her eyes look wet. "Did someone tell you not to call me *Mom* anymore?"

I shake my head no. "This isn't a Forever Home," I say.

I clamp my hands over my mouth. Fast. I want to take the words back because now Maura might figure out my secret plan. She might figure out that I know Gloria's phone number and that I'm going to call her to tell her it's time to go up to Canada. I just need to get a phone. I looked today at school but I didn't find one.

"Oh," she says. "It sounds like you're starting to put two and two together, then.

"So the cat is completely out of the bag. I might as well come to terms with it myself. With talking about it, I mean. After all— Anyway, I know Patrice showed you the pictures of Saint Genevieve's, so I guess it's okay. Do you want to talk about it now? Because we can, if you want. You have to leave pretty soon to catch the bus, but we can talk about it for a few minutes."

She looks at the clock on the stove.

I don't understand. I think hard.

"Ginny?"

"What?" I say. And cover my mouth again.

Maura gives a little smile. "It's okay," she says. "I'll make sure everyone knows that you're going back to calling us all by our first names. It makes me a little sad, you know. A lot sadder than I would have guessed. We had some good times for a while, when it was just the three of us. But you seem pretty comfortable with the idea. Are you really as comfortable as you seem?"

I take my hands down. "I'm not really comfortable," I say.

"Oh," she says. "Well, then. That's understandable. We don't have to discuss it at all today. Just so long as we have an understanding. We can deal with it some other time. For now, let's just get through the rest of this week."

Sometimes Ms. Carol helps Larry too. Like right now. We are in science working on a lab. Larry has to light a Bunsen burner with a metal tool called a *striker*. It has flint and steel in it. Then we have to see what color some chemicals turn in a bunch of test tubes when he puts them in the fire. Mr. Crew the science teacher said we have to *record the data* which means we have to write the colors down and see how long it takes for them to turn color. Right now they are all white.

Mr. Crew picked groups for the experiment. He put me and Larry in a group with Michelle Whipple. Michelle Whipple asked if she could go in another group because I attacked her once before but Mr. Crew said we all need to learn to get along.

"Put your arm braces here," says Ms. Carol to Larry. She touches the heater next to the wall. "Then you can lean on the counter and light the flame. I'll turn on the gas for you."

Michelle Whipple is in charge of writing down the data. She has a clipboard and pencil out. She is watching Larry closely.

I am watching her.

I have my Snoopy pad in my left hand and my Snoopy pencil in my right. Plus I am wearing my red sweatshirt with the pocket in the front. It is perfect for today which is why I wore it.

"Here we go," says Ms. Carol.

She turns on the gas. Larry starts squeezing the striker. It makes a clicking-scraping sound.

Michelle Whipple looks at the clock and writes down the time.

I take a step back and drop my Snoopy pencil into her backpack.

I bend down to pick it up. I feel around and grab something flat and rectangle-shaped. I put it in my pocket and stand up again.

"Good job," Ms. Carol says to Larry.

Larry starts singing about good vibrations. He moves his head back and forth like a chicken and his voice gets louder. He winks at me and then closes his eyes and keeps singing.

"Steady with that test tube, Larry," says Ms. Carol. "And keep your eyes open."

I walk behind Michelle Whipple and peek in my pocket. The flat rectangle-shaped thing is a candy bar.

In my brain I say, *Well dang!*

I bend down to try again. I put my hand back into the backpack. My fingers find my Snoopy pencil.

"Ginny?" says Michelle Whipple.

I stand up fast. "I dropped my pencil," I say. And hold it out to show her.

Michelle Whipple bends down and makes a mean face at me. The backpack is between us. She zips it shut and says, "Next time, tell me and I'll get it for you."

We finish the experiment. When the bell rings I go to my

locker to get my flute for band. I also get my music and my water bottle. Then I go to the band room and sit down in my chair to eat the candy bar. I will share it with Larry when he gets here.

Maura's eyes are thin like cuts. She leans forward. "I already know what happened," she says. "I'm only asking because I want to see whether or not you're going to lie to me. Now, did you steal someone's chocolate yesterday at school?"

I don't like it when people get close to my face. I don't like the feeling of people's breath on my lips and nose.

I remember what Patrice said about people who are yelling at me. I turn my head and close my eyes. I do not move forward at all.

"Yes!" I say. And open one eye to peek.

Maura leans back. Her eyes are regular again. I let out a breath. "Good," she says. "That was the smartest thing you could have possibly said. But I told you *no more incidents* the other day, and this is an incident. A big incident, Ginny. We don't steal in this family."

I want to say something but I decide not to. I want to say a lot of things but I will not.

"Grammy is coming over right now to watch Wendy. You and I are going to the store."

"Why?" I say.

"You're going to buy a new bar of chocolate for Michelle," she says. "With your own money."

"Why do I have to use my own money?"

"Because you stole. When you steal something, you have to give it back or replace it. Now, go get ready to go."

She makes a loud breathing sound and hits her hand on the counter. I jump.

"Why do you have to pull something like this? Don't you have any control over yourself at all? Don't you know right from wrong? We've taught you to have good habits and to respect other people. We've taught you how to— But, Ginny, I don't have time for any more nonsense! I don't have time to talk with guidance counselors or angry parents on the phone. I have an infant to take care of and a husband in the hospital. And you pull something like this?"

Baby Wendy is still asleep when Grammy comes. I put my scarf and gloves and hat and coat on. Then we get in the car and drive. Maura gives me my money. She keeps it in a box in the closet in her bedroom. She and Brian don't let me keep money in my room because they think I'll take it to school and might lose it. Or someone will take it from me.

At the drugstore we look through the candy aisle. I find a candy bar that matches the one I ate. It costs ninety-eight cents. I would like to eat it so I ask Maura if I can get two—one for me and one for Michelle Whipple—and she says no, that would defeat the whole point. Then I ask if I can split it with her and she still says no. So I pick up the candy bar and we bring it to the cash register. I don't want to put it down on the counter. I want to hold it and keep on holding it and open it and put it in my mouth. It will be delicious. But Maura looks at me and says, "Ginny, it's time to put the candy bar down." So I do.

The lady behind the counter picks it up and scans it with a red light. Then she says, "Ninety-eight cents." I take a twenty-dollar bill out of my pocket and say, "Here," and drop it on the counter.

"Ginny, that's not how we hand something to someone," Maura says. Then to the lady she says, "I'm sorry, my— Ginny is *special*."

The lady nods her head and makes a half smile with her mouth.

"She's *adopted*," Maura says.

"Really?" says the lady. "How long has she been with you?"

"About two years," says Maura.

"Wow!" says the lady. "I have a cousin who just adopted a baby from Korea. It's such a beautiful thing, adoption. It's the most unselfish thing a person can do. And you adopted a teenager! I don't think anyone could resist adopting a baby if they were in a position to do something like that, but it takes a really selfless person to adopt a teenager. And a *special* one to boot."

Then the lady looks at me. "Your mom is really awesome," she says. And then, "Do you call her that? *Mom*, I mean?"

Maura looks at me. "No," I say.

Then I pick up the money. I pinch a tiny corner and lift it. I hold it out to her. "Here," I say again.

The lady takes it and puts it in the drawer of her cash register. She gives me a ten-dollar bill and a five-dollar bill and then four one-dollar bills and two pennies.

And I say, "Seriously?"

"Is something wrong?" says the lady.

"What is it, Ginny?" Maura says.

"That woman gave me a ten-dollar bill and a five-dollar bill and four one-dollar bills and two pennies," I say.

"That's your change," Maura says. "Put it in your pocket so we can go home."

I put the money in my pocket and we go back to the car. Now I have a lot more money than I had before. Gloria will be excited. I'm guessing she never knew how to make money by buying things. My new trick will help us get money when we go up to Canada. Getting money was always hard for her. That was why she liked free things so much. When we were living in the Green Car before my Baby Doll came we used to go to the grocery store when it was time to eat. We would get free cookie samples from the bakery. Or slices of meat from the deli. Virginia smoked ham was my favorite. *Could I have another piece of that Virginia smoked ham?* Gloria used to say. *My daughter is a picky eater. I want to see if she likes it.*

But after a while the people in the grocery store stopped giving us free samples. A man in a blue coat came out from behind a door and asked Gloria to shop somewhere else so she got mad and yelled at him and in the parking lot she peeled out.

We'll just have to expand our range, she said to me when we were driving out of the parking lot.

"Ginny?"

I come up out of my brain. I am not in the Green Car. "What?"

"Do you understand that it's wrong to take things that aren't yours?"

I nod my head yes even though I know sometimes you have to.

"We have plenty to eat at the Blue House. You don't have to take food or hide it anymore. If you want to bring an extra snack to school, you have to tell me," she says. "We can't have any more incidents. It's all just too much. Okay?"

"Okay," I say.

EXACTLY 3:12 IN THE AFTERNOON, FRIDAY, JANUARY 14TH

I used to play *Flap, Flap, Flap, Tent!* with my Baby Doll. It was an easy game to play. You hold the edge of a shirt in two hands and flap it three times so that it makes wind on the baby's face and then on the third flap you let the shirt rest on its head. But you keep holding it so that it makes a tent and then you look under it so that both of you are inside. And the baby laughs. So you do it again.

But I don't have to use a shirt now because Baby Wendy has a family and nice things. It has a mom and a dad who take good care of it. It even has its own bed.

I am playing *Flap, Flap, Flap, Tent!* with Baby Wendy right now. We are using a white burp cloth.

Maura is on the couch. Asleep. She was sitting next to Baby Wendy while I did my homework at the kitchen table and then her eyes closed. Baby Wendy was next to her in its bouncy seat. It started to fuss so I picked up the burp cloth and started playing *Flap, Flap, Flap, Tent!* with it.

Now Baby Wendy is laughing and laughing. I am kneeling in front of it. It makes a surprised face when I make my mouth and eyes turn into round circles and it waves its arms while the cloth is flapping and then every time I say *Tent!* a laugh comes up from its belly. The laugh makes it smile and look into my eyes.

I play *Flap, Flap, Flap, Tent!* nine times with Baby Wendy. I am careful not to touch it because I remember the most important rule. It laughs and laughs and laughs. I look over at Maura. She is still asleep. Then when I look back at Baby Wendy Maura moves her arms. She stretches. Her eyes open.

I put the white cloth down on my lap and wait.

She doesn't move. "What's the most important rule?" she says.

"I will not touch Baby Wendy whatsoever," I say.

She sits up. She looks at the clock. "Did you touch her?"

I shake my head no.

"Then what are you doing with the burp cloth?"

"Playing *Flap, Flap, Flap, Tent!*" I say.

"What is that?"

"A game I used to play with my Baby Doll," I say. "You flap the cloth and make wind."

Maura sits up. "Let me clarify the rule for you," she says. "*Touching* means *touching with your hands* or *with an object.* Now, what's in your hand?"

"A white cloth," I say.

"And a white cloth is *an object*," she says. "So, are you allowed to play that game with Wendy?"

I think. Then I shake my head no. I put the white cloth down on the ground.

"Good," says Maura.

I stand up. Baby Wendy laughs when I move past it.

Maura looks surprised. "Did you just laugh?" she says to Baby Wendy.

Baby Wendy doesn't answer so I nod my head yes for it.

Maura gets down on the floor in front of the bouncy seat. Where I was. It is like she wants to take my place. She kisses

Baby Wendy on the head and says to it, "Can you laugh again for Mommy?" But Baby Wendy doesn't laugh. I am glad.

I know it won't laugh because I'm not playing *Flap, Flap, Flap, Tent!* with it anymore. I know it laughed when I stood up because it thought I was still playing. So I say, "It wants to play the game some more."

Maura looks at me then at Baby Wendy again. "Show me," she says.

So I kneel down in front of it and pick up the cloth. I make my mouth and eyes into big round circles. Baby Wendy picks up its hands. Then I lift the cloth high and bring it down nice and slow. The wind makes the baby's hair move. It closes its eyes and mouth and opens them again. Its feet and hands start to wave. After the third flap I say, *"Tent!"* and bend forward and let the cloth cover our heads.

When I take the cloth off the baby laughs and laughs again.

I look at Maura. She doesn't say anything. Her eyes look wet. "How long did you take care of your sister?" she says.

I am confused. "Do you mean Baby Wendy?"

"I mean your Baby Doll."

"For *approximately* one year," I say.

"One whole year," she says. "While your mother was taking drugs and selling cats and running from the police."

That wasn't a question so I don't say anything.

"And you used to scream whenever the baby wouldn't stop crying?"

I look at Baby Wendy. It is chewing on its hand. I don't want to answer but I have to. "Yes," I say. Because it's true, 100 percent. That was how I used to get Gloria and Donald to leave my Baby Doll alone.

Maura shakes her head. "It's too much," she says. "It's all just too much at once."

"Ginny, I have to feed the baby," says Maura.

I am in the dining room eating breakfast. I have my cereal and my grapes and my milk.

"So we're just going to try this, okay? We'll see if we can get through it. I can't go upstairs every single time Wendy needs to eat while keeping an eye on you at the same time. So I need you to keep eating. Just keep eating, and don't stop until you're done. And when you're done, bring your bowls and spoon into the kitchen and put them in the sink. Then rinse the bowls out and put the bowls in the dishwasher. Then you can go to your room and start cleaning it up."

I eat grape number six.

"And your cup, too. Don't forget your cup."

I eat grape number seven.

Now Maura is on the couch holding Baby Wendy. I'm not looking at them but I know they're there. Because I saw them sit down. I always know where Baby Wendy is.

I hear Maura moving. With my eyes I look. The white cloth is over the baby's head. It is breast-feeding.

"There," says Maura. "Now, like I said, just keep eating. And by the way, have you seen Wendy's bunny? The little one with the bow?"

I open my mouth to answer. Cereal falls out. I pick up my napkin quick.

"Never mind," says Maura. "Just keep eating for now. And when you're done, go into your room and start cleaning it."

I finish at 9:21 and stand up. I bring my bowls and spoon and cup into the kitchen. Then I go into the living room and stand in front of her.

"You l—"

"I said to go into your room and start cleaning," says Maura.

"But y—"

"Ginny, now."

I turn and walk out of the living room. When I get to the hallway she says, "Wait. I'm sorry. Stay there. Just tell me what you wanted to tell me."

I stop walking. "You left your purse in the car."

"In the car? What's it doing in the car?"

"You left it there."

"My purse? Wait—you mean the bunny is in the purse?"

I nod my head yes.

"When did I leave it in there? I mean the purse in the car, not the bunny."

"Yesterday when you picked me up from school."

"Ginny, just come here."

I walk into the living room. Maura turns her head and looks at me. Her hands are still under the blanket. "Are you sure my purse is in the car?"

I nod my head yes.

"Of course you are. You keep track of everything. But why didn't you tell me yesterday? Why did you wait this long?"

But that was two questions so I don't say anything.

"Sorry. Why did you wait?"

I make sure my mouth is shut tight. I think hard. Then I shrug.

Because after she left her purse in the car I went out to see if the charger to her phone was in it. Sometimes she keeps it in her purse. The phone I got from school yesterday won't turn on. It's the exact same kind as Maura's. I made sure.

So I went outside to the car to look for the charger when she was in the bathroom but when I got there I remembered that if I opened and shut the car door she would hear. But while I was standing next to the car looking through the window I saw the bunny's ears poking up out of her purse.

Maura is quiet. Then she says, "All right. I see now. When I said I was looking for the bunny, you remembered when I put it in my purse. And then you remembered that I left it in the car."

I am glad she didn't ask a question.

"Well, that makes sense. Do you think you could go outside and bring it in for me?"

I nod my head yes. I am excited because now I can look inside the purse. I go to the closet to get my coat.

There wasn't a charger in Maura's purse. I need to find it
soon. Or find someone else's.

We didn't go to church this morning because Brian is coming home. Grammy is staying with me while Maura goes to
get him. When Grammy told me that they would be home by
lunchtime I was glad. I have all morning to find a new hiding
place for the things in my backpack. So I told Grammy I was
going to make my list.

When I got into my room I made my list fast and then I took
Kayla Zadambidge's phone out of my backpack. Her wallet too.
I didn't want to get them from Kayla Zadambidge but I needed
to. Because Michelle Whipple pulls her backpack up close to
her every time I walk by. I took Kayla Zadambidge's phone and
wallet on Friday in Room Five when she was talking with Larry
because I'm guessing I might need some money when I leave
to go to Canada. Even though *it's wrong to steal*. Her phone and
her wallet were together in the front pocket of her book bag.
I need to find a better hiding place for both of them because

Brian always helps me clean my room. Maura never comes in here anymore.

The house is very quiet. I stand with the wallet and the cell phone in the middle of the room. I look around. I could hide them under my bed. I could put them in my closet. I could put them in one of my game boxes in my closet. I could pick Sorry! or Chutes and Ladders or Life, the Game of Chance. Or maybe even Chinese Checkers. I pick Chinese Checkers because it is my favorite game. Plus it's the game that Maura used to play with me all the time when I first came to live at the Blue House. Seeing Chinese Checkers makes me feel happy and sad at the same time which is what I feel when I think about stealing or running away or getting kidnapped.

I take the Chinese Checkers box down from the shelf and put the wallet and cell phone inside. Then I put the box back on the shelf and close the door. And sit down with my Snoopy pad to check over my list. It says,

Empty garbage in room
Clean room
Put laundry in dryer
Read for exactly 30 minutes
Listen to Michael Jackson
Go outside to get some air
Watch a movie
Do not play Chinese Checkers

When I go into the living room to see what Grammy is doing and to tell her that my list is done she is playing with Baby Wendy. It is on the couch with its feet up in the air laughing. It laughs all the time now. Grammy is making silly animal noises at it. I try to remember my Baby Doll laughing but I can't. It's been too long. And that makes me *anxious*. I need to be with it soon so I can help it learn things like the ABC's. I used to sing the ABC's to it all the time but it's still way too little to *sing with me*.

In the living room Grammy asks Baby Wendy what a cat says. I know she will answer the question herself so I say, "Meow," before she can. Then she asks Baby Wendy what a horse says so I say, "Neigh." And when she asks what sound a sheep makes I say, "Baa." Because I know. I know what *all* the animals say. I am fourteen years old and I know a lot more than Baby Wendy.

"It's great that you know all the animal noises, Ginny," says Grammy, "but I was trying to talk with your sister. She's just a baby, so she has a lot to learn. Isn't it great that she finally learned how to laugh?"

"I made my list," I say.

"Does that mean you want to read it to me?"

I nod my head yes.

"All right. Go ahead, then."

So I read my list and at the end Grammy says, "Why should we not play Chinese Checkers?"

I shut my mouth tight. Then really fast I say, "Because there's nothing in the box."

"You mean you forgot to put the game away when you last played it?"

I keep my mouth shut tight and wait for three seconds and hope she says something else.

"I think it's great that you're playing games with your mom again," says Grammy, "but you might want to put them back in so that you don't lose them. But it's fine if you don't want to play Chinese Checkers. By the time your movie is finished, your mom and dad should be home. I'll have lunch all ready."

"So they'll be home before *exactly* twelve o'clock?"

"As far as I know, yes. Do you have any homework that needs to be done for tomorrow?"

I shake my head no.

"Are there any projects that are due?"

I think because that's a different question and then I shake my head no again.

"Okay. Then I think you're ready to start working through your list."

In the kitchen her phone buzzes. She picks up Baby Wendy and walks into the kitchen. She looks around on the counter. Her phone is next to the coffeemaker.

Charging.

She finds it and answers it.

"Oh," she says. "That's a surprise. We'll be ready for you." She puts the phone back down on the counter. My eyes follow it. "Your mom and dad will be home even earlier than we thought. They're getting discharged right now. Let me go change Wendy's diaper, and then we'll start getting ready for them."

"I will wait downstairs," I say.

She goes upstairs. I walk right to the counter.

"I think you might be turning a corner," says Patrice. "Or someone might be turning one, anyway. Your mother says things are improving."

I put another pretzel in my mouth. I like the way the salt feels on my tongue.

"It was the day she fell asleep that did it, I think. You sat there playing with the baby while she slept, and when she opened her eyes, everything was fine."

She looks down. Then she looks back at me.

"But they still want to go have a look at Saint Genevieve's. Your mom knows how much work it is to take care of you, and how much attention you need. They want to make sure they explore all the options. It sounds like a really great place for you. The structure, the calm, the supervision—there aren't any small babies there at all. You have to be at least thirteen to live there."

I take a drink of water and look around the room for Agamemnon. He is hiding again. He hides mostly all the time. I wonder if he ever comes out.

"Are you glad that your dad is home?"

I nod my head. "Yes," I say. "Now I don't have to vacuum or empty the garbage."

Patrice laughs. "I wonder if it's nice to talk with him again, though," she says. "How is he doing?"

"He takes a lot more pills now. He lies down and takes naps and breaks. But we talked yesterday about going to the Special Olympics basketball tournament on Sunday, January 23rd."

"It will be nice for the two of you to go there together. I understand that you invited Rick, too."

I nod my head yes. "I wrote a letter on Wednesday to invite him. Then I gave it to Maura to type into an email," I say.

"Did he write back?"

"Yes. He said he couldn't make it because he's still down in Georgia."

"Well, that's sad. But it's nice that you can still email back and forth with him. I saw that in your letters you still call Krystal your Baby Doll."

"Krystal *with a K*," I say.

"Right," says Patrice. "Why don't you call her by her name? I hear you've started calling Wendy by her name. Or at least, *Baby Wendy.*"

I don't want Patrice to know the reason. I don't want her to know that I can't call Maura *my Forever Mom* or Brian *my Forever Dad* or Baby Wendy *my Forever Sister* because I'm not going to be with them forever. I'm going up to Canada with Gloria to take care of my Baby Doll. All I have to do is make the call.

So I don't say anything. Instead I make my shoulders go up and down. Sometimes that means *I don't know.* And sometimes it's just your shoulders going up and down.

"At any rate, I think you might have bought yourself some time. Just keep doing whatever it is you're doing. I don't think it's too much for me to tell you that I'd like you to stay with Maura and Brian. Saint Genevieve's is a great place, but— Let's just see what happens, all right? Let's just keep letting things get better, and we'll all just see. Okay?"

"Okay," I say.

Patrice looks at a pad of paper. "And I have some more news for you from some of my social worker friends."

I sit up straight and listen.

"They said that they helped Gloria register Krystal with a K with Social Security. They helped Gloria get her to a doctor and to an ophthalmologist. It turns out she needs glasses, just like you."

"Is Gloria hitting it?" I say.

Patrice bites her lip. "It's hard to say," she says. "Hitting doesn't always leave marks. And there are different kinds of abuse, too, that are harder to detect. But for right now, the social workers didn't see a reason to remove Krystal fro—"

"Krystal *with a K*," I interrupt. I am picking at my hands.

"—*Krystal with a K*," says Patrice, "from Gloria's care. I'm sorry that I don't have more information than that. But you know, I was hoping we could talk a little more about her today. It must be frustrating to know that she's still living with Gloria."

"It is very *tedious*," I say.

"I can only imagine," says Patrice.

"Gloria doesn't know how to take care of babies."

Patrice makes a big smile with her teeth and lets out a breath. "Right, well—"

I interrupt. "She doesn't remember to change diapers. Or give it food."

Then Patrice interrupts me. "I know Gloria was abusive and neglectful when you were with her," she says. "You kept Krystal with a K alive. You kept her safe and fed. You were a really good girl, Ginny, and I'm proud of you. But things are different now."

So I say, "How are things different now? Gloria used to get really, really mad. She forgot to bring food home."

"I know it," says Patrice. "I remember how thin you were when we first met at the hospital."

"They put a needle and tubes in me," I say. "Plus a cast on my arm. Then they let me eat a lot of food."

"I'm sorry that you still remember all that," says Patrice. "It was a scary time. But like I said, things are different now."

I remember that Patrice didn't answer my question. So I ask it again. "How are things different now?"

"There are two reasons," she says. She looks up at the ceiling and counts. "Actually, three."

I wait.

"The first reason is that Crystal with a C did a good job of taking care of Krystal with a K. She made sure she had plenty of food after you left."

I wait for the second reason.

"The second reason is what I already told you. There weren't any marks on little Krystal with a K's body when she went to the doctor's," says Patrice. "The doctor couldn't find any signs of physical abuse."

"There were signs on my body," I say.

Patrice touches her eye. "Yes, there were," she says. "And now that we know about Krystal with a K, we know why. Little babies cry a lot. You were protecting her."

"Gloria used to come downstairs to yell and hit when there was too much noise. And Donald—"

And then I stop talking.

Now Patrice is crying. I don't know why. "You were a good girl, Ginny," she says. "You kept the baby safe from them. And all this time we didn't know it. Thank goodness your aunt stepped in and took charge. Did you know she kept the baby for a few months after you left? She took care of little Krystal with a K while Gloria got some help. Then a few years passed, and—"

Patrice stops.

"How many years have passed since you were taken out of the apartment?" she says.

"Five years," I say.

"Five years?" says Patrice. She is still crying. "Are you *sure* it's been that long?"

"Yes," I say. "Crystal with a C took care of it after I left but now she's in jail. I need to go keep it quiet or—"

"Ginny," says Patrice, "it's time to tell you the third reason. I'm going to tell it to you straight."

I listen.

Patrice swallows. "I know it's a lot to take in all at once. I know this is probably the worst possible time for you to have something else to deal with, but it's causing you a ton of stress. So I have to tell you." She stops and her face changes. "Ginny, your Baby Doll is six years old."

I don't say anything. I am thinking.

"Does that make sense?" says Patrice.

"My Baby Doll is a baby," I say.

"No," says Patrice, "she isn't. She's a big girl now. She doesn't wear diapers anymore. And if there's food in the apartment, she can get it herself."

I shake my head. "That's not true," I say.

"It *is* true. A baby who was one year old five years ago needs to be six years old today. Because five years have passed. Right?"

In my brain I check the math.

$$5 + 1 = 6$$

But I also know my Baby Doll is way too little to be six.

I shake my head again. "No," I say. "Crystal with a C said *she'll always be your little baby.* It needs me."

"Ginny, that's just an expression. Krystal with a K is six."

"No, she isn't!"

I cover my face with my hands. Crystal with a C knows I don't like expressions. She doesn't lie. She's the one who tells the truth. If the truth is that my Baby Doll is six then I'm too late to stop all the things that happened to me from happening to it. Because Gloria is completely *unreliable* and Crystal with a C does her thinking for her.

And now Crystal with a C is in jail.

"The Special Olympics basketball tournament will be on Sunday, January 23rd," says Maura. "Then, the day after that, we're going to Saint Genevieve's. We're really hoping you like it. The pictures Sister Josephine sent sure are nice."

That wasn't a question so I don't say anything.

"Ginny?"

"What?" I say.

"Are you...excited about going to Saint Genevieve's? It will be nice to meet some new kids. Kids who are special like you."

"The kids at Special Olympics are special like me," I say. "And Room Five."

"That's right!" says Maura. "It will be a lot like Special Olympics. Everyone will be special."

I look at Brian. He is sitting across from me at the table. Not talking. Maura stays downstairs now with Baby Wendy during the day and Brian stays home too. He is *taking it easy* until he gets 100 percent better, Maura said on Sunday when he got home.

Brian drinks some wine. He drinks red wine every night at

supper now. And doesn't eat things with lots of salt. He isn't going back to work this year. "I'm looking forward to the basketball tournament, Ginny," he says. "It will be nice to see the team again."

"Rick said in his email that we should take pictures," I say.

"Oh, I'll take lots of pictures," says Brian. "And I promise I'll send some to good old Rick."

I wonder if Rick will come up to Canada with me and Gloria. I don't think he will but I really want to thank him. Because he gave me *Return of the Jedi* and Gloria's phone number. I wanted to call Gloria last night but I know people can hear me when I talk in my room. So I need to find a quiet place when no one is around. I need to find a place that's private. There aren't any private places at school. There aren't any private places here at the Blue House. There's always someone here.

"Ginny?"

"What?"

It is Brian. "What's on your mind tonight? You seem awfully distracted."

"Is everything all right at school?" says Maura.

"Yes," I say.

"It's the trip to Saint Genevieve's, isn't it," says Brian. His voice didn't go up so he didn't ask a question. Then he says, "How do you feel about going there?"

"We are going there on Monday, January 24th," I say.

"Yes, but how do you feel about maybe going *to live* there?"

I don't want to answer so I wait. Because sometimes if you don't answer then someone will answer for you or someone will say something else to help you know what to say.

"It's going to be hard for us, too," says Maura. "Like I said the other day, we've had some good times together. But I'm glad that you'll be in a place where people can give you what you need. You're going to be very happy."

"What was the question?" I say because now I don't remember.

"I asked how you feel about going to live at Saint Gene-vieve's," says Brian.

"I feel like I would like to go to my room now," I say.

He nods his head. "All right," he says. "You can go to your room. I understand."

I get up from the table.

"I'm really looking forward to the tournament," he says. "Aren't you? It will be like one last good time." His eyes are wet.

"Yes," I say. "It will be the last good time."

There are woods behind the Blue House.

I can't see them because it's dark outside. I can see only myself. My reflection is looking back at me from the dark, dark window. I see a skinny, skinny girl with long hair and glasses. She is wearing her hat and coat and boots. She is wearing her gloves and scarf. She is a big girl, not the little girl she used to be. Not the little girl she's *supposed* to be. She isn't nine years old anymore. She is (-Ginny) and she has a lot of work to do. She has to be really, really smart and not be a cave girl at all.

I open the window as quietly as I can. The screen is already up because I got it ready before I put on my gloves. I put my backpack out the window and drop it in the snow. It falls only thirty-two inches to the ground. I know because I measured the distance two years ago when I first came to the Blue House.

Next I put my leg out the window and let it hang there. I think.

Because there isn't a ladder.

When I read the poem by Robert Frost about apple-picking there was a ladder and Mrs. Carter said the ladder meant *heaven*.

Then when I drew the picture of me climbing out my bedroom window there was a ladder. Because when I escape and find my Baby Doll it will be like everything is good and okay and safe.

But thirty-two inches is easy to jump, no problem. I don't need a ladder at all. So if I don't need a ladder and a ladder means heaven then maybe it won't be like heaven when I call Gloria and tell her to come pick me up. Or maybe no ladder means someone will stop me. Maybe someone will grab my arm right now and say, *No, Ginny! Don't climb out that window! Don't try to call Gloria!*

I look back fast at my door. It is shut and everything is quiet. Then I look outside. It is dark and there are no more reflections. No more (-Ginny) looking at me while I get ready. Instead I see the dark woodpile and the darker trees behind it. The open space of the yard under my feet. Empty and white. With or without a ladder I need to do this.

I need to go.

The snow is clean and waiting. I hop down and pick up my backpack and walk across the snow.

EXACTLY 5:36,
TUESDAY, JANUARY 18TH

Kayla Zadambidge's phone tells the time when I push a small button at the bottom of it. It also shows the exact date. It is all charged up now. Sometimes I wonder if I love dates and numbers because when I'm deep in my brain they help me remember where I really am. They are like handles I can use to pull myself back up.

The time right now is *exactly* 5:37 and I am on a path behind the woodpile.

I put the phone back in my coat pocket and keep going. The path is easy to see even though the sky is dark. Because the snow is bright. I walk for *exactly* nine seconds and then take the phone out and press the button and slide to the main screen. I touch the words Address Book.

I don't know the names of the people listed there. One of them says "Mom" but I know that that isn't Maura. One says "Dad" but I know that that isn't Brian. One says "Grandma" but I know that that isn't Grammy. I don't see "Gloria" or "Rick" anywhere.

I put the phone away again. I have to go deep into the woods to call Gloria quickly because I don't want them to see me. Brian and Maura won't go in my bedroom right away but I think they might if they call me and I'm not there to answer. So I keep walking. The path turns. When I look behind me I don't see the Blue House anymore. I don't see the woodpile or anything.

In my backpack I have my videos. I have my DVD player too but nothing else. It's all charged up just in case someone finds me. It is part of my secret plan. When I call Gloria I will have my movie playing. That way if someone finds me and says, "What are you doing in the woods, Ginny?" I can say, "I am watching a movie."

That way I will be telling the truth. That way I will still be a good girl.

The snow comes up past my ankles. The air is so cold that the inside of my nose hurts and my eyes are watery. I walk over old tree trunks. I walk between rocks. I walk for nine seconds.

I put my backpack down in the snow and take my DVD player out. I put it on top of the backpack and take out *The Sound of Music* which is about a lady with short hair named Frogline Maria. I put the DVD in the DVD player and press the power button. The screen lights up. I see words on the screen but I'm so *distracted* and *anxious* that I can't read them.

The moon is high up in the sky above me. It is as bright as the screen. I take out the cell phone. The time is *exactly* 5:39 now. I look inside my eyes and see Gloria's number: *555-730-9952*. I press the numbers and then I press the green button but I don't hear a ringing sound. I press the red button and try again but I still don't hear anything. Then I see that the phone says *No Signal*.

So I say, "Well dang!"

And slam the DVD player shut. I grab it and throw everything in my backpack. I pick my backpack up and put it on and start walking. Back the way I came.

But not to the Blue House.

Because I know that sometimes people walk on the road past the Blue House talking on their cell phones. I saw them do it when the weather was warmer. In the spring and summer and fall. I'm guessing they had a signal.

The time is 5:42.

I follow the path until I see the woodpile and the lights from the Blue House behind it. I walk around the house and up the driveway. When I get to the road I go left.

There are no streetlights because we live out in the woods. I see the sky and the moon above the road. I walk fast for another nine seconds and turn around.

The Blue House is still too close.

I walk fast for nine seconds more. The road turns. I go around the corner and look back. I don't see anything. I take out the cell phone and call.

This time the phone is ringing. It rings four times and then Gloria picks up. "Hello?" she says.

"Hello, this is Ginny. I'm your daughter. Remember?"

"Ginny?" Gloria says. Her voice sounds just like it did five years ago when the police came to take me away and she said, "I'm so sorry! I'm so sorry, Ginny!" but she is not screaming and I am not screaming either. I want to yell or grab my socks because I'm so excited but I can't because I am walking on the icy road and I can't see the edges. Plus I am worried that a car will come the other way. I am so excited and anxious that my name sounds like it's not mine when Gloria says it.

"Ginny? Ginny?" says Gloria.

"Yes, I am here," I say.

"Holy shit, Ginny, this is great! But how the hell did you get my number? This is a track phone. I only use it for business."

I don't know what a track phone is but I know that her business is selling Maine coons. "It was in *Return of the Jedi*," I say.

"*Return of the Jedi*? You mean the movie?"

I nod my head yes.

"Ginny?"

"What?" I say.

"Who gave you my number? Holy shit!"

"Rick."

"Rick? But that doesn't make any sense. Oh, wait, yes, it does! He got my address from the police and came to talk with me a few weeks ago. We exchanged phone numbers."

That was not a question so I don't say anything. I am still remembering the way Gloria's voice sounds when her face is squashed.

She takes a deep breath. "All right, let's focus. It's great that Rick gave you my phone number, but I need to ask some questions. I need to figure out what's going on. First, does anyone know where you are?"

"No."

"Where are you?"

"I'm walking down the road."

"You mean Cedar Lane?"

"Yes."

"So you're out by yourself and no one knows it. Whose cell phone are you using?"

"Kayla Zadambidge's," I say.

"She's someone from school?"

"Yes."

"All right," says Gloria. "Wait. Does that mean you ran away?"

"No," I say.

"You just took your friend's phone home and then sneaked outside to call me?"

"Right," I say.

Gloria laughs. "Leave it to my kid to know how to get the job done," she says. "Okay. So you probably don't have a lot of time to talk before someone finds out you're missing. We have to figure out what to do. But first, I want to tell you what I didn't get to tell you online before those assholes shut me down."

She takes another breath.

"I want you to know that I've been looking for you nonstop ever since you left. For four whole years. No one would tell me where you were. Not even the social worker or the therapist. You know what *therapist* spells if you divide the word up, right? Anyway, I've been looking and looking for you, and then you found me on Facebook. It was the best day I had since Donald got arrested. And—"

"Wait," I say. "Donald got arrested?"

"Yep," says Gloria. "And then Crystal got involved without me even knowing it. If she'd just told me what she was up to, I could have helped. Man, I have a lot to say to her. She'll be allowed to send emails when the trial is over, but I haven't been in touch with her yet. But you belong with us, Gin. With me and your sister, I mean. You know that, right? And did you get the Christmas present I sent? What about the pizza?"

But that is three questions at once and my brain is thinking *Donald got arrested, Donald got arrested* so I don't say anything even though the answers are *yes, yes* and *yes*.

"Ginny?"

"What?"

"Remember, I said we need to focus. Now, tell me what you want. Because I know what my plan is, and I want to make sure yours and mine are the same thing. I need to hear you say the words."

"I want to go up to Canada to live with you," I say. "We can disappear in Quebec and I can take care of my Baby Doll again. But you can't come kidnap me or you'll get arrested. So I'll need a ride."

I want to also say *I need to make sure you're feeding my Baby Doll and that you don't hit it* but I don't.

Gloria waits a few seconds before talking and when she talks again her voice is shaky. "That's great to hear, Ginny. Shit, that's great. That's exactly what I want, too. And you're right that if I try to come get you at home or school I'll get arrested."

"Who will come pick me up?" I say.

"That's the tricky part. I'm not supposed to see you. The people you live with got really pissy when I came to your house and school. Venomous, you might say."

"Why might I say that?"

"What, venomous? It's just an expression. You really haven't changed at all, have you?"

"I still have the same head," I say. "Plus my eyes are still green."

Then Gloria says, "All right. Let's think this through. Just because it sounds impossible for me to come pick you up doesn't mean I shouldn't try. I mean, where there's a will, there's a way, right?"

She is talking *really* fast now. So fast I almost don't understand her. It is like we have the same head. Only I'm not so good at sharing.

"But I really don't want to end up in jail. That wouldn't be good at all. So we're going to have to make some adjustments, Gin. Some big adjustments."

I'm guessing that *adjustments* are like *modifications* at school which means someone makes my homework a lot easier. I keep listening and walking down the cold sandy road. The back of my pant legs are getting wet and stiff and I am shivering but I don't care. Because I am talking with Gloria and Donald is in jail. My secret plan is going to work.

"Let's see, let's see," says Gloria. "Who can I get to pick you up? I obviously can't do it. Not at the house. The cops would be onto us in two seconds flat."

So I say, "My Old Dad Rick can give me a ride."

"Rick? No. We can't trust him. I know he gave you my phone number, but he also got my sister thrown in jail. Besides, I don't think he'd do it."

I am shocked. Rick was going to bring me to Canada. He is my Birth Dad and I know he loves me so that means Gloria is wrong. But I don't want to *contradict* her because if I do I'll make her angry. And I can't, can't, can't make Gloria angry.

So I say, "Who else can bring me? I'm not allowed to drive. Plus I don't have a car."

"I know you can't drive, honey. Just give me a minute to think."

I wait for her to finish thinking but Gloria thinks out loud which is not how I think at all and it hurts my head. She keeps talking and talking.

"If you didn't live so far away from town, you could just run away again, and I could pick you up at a meeting place," she says. "You know, a little *rendezvous*. That's what my old Frenchy mom used to say. You're going to love her! Now, what would be a good meeting place?"

"People sometimes meet at the mall," I say.

"Right, but you'd have to get someone to bring you there, and it would be hard for us to find each other with so many people around. Where else do people meet?"

"We met Rick at the park," I say. We are thinking our thoughts together with our mouths instead of in our brains. I have never done this before and it is just too fast. It makes me *anxious* but I don't tell her that because she'll get angry and making Gloria angry can be scary. I pick hard at my fingers.

"I'm afraid that won't work, either," says Gloria. "Remember, you'd have to get a ride there, too. We have to think of a place that you can get to without anyone driving you. Okay? What about a grocery store? Or a church or something?"

"I could ask Maura to bring me."

"Who's Maura?"

"She was my Forever Mom but I don't call her that anymore."

Gloria stops talking for a second. Then she says, "Your what?"

"My Forever Mom," I say.

"You mean the woman you live with? Is that what they make you call her?"

I don't know what to say. I called Maura my Forever Mom because all the social workers said I was going to stay with her forever. That was what they called her too.

"And I suppose her husband is your *Forever Dad*," says Gloria.

I nod my head yes.

"Ginny?"

"What?"

"I asked if they *make* you call them that."

I want to say no but I know Gloria wants me to say yes. So I don't say anything. I don't want her to get mad and she's going to get mad either way. I really hope she doesn't ask about my new name.

"Ginny, *I* am your *Forever Mom*. Got that? You know that, don't you?"

I think. "I thought you were my Birth Mom," I say.

"I *am*. But I'm your Birth Mom *forever*, right? Don't you see that?"

That was two questions so I don't say anything.

"All right, let's just start over. I can't come get you at the house, and I can't come get you at school. By the way, it was great to see you when I came there in September. But I can't believe how fast those bastards called the police."

I nod. "Yes," I say. "There was a lot of *drama*. I saw you

standing next to the Green Car. I stood at the window and slapped the glass. Then I had to go see Patrice."

"Patrice? That's that therapist lady, right? I'm surprised she's still in the picture."

In my brain I see my picture of Michael Jackson. He is dancing on the stage and holding his hat and standing on his tippy-toes. "She's not," I say.

"But you just said you went to see her."

"I *did* go to see her," I say.

"All right, listen," says Gloria. "We need to focus. We need to find a way to get you the hell out of there. And I think we're thinking way too hard about it. It needs to be smoother. Simpler. So here's what we'll do. Go home. Just go back, I mean. Then on Monday when you get off the bus at school, don't go inside. Just walk down the sidewalk as fast as you can, and when you get to the corner, cross the street. I'll meet you right there at Cumberland Farms. Then we'll make a run for it."

"A run for what?" I say.

"For the border."

"On Monday, January 24th?"

"Yes. I think so. Today is Tuesday, so that's just six days from now, right? I know that seems like an awfully long time to wait, but I need some time to get things in order. The hard part will be giving the social workers the slip. They won't leave me alone."

"I can't go on Monday, January 24th," I say. "That's when I'm going to Saint Genevieve's Home for Girls Who Aren't Safe."

"Saint Genevieve's Home for—what?" says Gloria. "What do you mean?"

"Brian and Maura are bringing me down to Connecticut on Monday," I say. "To visit Saint Genevieve's Home for Girls Who Aren't Safe."

"Are you going to school at all that day?"

"No."

"It won't work, then. We need to do it on a day when you're at school. What about Tuesday?"

I nod my head yes and now I am even more excited. I feel like my brain isn't in my head anymore. I feel like it is floating around in the air. "Yes," I say. "On Tuesday, January 25th, I will go to school. The day after I get back from Saint Genevieve's. Two days after the Special Olympics basketball tournament. Will you have my Baby Doll in the car?" Then my brain makes me remember that she wants me to go to Cumberland Farms. Which is at the end of the road that goes to school on the other side of the street. "But I'm not allowed to cross the street by myself."

"Oh, come on," says Gloria. "You can figure out how to cross the street. You won't have to do what those people say anymore, so you can just wait for all the cars to stop and then run across. Don't you want to come home with me and Krystal with a K?"

"I want to pick it up and let it chew on my finger and get it something to eat," I say.

Gloria starts to laugh. Then she stops. "Wait. You want to—"

"Pick it up and let it chew on my finger," I say, "and get it something to eat."

"Okay," she says. Very slowly. "We'll talk about that some other time. But right now I think we really need to stop talking so you can go back and get ready. For our little *rendezvous*. With a little luck, no one will even know you were gone. Sneak back in, if you have to. And then this week make sure no one sees what you're packing. Get all your money together, if you have any. Put some clothes and all your favorite things in your backpack or whatever you carry to school, and be sure to hide the cell phone. Actually, no—it would be better if you got rid of the phone completely. Turn it off and throw it in the woods. And then if you could get a few *new* phones, that would be great, too. You can never have enough phones when you're on the run. The police can trace them sometimes, so it's good to use each one once and then get rid of it. And remember to bring the money. And it's extremely important that you *not* tell anyone what you're doing. Don't let anyone know that you called me and that we talked. If anyone finds out, none of this will work, right? Do you think you can remember all that?"

Gloria doesn't like to hear the word *no* so I nod my head yes even though it is way too much to remember.

"Have you ever dyed your hair before? We'll have to move fast as soon as you get in the car, but we should probably dye your hair. I'll stash my car somewhere to throw the cops off our trail. Point is, I'll be driving something else. Then we'll ditch that and get on a bus. It's going to be tricky while we're still in the States, but once we get across the border, it will be easier. It's so much easier to hide up there in Canada. I already know a place where we can stay, and then after the dust settles, we can start to build a new life, just me and my two girls, just like we're supposed to."

"And I'll take excellent care of my Baby Doll."

Gloria laughs. "Right. Like I said, we gotta talk about that sometime. Shit, you've been through a lot. I can't believe— No. We have to stop talking now, or you're going to get caught. So let's say goodbye, and then I want you to start walking back to the house. When we hang up, you should turn the phone off and then throw it as far into the woods as you can, okay? Then go back inside. Like I said, with a little luck, no one will even know that you were gone. And wait—did you say you had a tournament coming up?"

I nod my head yes. "On Sunday, January 23rd. It's in the gym."

"Sunday in the gym. Got it. All right, then. Is there anything else you want to say before we hang up?"

I think. "No," I say.

"Great. So remember, get as much money as you can, and a few phones, and then walk straight to Cumberland Farms on Tuesday when you get off the bus. That's where we'll have our little *rendezvous*. Be sure to walk, nice and steady. Don't go slinking around all careful. People notice that sort of thing. Walk with purpose, okay?"

"Okay," I say.

"Good," she says. "Now let's say goodbye. I love you, Ginny."

"Goodbye," I say. Then I press the red button on the phone and I stop walking.

I look around at where I am. It is darker than ever now and the road is still sandy and so are my pants and there are piles of snow on the side of the road. Everything is black and white and colder than it was before. So cold that I can't feel my fingers when I pick at them.

The time is 6:03. I shut the phone off and throw it deep into the woods where no one will find it. Then I turn around and keep walking back to the Blue House.

EXACTLY 3:31 IN THE AFTERNOON, WEDNESDAY, JANUARY 19TH

I am in Patrice's office again sitting in the flower chair. Agamemnon is lying in a sunbeam on the carpet near the heat register. His eyes are closed but sometimes he moves his tail back and forth.

I take a bite of graham cracker.

"What are you thinking, Ginny?" says Patrice.

"I am thinking about Agamemnon," I say.

"What about him?"

"He isn't hiding today."

"No, he isn't."

"His tail is moving but his eyes are shut."

Patrice looks. Agamemnon's tail twitches from right to left. "You're right," she says. "Sometimes animals do that. They look like they're asleep, but their minds are moving. In his dreams Agamemnon might be chasing a mouse."

"Or a chipmunk," I say. "Or a squirrel." Because I remember that the Maine coons were great hunters.

Patrice stands up. She picks up Agamemnon and turns to me. "Is it all right if I put him on your lap?"

I nod my head yes. I haven't held a cat in a long, long time. I wonder if I remember how to do it. The last alive thing I held was my Baby Doll. Five years ago when I picked it up to put it in the suitcase. Then before I can think any more Patrice puts Agamemnon on my lap. His head is near my knees. I put my arms around his sides. With my right hand I start to pet him. He purrs.

My eyes are wet. It is hard to see.

"There," says Patrice. "Now, that's a surprise, isn't it? You're pretty good at holding cats. Now the two of you can get to know each other. He'll just keep on dreaming, if you let him. I wonder if we could talk about what happened last night. Brian and Maura tell me that they found you climbing back into your window."

I wipe my eyes and go back to petting Agamemnon. "I went outside," I say.

"Yes, I'd gathered that," says Patrice. "They said that you wouldn't tell them why, though. They said that you had your backpack with you, and your DVD player and fourteen movies inside it."

"I am fourteen years old," I say.

"Right. You're fourteen years old, so of course that's how many movies you would bring. Did you watch a movie while you were outside?"

"I was going to watch *The Sound of Music* but then I didn't."

"What made you stop?"

I make sure my mouth is closed tight. I think. And keep moving my hands deep in Agamemnon's fur.

"I'm going to wait until you're ready to answer," says Patrice. She picks up some blue-and-white yarn from a basket next to her chair. There are two long silver needles in the yarn. She starts to knit. "But I'll ask the question again in case you forgot it. What made you stop watching the movie?"

"I got angry," I say. And clamp my hand over my mouth.

The knitting needles make a clicking sound. "I see," says Patrice. "I bet you were angry about the conversation you'd just had with Brian and Maura. What was it about?"

I am shocked. Because she gave me the thing I have to say and it's true, mostly. Now I can just say it. I take my hand away and breathe. "They're going to bring me to visit the home for girls who aren't safe," I say.

Patrice starts nodding her head. "Saint Genevieve's. And you don't want to go there?"

I think. Then I say, "No, I don't want to go there."

"It sounds like you got angry about having to leave the Blue House, and so you needed to get away for a little while to be by yourself. Have you thought about telling Brian and Maura that you're angry and that you don't want to go?"

I am confused. "No," I say.

"Well, maybe you should. When you tell people that you're angry, or that you don't want to do something, then it shows that you care. And that's what they've wanted all along, Ginny. Brian and Maura want to know that you like living with them. That you'd miss them if you had to go away. That *it's worth* trying to get you to stay. The only thing they've seen you care about since you contacted Gloria on Facebook is your sister. About Krystal with a K, I mean. Now, that's understandable, considering the circumstances, but aside from that, you haven't shown anyone that you care about anything. You haven't shown any interest in staying at the Blue House at all. I mean, your behavior has gotten a lot better, but you still don't seem to want to stay."

What this means is that Patrice doesn't know anything about the reason I climbed out the window. She isn't going to talk about Gloria or phones at all.

I smile.

"Why are you smiling?"

I want to clamp my hand over my mouth but I don't. I don't need to.

"Ginny, I asked why you're smiling."

"We are going to the Special Olympics basketball tournament on Sunday, January 23rd," I say. Because it's true even if it isn't the answer to Patrice's question.

"That's great," says Patrice. "I think it's great that you've kept up with all the practices each week, even while Brian was in the hospital. I know he's glad to be home. Are you still glad he's home, too?"

I nod my head yes.

"Good," says Patrice. "You and Brian have a special bond. It will be hard to go away to Saint Genevieve's and leave him behind, don't you think?"

I think. Then I nod my head yes.

"I bet you'll miss the way he used to take you sledding, and all the fun you had going to the lake this past summer."

That still wasn't a question so I still don't say anything.

"You won't be able to do any of those things if you move to Saint Genevieve's. How does that make you feel?"

I start picking at my fingers. I know what she wants me to say. There is only one answer that will make her happy and the answer is true even though I never have time to think about it. "It makes me feel sad," I say.

Patrice keeps knitting. "I wonder if we could write down just how sad it makes you feel," she says. "You know, on a piece of paper. I could do the writing for you, if you like. We could write a little note to Brian telling him how much you're going to miss him. But Brian isn't the only one in the Blue House who you'll miss, I bet."

"I'll miss Maura and Baby Wendy too," I say.

"Of course you will," Patrice says. "Should we write to them all in the same note? Or do you think that we should write separate notes to each of them?"

But that was two questions. In my brain I see my Baby Doll on one side of the equal sign and on the other I see Brian and Maura and Baby Wendy. But one does not equal three at all. One is *less* than three, like this:

$$1 < 3$$

I can't miss Brian and Maura and Baby Wendy as much as my Baby Doll because my Baby Doll needs me a lot more than they do. Because they're safe. No one will hit them or hurt them. Brian and Maura and Baby Wendy don't need me. So really one is *greater than* three this time even though the math isn't right. Because taking care of my Baby Doll is greater than everything. Even math.

"What are you thinking, Ginny?" says Patrice's voice.

"I am thinking about my Baby Doll," I say without moving my head or eyes.

"Yes, well, I think we should probably talk about that a little, as well. I heard from my social worker friends again."

I come up fast out of my brain. I look straight at her. Agamemnon grips my leg with his paws.

"They let me know that they've been having some meetings with Gloria, and the doctors who've been looking at Krystal with a K say she's losing weight."

"That's because Crystal with a C is in jail," I say. "She knows how to take care of it."

"You may be right," says Patrice. "The social workers are doing the best they can to help Gloria be a better mom. But—"

I interrupt. "Is she hitting it?"

"Not that anyone can tell. But—"

"Is she changing its diaper?" I say. "Is she staying with it at night?"

Agamemnon jumps down on the floor. He runs out of the room.

"Ginny, I knew this news would be surprising to you, but I need you to stay calm and listen. I have more to say."

I grab the arms of the chair tight and wait.

"The social workers said that if Krystal with a K doesn't stop losing weight, they're going to have to take her out of the apartment. They're going to have to take her away from Gloria."

Everything stops. In my brain I remember the first time the police came. The day the first Forever started. The whole thing all at once. The knocking and yelling. The flashing lights.

I shake my head and look at my watch and come back up again. "When are the police coming?" I say.

"I don't know yet," says Patrice. "And remember, it's not definite. It's a possibility, if things don't improve."

"When will you know?"

"Again, I'm not sure," says Patrice. "Probably sooner than later, though. We should know something by the end of this week. Maybe even this weekend."

I pick at my fingers. I stand. Then I sit again. Then I stand up and stay standing.

"Ginny, do you want to have a beverage?" says Patrice.

"No," I say. "I want—"

I stop talking. I shut my mouth tight, tight, tight.

"Brian and Maura wanted me to share these things with you," says Patrice. "They think you have a right to know. And I agree with them. I know it's hard to hear that Krystal with a K isn't doing well, but I hope you see that people are doing something about it. The social workers are involved, and if it comes to it, they'll do their best to place her in a good home."

"Will I be able to go see it?"

"I'm not sure, but when you're at Saint Genevieve's, you're going to be pretty far away. The social workers try to place children locally, when they can. If you're in Connecticut, visits will be tough. Krystal with a K will be in foster care until a judge decides whether or not reunification is possible, and then—" She stops. "So it's a big mess, and I know you're going to want to be around to get updates. Now, if you tell me that you want to stay at the Blue House, I can help you work toward that. But we need to tell these things to Maura and Brian. So let's write that letter, okay? We need to make it clear how much you'll miss everyone. How much you care. And above all, we can't have any more *incidents*. No more running off into the woods or running away. You have to stay put."

I don't know what *stay put* means. I don't understand it at all but Patrice already has paper out and a pen. She tells me to say what I want to say while she writes it. So I start talking in my brain. I talk fast in my brain and then talk very, very slowly. So that I'm not telling any lies. It is extremely hard and *tedious* to do.

But I have to do it.

Patrice writes and writes and then she reads it back to me.

Dear Maura and Brian and Baby Wendy,
I don't want to go to Saint Genevieve's Home for Girls Who Aren't Safe. I'm guessing I want to stay put instead even though I don't really understand what that means. But I promise while I'm here I won't tell any more lies with my mouth. I won't have any more incidents. I won't get into fights at school. I will not steal things. Every time you see me I will be a very good girl.
Love,
Ginny Moon

I have a lot of things to think about and it is making my head hurt. It hurts so much that I keep putting my hands on the sides of my head and squeezing. When Brian saw me that way this morning at the dining room table he asked me what was wrong but I just made an angry face. Because I'm supposed to get ready for the little *rendezvous* on Tuesday, January 25th, but the police might come to take my Baby Doll away from Gloria before that. Which means I have to call Gloria to tell her right away. I have to call her now.

But I don't have a phone anymore.

"So your mom can't go because of your baby sister?" says Kayla Zadambidge. We are in Room Five working on a puzzle together. The pieces don't feel like pieces that go to anything. They feel like pieces of a broken sidewalk or broken glass.

"Ginny?"

It is Brenda Richardson. I think hard. She has a phone but her mom won't let her take it to school every day. Only on days when she has tumbling lessons after school. She has tumbling lessons today.

"Will it be just your dad there on Sunday, or your mom and little sister, too?"

I nod my head yes.

"What about your other dad? You know, that Rick dude," says Larry. "Is he going?"

"No."

"Why not?" Larry says. His dad won't let him have a phone until he gets to high school.

"He's driving truck down to Georgia," I say. "But he sends me emails."

"Are you going to, oh, I don't know, meet him anywhere sometime soon?" says Larry. Because Larry knows about my secret plan. He's going to help me on Tuesday, January 25th. Because he said he would *do anything* for me.

"So your mom isn't going to be there at all because she has to watch the baby?" says Alison Hill.

Alison Hill has a phone. It is *exactly* the same kind as Brenda Richardson's. She keeps it in her locker. I don't know the combination but her locker is right next to mine. I don't want to take Alison Hill's phone or Brenda Richardson's because they are my friends but Gloria said to get *a few cell phones*. Plus if I don't call Gloria to tell her that the social workers are going to take my Baby Doll away then it might happen. The police will come to get it. Maybe today or tomorrow or this weekend. They might already have it.

I try to remember what Alison Hill asked. I shake my head no.

"That must make you sad," she says.

I nod.

"When she grows up, will she be able to go?"

"Mostly," I say.

"I love your little sister," says Kayla Zadambidge. "Remember how she was holding my finger and your mom let me wipe her mouth with that white cloth? I love babies."

Kayla Zadambidge's cell phone is in the woods. I don't think I can find it again and I don't have time to look. Alison Hill's will be the one I try to take first. Then Brenda Richardson's.

"I love my Baby Doll," I say.

Larry starts singing a song about not hesitating and love that won't wait and then something about a baby. I give him a look but he doesn't stop.

"I want to do a layup on Sunday," says Alison Hill.

"Me, too!" says Brenda Richardson.

"I'm going to make five baskets," says Larry. "Five."

"I'm going to box the other team out."

"I'm going to use my hook shot."

"At the end we'll have to take a picture of us all standing together with our medals."

There are too many people talking all at once and I can't take it anymore. I want to get up and walk into the hallway but Ms. Carol points to the clock. "Time to start putting things away, everyone," she says. So we put the puzzle away and then we get our things. It is time to get ready for science. I get my backpack and line up at the door. Then the bell rings and I follow Alison Hill into the hallway.

EXACTLY 4:48 IN THE AFTERNOON,
THURSDAY, JANUARY 20TH

"Hello?" says Gloria.

"Is my Baby Doll still there?" I say. Brian and Maura are upstairs giving Baby Wendy a bath. I am in my bedroom with the door shut.

"Ginny? Why are you calling? Yes, of course your sister is still here. What's the matter?"

"Patrice says the police are going to come take it away. At the end of this week or maybe this weekend. You aren't feeding it enough."

Gloria stops. "Shit," she says. "Shit, shit, shit! I knew those— Listen. Just listen! It's great that you called me, but I have to go now. I have to get the hell out of here. I have to pack everything and get us moving before they show up."

"Are you still coming to the little *rendezvous* on Tuesday, January 25th, at Cumberland Farms?" I say.

"Yes, yes, of course," says Gloria. "But I have to figure out where to go for the next three days."

"*Four* days," I say.

"Right. Four days. Whatever. Holy shit, not *two* of you taken from me! I could really use my sister's help right now! The fuckers!"

"You have to give it more food," I say but then I hear footsteps coming down the hallway. "Someone is coming."

"She's just a picky eater! Like you were! Listen, keep the phone this time," Gloria says. "I might try to call if something happens. Just keep it and hide it. Turn it off, and then check to see if I left a message after you go to bed. But don't hide it in your room. Hide it someplace else. Outside, if you can."

She doesn't say which phone to keep. Brenda Richardson's or Alison Hill's. I start to pick at my fingers.

But then the door opens.

It is Maura. "Ginny, supper is going to be a little later than usual tonight," she says.

The phone is behind my back. I slip it into my pocket.

"Wendy had a diaper blowout, so we're washing her up. Then I'm going to feed her and put her down for a rest. We'll eat at six tonight. *Approximately* six, okay?"

"Okay," I say.

She shuts the door.

I take the phone out and put it to my ear. "Hello?" I say but Gloria is already gone.

I turn the phone off and open my closet door and reach for Chinese Checkers. Then I remember that Gloria said *don't hide it in your room*. I don't think I could get my hat and coat and boots without Brian and Maura hearing. I don't think I could open the door to go outside without someone hearing me.

So I go into the kitchen and open a drawer and get some duct tape. I return to my room and open the window. I open the screen and tape Alison Hill's phone to the side of the house. Then I shut the screen and window and sit down on my bed.

I hold my quilt close to my nose and go inside my brain. *Just a little bit longer,* I say to my Baby Doll. *I'll be there soon to make sure you're safe.*

"That's two cell phones missing this week, both from Room Five kids," says Ms. Carol. Her big eyes squint behind her glasses. "And Kayla's phone disappeared as well a week ago. And I remember that Michelle Whipple said you were going through her backpack."

We are at a table in the back of the room in math class. Everyone is working on something called *slope*. "I was not looking through Michelle Whipple's backpack," I say. "I was picking up my pencil."

"Yes, I remember that, too," says Ms. Carol. "But you managed to find a candy bar while you were picking it up. Ms. Dana says she needs to search everyone's lockers today after school. How do you feel about that?"

She said two different things so I pick the second one and say, "I feel fine about that."

"And she's making phone calls home, as well," she says. "She's going to ask your parents to look through your bedroom. How do you feel about *that*?"

This time I don't say anything. I make sure my mouth is shut tight.

"That's what I thought," says Ms. Carol. She writes something down. "We'll just have to wait and see what happens."

I open my mouth. "How long will we wait?" I say. Then I shut it tight again.

"Probably not very long," says Ms. Carol. "I imagine your parents will talk with you about it when you get home. Ms. Dana already called them. She met with the police in her office right after lunch to discuss the stolen cell phones. But I think they left about an hour ago."

We are in the car on the way to see Patrice.

"We aren't accusing you of stealing," says Brian, "but you did take that candy bar last week while I was in the hospital."

I make sure my mouth is shut tight.

"So I'm just going to ask you straight out. Did you steal Alison's cell phone?"

I can't lie to him. I can't lie to anybody because lies aren't true. Words have to tell the truth. They have to *add up* just like numbers. It's a rule.

He looks at me and looks back at the road. I shake my head no.

"Well, I believe you. I really do," he says.

I get a funny feeling deep inside my chest. Patrice says that people feel things with their bodies. With their hearts and bellies, mostly. She is right. Because I really like Brian and now I feel sick, sick, sick. I really wanted him to be my Forever Dad and right now my chest feels as heavy and cold as a gallon of human milk.

"Your m—I mean, Maura looked through your room today. She didn't find anything. We haven't called Ms. Dana back to tell her because I wanted to talk with you first. But I'm sorry about all this, kiddo. About all of it. The timing was just awful. Then all the confusion with the Baby Doll—who knew? Things are different now."

"I am sorry too," I say. And it's true. I'm sorry about everything I did and for what I'm going to do on Tuesday, January 25th. I don't like any of it but I have to do it.

"Are you crying?" Brian says. He looks at me again and looks back to the road.

We slow down and turn a corner. I nod my head yes. My eyes are wet but that still doesn't make the human milk go away.

"You're a good girl, Ginny. No matter what anybody else might say."

I am at the Special Olympics basketball tournament. There
are police officers in the building. I counted three when we
were walking to the court. Then two more when I was sitting
on the bench waiting for the first game to start. I am okay because I knew the police officers would be here. They come to
all the Special Olympics tournaments. They aren't here to keep
me safe from Gloria.

I walk onto the court with Brenda Richardson and Larry and
Kayla Zadambidge. There are two partners as well. Partners are
not special kids. They can keep their mouths closed when they're
thinking and can tie their own shoes. They play on the same
team as the special kids but they don't shoot baskets. So it is the
six of us on Court Three against the Hamden Hornets. We are
the Lee Lancers. On our banners and shirts there is a picture of
a knight with a long pointy spear.

In the bleachers I see Brian. He is watching the game with
Brenda Richardson's parents and some of the other parents too.
Rick is not there. I want to wave to Brian but then I see the

ball go bouncing past me. Then someone yells, "Ginny!" and
I see that Kayla Zadambidge is looking at me with a mad face.

Which means I got distracted again.

"Ginny, let's keep your eyes on the ball," says Coach Dan. He
is wearing a blue-and-yellow T-shirt and a blue-and-yellow hat.
My uniform is blue and yellow. Everyone on the Lee Lancers
has a blue-and-yellow uniform. But the Hamden Hornets have
black-and-yellow uniforms like they are bees.

"Ginny?" says Brenda Richardson.

She is standing next to me but I don't remember how she got
there. "I think you need to take the ball out."

She is pointing to the other side of the court where I see
Coach Dan. He is pointing to a spot on the ground and making
a hand motion to me with his other hand. I go to see what he's
looking at and when I get there he says, "Stand here, okay?" So
I do. I stand there and the referee gives me the ball. I like the
referee because he always knows the rules and he has a whistle
and he always wears black and white.

"Pass the ball to the player in front of you," says Coach Dan.

"But that's a Hamden Hornet," I say.

"I know," says Coach Dan. "I promise he'll give it back."

So I pass the ball to the player in front of me and he catches
it and bounces it to me. I catch it. "Now pass the ball to one
of *our* players!" says Coach Dan and moves away fast. So I look
and I see Brenda Richardson and Larry and three players from
the Hamden Hornets. I throw the ball to Larry who is in his
wheelchair today. He catches it and starts to bounce and sing.
I can't hear the words.

"Get down court!" says Coach Dan. Everyone starts to run.
I run with them. Then I look up to see Brian again but my eyes
look in a different place on the bleachers and I see someone else.

It is Gloria.

I am confused. I don't know why she's here. It isn't time for

our little *rendezvous* yet. She is wearing a purple sweatshirt but
her head is the same as the one from the parking lot. Plus there
is a little girl sitting next to her. A little girl with long brown
hair. She is shorter than I was when I was nine years old but
I'm guessing her eyes are green even though I can't see them
from so far away.

Which means I have been replaced.

Gloria got an *Other Ginny*. Or *Another Ginny*. I don't know
which. I don't know if the Other Ginny is adopted or if she was
hiding someplace in the apartment or if she is a ghost.

Gloria stands up. She waves at me slowly and with no noise.
Back and forth, back and forth. She gives me the thumbs-up
and then waves some more.

The Other Ginny just sits there. Not moving. I'm guessing
she has nothing inside her to say. I'm guessing she is an empty
girl. A girl with a face I don't know.

Gloria looks down and puts her hand on the girl's head. Then
Gloria points at me. The Other Ginny stands up with her and
Gloria puts her arm around her shoulders. Gloria points at me
again and then they both wave. Slowly so that no one will hear
them.

I start to *hyperventilate*. Which means breathing too fast. Because I am angry. Because I want to get the Other Ginny's eyes
so she can't look at me. Because I have been *replaced* which is
what happens when your old earbuds are broken and you get
new ones and throw the first ones out.

Someone yells my name.

I look around but I don't want to see who it is. People run
past me. I look back at Gloria and the Other Ginny to see what
they'll do next. I don't see them at first but when I finally find
them Gloria puts her finger in front of her lips. That means she
wants me to be quiet. She did that once when Donald came out
of the bathroom yelling bad words. I was behind the couch and

when Gloria saw me she put her finger in front of her mouth so I was quiet and she started yelling and then Donald beat the hell out of her instead of me and then—

"Ginny!" someone else yells again and before I see who it is I get knocked over. By Brenda Richardson and some people I don't know. There are lots of sneakers and legs and arms on top of me and I try to push them away but I can't. Finally they get off and I roll over and fix my glasses and stand and try to see where Gloria is. I see her again. I start to put my hand up to wave but then I clamp it over my mouth instead.

"Ginny?" says Coach Dan. I don't see him but when I turn around there he is. "Are you all right?" he says.

I nod my head yes. When I look back up into the stands I see that Gloria and the Other Ginny are walking down the bleachers toward the floor.

"Ginny, why don't you take a break?" says Coach Dan. "Go have a seat on the bench. We'll put you in a little later when you're feeling better. Have some water and maybe go to the bathroom."

The bathroom. That is where Gloria is going, I'm guessing. She is going to the bathroom because that is where she used to meet me when we were in a supermarket or a store or a place where she had to talk with her dealer. *If you lose track of me, go to the bathroom,* she used to say. She wants me to go there now, I'm guessing. I will go see her. I will ask her where my Baby Doll is. I will tell her she has to feed it more because it's losing weight. If it's out in the parking lot I'll run out there and take it.

I make my hands into tight, tight fists. I have to be strong.

There are a lot of people walking around in the gym. I walk between them and around them and I am not going in a straight line but I will be okay because my brain remembers where it is bringing me.

When I get to the bathroom I go right in. I see four white

sinks and six green bathroom stalls and some ladies who I don't know. I don't see Gloria or the Other Ginny. I look and I look but they are not here. So I leave the bathroom and walk back out into the hallway and someone says my name.

I look. I still see lots of people but I don't see who called me. "Ginny?" the voice calls again.

It is a small voice. I turn and look. A little girl is standing far away next to a popcorn machine. She has hair that looks just like mine used to look. Her eyes are green.

It is the Other Ginny.

I'm guessing she's mostly in kindergarten or in first grade. She is small enough to make an acorn out of construction paper and to paste her picture on it to put on a bulletin board. She is too small for me to be mad at. Even if she replaced me I don't want to get her eyes out like Michelle Whipple's.

The Other Ginny starts walking. Toward me. Closer and closer.

When she gets to me she smiles.

She isn't teasing or making fun. She is in front of me just smiling. Then I see that she's holding something in her hand. She holds it up for me to see.

It is a picture of me when I was nine years old. In it I am holding my Baby Doll.

I want to grab it. I want to put it near my eyes and look and look and look. I want to see my Baby Doll's tiny face and hands but the Other Ginny takes the picture away and runs back the way she came. She moves out of people's way like a squirrel or a cat. She runs down the hall and ducks and then stops. And looks back at me. She is standing next to the popcorn machine again.

With Gloria.

I don't hear any sound at all. The ground is flat and hard under my feet. It is like I am standing on the back of a giant equal sign even though I can't see it. So I take a step toward them. Gloria

looks at me and puts her finger in front of her mouth. I want to
yell *What are you doing here? You should be taking care of my Baby
Doll!* but no sound comes out. I try again but I can't talk. So
instead I start walking toward them. Fast.

A police officer walks in front of me. I *recoil*. He crouches
down next to me and asks if I'm all right. With my eyes closed
I nod my head yes. He asks if I need help. I shake my head no.
He stands up and says he's sorry and asks if I know where I'm
supposed to be. I nod my head yes again. He asks if I need help
getting back to the game. I shake my head no. Then he says
again that he's sorry that he startled me. He wishes me good
luck and walks away.

I look back to where Gloria was standing with the Other
Ginny. She is gone. I look in every direction. I look at the doorway to the bathroom. I look at the exit sign.

The exit sign.

I run to it. I push past two people coming in and run outside
into the parking lot. I slip on slushy ice but someone catches
me. "Sorry," I say in a quiet voice. Because it is freezing and the
cold makes it hard to talk. I don't have my coat or boots but I
don't care. I look across the sidewalk at all the cars in the parking lot. I look hard to find Gloria or the Other Ginny or the
Green Car but I don't see them.

Which means I am alone again. I am fourteen years old and
still on the wrong side of the equal sign.

My hands are shaking and I am breathing fast because Gloria
was here with another Ginny and neither of them had my Baby
Doll but the Other Ginny had a picture of her. And of me. The
Other Ginny smiled and showed me the picture but she didn't
let me have it. But where did they put my Baby Doll? Did they
leave it in the car while they came inside?

Then I wonder if maybe Gloria is still in the building. Maybe
she didn't come out to the parking lot. I go back in.

302   BENJAMIN LUDWIG

Steam covers my glasses. I wipe them on my shirt and put them back on. I look and look but I don't see Gloria or the Other Ginny anywhere.

"Hey there, Ginny," someone says.

I look. Maura is coming toward me from down the hallway. Pushing a baby stroller. People move out of her way.

"I didn't know if Wendy's schedule would let us come, so I didn't say anything," she says, "but we really wanted to see you play. What are you doing out here? Is the first game over already?"

I look behind her. I look back at the exit sign. I look behind me and at the bathroom again.

"Ginny? Is the game over?"

"No," I say.

"That's great! Why don't you walk me to the bleachers to find Brian? Wendy and I will stay as long as we possibly can."

I look at Baby Wendy and grab my hair. I take three deep breaths just like Patrice taught me to do and then start walking back to the court. Maura follows me with the stroller. When I get there I see Brian. He is next to the bench holding out my water bottle. He waves to Maura and Baby Wendy.

"Here you go, Ginny," he says. "Have some water. That was quite a fall you took! What happened out there?"

"I don't know," I say.

"Did you get confused?"

"Yes," I say and look back up to where Gloria and the Other Ginny were sitting. The space is empty. I wonder if she saw Maura and decided to leave. Or if she got scared by the police.

"Hey, Ginny. Are you ready to play again?" says Coach Dan's voice. I look up. He is standing with me and Maura and Brian. "Alison came in when you left, but Brenda is ready for a break. What do you say?"

I know that I look like a cave girl. I know that my mouth is open and my head is down and that I am thinking. I am not interacting. I am *withdrawing*. That's what Patrice says. She says I withdraw when I am upset and that I don't think of anything when I *withdraw* but what I'm really doing is thinking really, really hard.

Someone says, "Ginny, let's go sit down in the stands. Did you hurt your head when you fell?"

Someone else's voice says, "Come with us and take a break. You've done a great job so far. You've made your dad and sister and me really proud."

It is Maura. She is talking to me. About Brian and Baby Wendy.

I shake my head no. "I want to play," I say.

"You do?" says Brian.

I look at the numbers on my watch and nod my head yes. "I want to play basketball with the Lee Lancers. I want to help us win." Even though there is no *us*. There is only *them*. I stole three cell phones from people on the team and I don't care about Larry at all. I made Mrs. Wake go away at school and made Crystal with a C go to jail. And now Brian and Maura might send me away to Saint Genevieve's Home for Girls Who Aren't Safe. I have been replaced by a new Ginny. I am *(-Ginny)* and I don't belong anywhere. I'm not allowed to be part of something but I still want to win. At anything. Just once.

Coach Dan looks in my eyes and asks me to follow his finger. I follow it. I growl a little like a Maine coon and then he does a shoulder shrug and says, "She looks fine to me. It's all up to you."

"It's all up to you," I say as well because this is like part of a movie. Only I don't remember the name. It might be *Teen Wolf* or *The Empire Strikes Back* or *High School Musical*.

They let me play.

At Grammy's house we are having a celebration dinner. Because we won gold medals at the tournament. We beat all the teams we played except one and that team won gold medals too. I am wearing mine right now.

After supper we are having a cake that says *Congratulations, Ginny!* on it. I saw it when I went to count how many bottles of soda were in the refrigerator. The cake is a chocolate cake with white frosting and red writing on it.

I am sitting in the living room watching Baby Wendy hold big fat Legos on the floor. It doesn't know how to sit up yet. It doesn't even know how to put the Legos together. I want to help it but I remember the most important rule. *There is no reason for you to touch Baby Wendy whatsoever.*

I brought my backpack with some things in it like my iPod and a puzzle and some maze books and some coloring books from Christmas in case I get bored. I brought Brenda Richardson's phone too. It is in my pocket. I put it there when we took our coats off at *approximately* 2:32. Because I need to find a place to call Gloria. I need to ask her why she got the Other Ginny

and why she came to Special Olympics and where my Baby Doll
was but the house is full of people and I can't find a quiet place.

My coat and hat and gloves are in the mudroom which is on
the other side of the kitchen. My boots too. I will need those
things to go outside into the yard. Outside is the only place
where I can make the call, I'm guessing.

I walk into the kitchen. Everyone is talking. Maura is sitting
at the table and Grammy is cooking and Uncle Will is leaning
on the counter. They talk, talk, talk. And laugh too. They are
having a great time. Granddad is in the other room with Aunt
Jillian and Baby Wendy. Brian and Uncle John and Aunt Megan
are somewhere in the house. I don't know where.

I walk past everyone into the mudroom. I stand around the
corner and put my things on. I don't zip or snap my coat because I don't want to make any noise. I am as quiet as a Maine
coon walking on a carpet.

I walk out and shut the door behind me. It is colder than ever.
I zip my coat and run down the steps and stand right next to
the house where no one can see me from the windows. I take
out Brenda Richardson's cell phone and turn it on and dial Gloria's number.

Gloria picks up. "Holy shit, I'm sorry! We're sort of on the run
at this point, and we needed a place to come in and get warm.
Plus, I wanted a chance to see you! It's like the old days—we're
living in the car. The tournament was the perfect place, since
we need to be in town on Tuesday anyway. But, girl, I wanted
to grab you and hug you so bad, but that cop was right there! I
was afraid he'd recognize me or ask something, so we ducked
out. Why are you calling? Is everything okay?"

I start picking at my fingers. I really, really want to say something but she asked two questions. I don't know which one to
answer first. Which makes me confused and anxious.

"Ginny?"

"What?"

"Why aren't you saying anything?"

"Because you asked two questions."

"I did?" Gloria laughs. "Good old Ginny."

But that is not true. I've changed a lot because I'm taller now and my hair is longer. I even wear a training bra. Plus I'm not who I'm supposed to be. So I say, "But my eyes are still green."

She laughs again. "I'm sure they are, girlfriend," she says. "So why are you calling?"

"You have to feed my Baby Doll," I say.

Gloria makes a breathing sound. "Yeah, yeah, yeah. I know," she says. "Are you going to start riding my ass like the social workers? I kept her alive this long. Doesn't anyone get that? She's a skinny little girl, okay? Didn't you see her today? It was just a few hours ago. All the girls in my family are skinny. You included."

I want to say *No, Crystal with a C kept her alive this long.* But I don't care because I am confused. Because Gloria said *Didn't you see her today?* and *It was just a few hours ago.* I don't know what she means.

I swallow. "I didn't see her *today*. Or *a few hours ago*. I saw the Other Ginny."

"Excuse me?"

So I say, "I saw the Other Ginny. You left my Baby Doll in the Green Car and brought the Other Ginny to the tournament. But you can't do that, Gloria. You can't leave a tiny baby in the car. It's way too cold to leave a baby in the car. You have to take excellent care of it."

"Wait," says Gloria. "Even after seeing her, you still don't get it?"

"Even after I saw *who*, Gloria? Did you get the Other Ginny so that she could take care of my Baby Doll when you go to see your dealer? Does she sleep in my room? Why didn't she bring my Baby Doll into the gym?"

"The Other Ginny?" says Gloria. She doesn't sound angry anymore. "Are you seriously serious? You think the little girl you saw earlier today is some sort of replacement? You really are— Listen, I'm really, really sorry that those assholes took you away when they did. So much has changed, you aren't going to be- lieve it. I mean, you're *really not* going to believe it. And I know you don't like change, so this is going to be...a little surprising."

"I don't like surprises," I say.

"I know. I got an email from Crystal with a C. They let her write to me from jail. She said you don't understand how much time has passed or how much people might have changed since then. I told her it wasn't a big deal, but now I see it is. It's going to take a lot of explaining in order for you to get it. But lis- ten, we can't stay on the phone right now. You're going to get caught if you do. So we can't talk about this right now. Do you understand?"

"No," I say.

"Well, then you're just going to have to not understand. Until Tuesday. Because Tuesday morning is our little *rendezvous*. But the *Other Ginny* isn't what you think. I mean, she's not like some kind of clone or something. You could never be replaced. But like I said, we can't talk about that now. I have to go switch cars. Now, do you remember what to do?"

I nod my head yes.

"Ginny?"

"What?"

"I asked if you remember what to do on Tuesday."

"Yes," I say. "I'll bring all my things on the bus in the morn- ing and when I get off the bus I'll walk on the sidewalk past school and then I'll cross the street by myself when I see Cum- berland Farms."

"And you won't run," she says.

"And I won't run," I say.

"I'll be waiting for you right there. Just remember not to run. Running attracts attention. When you get to Cumberland Farms, you'll hop in the back of the car, and then we'll zip the hell out of town. Do you like black hair or red?"

"Red is my favorite color," I say. I am shocked that she doesn't remember.

"Red it is, then."

"Gloria?"

"What?"

"You have to watch out for the police. Crystal with a C says that if the police find me with you they'll put you in prison."

"Believe me, I know all about that, girlfriend," says Gloria. "I know how and why Crystal with a C got caught, and I won't let the same thing happen to me. She might have been the smarter one, but she always tried to do everything herself. That was her downfall. I survived because I know how to ask for help. How to network. The police have been on my case for years for all sorts of things. I know how to snake my way around and avoid them. Traffic is going to be pretty heavy at the school Tuesday morning, but we'll be pointed out of town and I'll have the engine running."

"Will you bring my Baby Doll?" I say.

Gloria pauses again. She makes a breathing sound. "This is all too much for you, isn't it? Honey, we've got a lot to talk about, but we're going to make it all right. But yes, your Baby Doll is fine. And yes, I promise I'll bring it and give it some food and keep it plenty warm. This will all be a lot easier to explain when we're all together in the car and we can actually see each other and talk. Then you'll understand. But again, yes, I promise I'll have your Baby Doll with me. You can count on it."

I look down at my fingers. I remember all the promises she broke. "I'm good at math," I say.

"Right. Well, I'll see you in two days, okay? You'd better get off the phone before someone finds you. Did you manage to get a few extra phones?"

I shake my head no because I have only one. Even though I found two.

"Ginny?"

"No."

"Well, we'll still manage. How about some money? Did you get any money?"

"No," I say, "but I learned a trick that you do at the cash register."

"You mean where you ask for change a bunch of times and the cashier gets confused? That's a great one. Surprised you can pull it off, though. I've been working it since I was in high school. We'll work on it together." She stops. I listen to the quiet between us. "All right, then," she says. "I love you. See you on Tuesday."

Then she hangs up.

I stand in the yard by myself with the phone in my hand looking at the snow. There are no marks in it. The whole yard is clean and white. On Tuesday I'll have a little *rendezvous* with Gloria and I will get in her new car and see my Baby Doll. I will have a bottle of milk ready for it.

EXACTLY 10:47 IN THE MORNING,
MONDAY, JANUARY 24ᵀᴴ

Everyone calls it *Saint Genevieve's Home for Girls* but in my brain I know it's *Saint Genevieve's Home for Girls Who Aren't Safe*.

We are in a bedroom that has a bed and a dresser and a desk and a little sink with a mirror over it. Girls who live at Saint Genevieve's Home for Girls Who Aren't Safe get their own sink and mirror. They get a crucifix on the wall over their bed next to the window. Brian and Maura want to see if I like it here. To see *if it can accommodate my needs*. Which is fine because I'm going to the little *rendezvous* instead to see Gloria and my Baby Doll and maybe, I'm guessing, the Other Ginny. I don't like her one bit. I wonder if my Baby Doll does. I want to talk with Brian about it. We used to talk a lot about all the things in my brain. He mostly didn't understand but it was okay because we were still talking. Now I can't say anything to him. I have to keep my mouth shut and not say anything about anything at all.

"What do you think of the room?" Brian says.

I don't answer because he is behind me and I don't see him. I can pretend I didn't know he was talking to me.

"Do you like it, Ginny?"

In my brain I say, *Well dang!* With my mouth I say, "Mostly."

"What about the food? That was a pretty good breakfast we had."

"I ate every bit of it."

"Yes, but you eat every bit of everything. Did you like it?"

"My belly is full."

I look out the window. I hear Brian let his arms flap down on his sides. He does that when he doesn't know what else to say.

"The girls we met were very friendly," says Maura. "I bet you could make some good friends here."

She wants me to say *Yes, you are right, Maura.* They both want me to say something like *Yes, I like it* or maybe *You know, this place is pretty okay if you like white walls and brown carpet and people nailed to crosses.* Or that I don't like it and would like to go back to stay at the Blue House. They want me to say anything.

I put my hands on my ears so I can't hear their questions. I don't want to think about Saint Genevieve's Home for Girls Who Aren't Safe. I want to think about the little *rendezvous* with Gloria and my Baby Doll. About the Other Ginny. And about Gloria's surprise.

Then Maura says, "Ginny, are you all right? What are you thinking?"

She stands close so I hear her right through my hands.

"Sorry," she says. "Ginny, what are you thinking about?"

I close my eyes and think of something else. Quickly. I remember what happened at the Special Olympics basketball tournament yesterday. I take my hands down. "I am thinking about Baby Wendy," I say.

"Really? What are you thinking about her? Specifically, I mean."

I look down at my watch. "It's almost eleven o'clock. It should be waking up soon."

Maura looks surprised. "You know, you're right. You sure have a good handle on her schedule."

"I was really proud of you for playing that tent game with her the other day," says Brian. "You've been doing a great job of helping out your mom."

He is talking about Maura, not Gloria. But still he didn't ask a question.

Sister Josephine walks in. She's the lady in charge of Saint Genevieve's Home for Girls Who Aren't Safe. Sister Josephine wears a big black sheet with a pillowcase hanging from her head. She calls it a *habit*.

"Well, I hope you've enjoyed having a look around the dormitory," she says. "Lunch is at twelve-thirty, so we have some time on our hands. Brian and Maura, why don't you stop by the office and talk with Sister Mary Constance? She can answer some of the financing questions you mentioned." Then to me she says, "As for you, young lady, why don't the two of us go for a walk? I think you'll enjoy seeing the gardens."

Outside we walk down a shoveled walkway through lots of bushes and trees. Everything is wet and there are piles of snow next to the walkway. "In the summer all these rose-bushes are in bloom," says Sister Josephine. "There are five different varieties."

At the end of the walkway I see a statue. There are bushes around it so I can't see the bottom. A stone bench is in front.

The statue is of a girl wearing a *habit* or maybe some kind of hood or blanket. She doesn't have a face. The stone is smooth and round where her eyes and mouth should be. Her head is looking down at something in her lap. I can't see because the bushes are in the way.

Sister Josephine points. "Do you see her, there? Wearing the shawl? That's our Blessed Mother. You know, the Virgin Mary. She was just a girl when she had her baby," she says.

"How old was she?" I ask.

"No one really knows," says Sister Josephine, "but a lot of people think she was as young as fourteen."

"Fourteen?" I say.

Sister Josephine nods.

I walk closer to the statue, past the stone bench and right up to the bushes. I rise up on my tippy-toes and look to see what the girl is holding.

It is a baby.

A stone baby with tiny hands and feet. A stone baby with no face. It is looking right at me.

For *approximately* three seconds I can't breathe.

"Why doesn't it have a face?" I say.

"Ah," says Sister Josephine. "I've often wondered that myself. The real Blessed Mother certainly ha—"

I interrupt. "No," I say. "The baby. Why doesn't the baby have a face?"

Sister Josephine looks at me funny. "Oh. I think it's the same reason for both figures. The artist probably wanted us to see that the beauty of our Lord and our Blessed Mother is unimaginable. How does that sound?"

I don't answer. I *can't* answer. "Does...does—" I try to say but I can't finish my question.

"Does what, Ginny?"

"Does the baby know who she is?" I say. I need to know because the baby can't see the fourteen-year-old girl's face. It can't tell what color her eyes are. It's like the girl changed and now she has a different head.

"Of course the baby knows who she is. She's his mother. Babies always recognize their mothers. He's all grown up now, of course."

But Sister Josephine doesn't understand. She *doesn't get it.* "What about sisters?" I say. "Do babies recognize their sisters? Do they remember their sister's face?"

Sister Josephine leans back. "I don't know," she says. "Our Lord didn't have any sisters."

She keeps talking but I can't listen to her. Instead I cover my face with my hands. I don't want anyone to see me. To see my face. Because I'm not who I used to be. I am (–Ginny) and I'm fourteen years old now and my Baby Doll isn't going to remember me when I go to the little *rendezvous*.

"Ginny?"

I put my hands down. Sister Josephine is standing on my right.

"Ginny, why were you covering your face?"

"I want to go inside now," I say.

"Are you upset? What's going on?"

"It is cold."

"All right," says Sister Josephine. "We can talk some more inside."

I am on the bus. We are driving into the front bus loop. Outside I see the space where the Green Car parked when Gloria came to school. I remind myself again and again that she'll be driving a different car today. I don't know what kind yet but I know the motor is running and when I hop in the car Gloria will *zip the hell out of town*. Which I'm guessing means she'll drive really, really fast before the police come. She might even peel out.

I have my backpack. It is packed for our little *rendezvous* which really isn't little at all. Inside there is a pair of jeans and four pairs of underwear and nine training bras and three pairs of socks and three shirts and one pair of jammies. Plus my quilt. I wanted to bring nine movies and my DVD player too but I had to take them out to fit the gallon of milk I took from the refrigerator. In the front pocket is my Snoopy pad and Michael Jackson calendar. In the left side pocket there are *exactly* three one-dollar bills and two quarters and five dimes and thirteen nickels and four pennies. All of the money is for Gloria. To make her happy. In the secret inside pocket is Brenda Richardson's phone. It is turned off. In the right side pocket is a baby bottle that I found in one of the kitchen cabinets.

The bus stops. Everyone stands up. I look outside and see the first few kids walking to the glass doors. I see Ms. Carol waiting next to the bus like she always does.

I look down at Larry who is still sitting. Getting off the bus isn't easy for him. He nods his head. "I'm ready, babe," he says.

I don't correct him. Instead I say, "Thank you, Larry."

Larry climbs down on the floor and slides his legs under the seat in front of us. He pushes one of his arm braces way down with him. He shoves the other one under the seat across the aisle.

When he finishes he says, "Maybe someday we'll see each other again. When we're older. You'll come back to find me, right?"

"I'll come back to find you," I say but my brain is too distracted to think right now.

He puts his hand up for me to squeeze. I squeeze it.

All the other kids are already at the front of the bus. I follow them and hurry down the steps. When I get to Ms. Carol I stop. "Larry is on the floor," I say.

"What do you mean?" she says.

"His braces are under the seat. I'm guessing he needs help."

"Is he hurt?"

I make sure my mouth is closed. Larry *could* have gotten hurt when I was getting off the bus. He *could* have hit his head on the seat or gotten his hand stuck in a spring. "I don't know," I say.

Ms. Carol stands on her tippy-toes. She looks with her too-big eyes into the bus. "Ginny, just stay here," she says. "Just stay right here for a minute while I go check on him."

She gets on the bus and says something to the bus driver. The bus driver looks in the mirror. Ms. Carol walks down the aisle.

I move up close to the bus under the windows. So close that

I see the yellow screws in the yellow paint. So close that I can't see who's inside.

And they can't see me.

I run.

I run until I get to the end of the bus. Then I remember to slow down and walk like Gloria said. I walk slow and steady down the sidewalk. Past cars with parents in them. Past the flag-pole. Past the end of the bus loop. Past the *Drug Free School Zone* sign. Past the whole school.

I turn around one last time to see if anyone is chasing me and yelling, *"Ginny! No! Don't do it! Don't cross the street!"*

But no one is there. I am going to the little *rendezvous* all by myself.

I walk past the parking lot and some bushes and trees. Then in front of me I see cars driving fast on the road in both di-rections. On the other side of them is the gas station. The sign above it says *Cumberland Farms*.

I get to the corner. There is a white crosswalk in front of me made of two parallel lines. *Parallel* means two things that are next to one another but don't touch. The lines are white, white, white.

I put my toes at the edge of the curb and look across. The cars are going by very fast right in front of me and I don't think I can get between them. I want to pick at my hands and fingers but I am wearing mittens. Then a black car stops and the driver starts waving. Only he isn't waving like he's saying hello. He is waving like he's angry. Then I see that he is telling me to walk. He has stopped the cars going one way. I step onto the road.

And I see that I am walking on a giant, giant equal sign.

Something in my chest jumps. I'm guessing it is my heart. The equal sign is right under my feet. I am crossing to the other

side of Forever. To the place where I am nine years old and my
Baby Doll is waiting.

The driver honks. I come up out of my brain and see that
I'm standing right in front of the black car. Still not moving.
The man in the driver's seat yells and bangs the steering wheel.
I hurry past him and see other cars stopped in the other lane.
The one in front is white. The driver in it is waving her hand
at me like the first. I run as fast as I can all the way across the
rest of the road.

Now the road and the cars and the bus are behind me. Ms.
Carol and Larry and Brian and Maura are all behind me now
because I have crossed the giant equal sign to the other side. To
the place where I belong.

I look down to see if I'm shorter. If my clothes still fit. Nothing looks different so I look around me instead. I see *exactly* four
gas pumps with a big roof over them and the gas station. There
are cars parked outside the building. Two of them are green
but in my brain I remember neither of them is Gloria's because
Gloria said she was going to drive a different one. I stand here
looking and looking and thinking hard. Then someone calls
my name.

It is Gloria. She is at the corner of the store wearing a yellow
hat with a pom-pom on top. I start walking toward her but then
there is a loud noise and a car stops fast right next to me. The
driver puts his hands up and shakes them. Through the glass I
hear him yell.

Gloria runs to me. She takes my hand and we hurry past the
gas pumps. She brings me behind the building to a blue car.

"Ginny, you need to look where you're going!" Gloria says
to me. "Shit. I need to hug you."

She gives me the biggest hug I have ever had. She is hugging me so tight that I can't move. I feel her bones under her coat. Her shoulder bones and her back. She's still really, really skinny.

Finally Gloria lets go. She pushes back from me. "Honey, you can't walk out in front of cars! You have to look both ways. Shit, you got tall," she says. "You haven't really filled out yet, though. How many boyfriends have you had?"

I start to say that I have had *zero* boyfriends but I hear a tapping sound and when I look I see the Other Ginny right there in the car. She sees me and I see her. She puts her hand flat against the window.

"Do you recognize her now?" says Gloria. "It's Krystal with a K. *That's* your sister."

I shake my head. "No," I say. "Krystal with a K is my Baby Doll."

And Gloria says, "Right. That's what I'm trying to tell you. That's Krystal with a K. Don't you see? That's the surprise I was talking about on the phone. She grew up. Well, got older, anyway. Just like you did."

I don't know if Gloria is teasing me or not because the Other Ginny is way too old to be my Baby Doll. My little sister *will always be my little baby* and this girl is much, much older than that. I shake my head no. "That's the Other Ginny," I say.

Gloria laughs. She makes a motion in the air with her hand and then the Other Ginny opens the car door and walks to us. She is skinny and her hair is brown and her eyes are green.

Which means she looks *approximately* like me.

"Hi, Ginny," she says.

That was not a question so I don't say anything. I don't have to say *anything at all* to the Other Ginny unless she asks a question.

"There," says Gloria. "You recognize your Baby Doll, don't you?"

"That's not it," I say.

"Don't you remember me?" says the Other Ginny. "I have your picture. Mom gave it to me, and I've been carrying it with me everywhere. I showed it to you on Sunday."

I want to say *Well Dang!* because she asked me something. So I say, "I don't remember you. My Baby Doll is one year old."

"Not anymore I'm not," she says.

"Ginny," says Gloria, "I know it's been a long time, but you have to accept this. Your sister isn't a year old anymore. What your aunt said was just an expression. When we talked on the phone after her trial, she told me all about how you took her at her word when she said your sister would always be a baby. But that's not what she meant, Gin. That's not what she meant at all."

I am breathing faster and faster. "Crystal with a C doesn't use expressions," I say. "Crystal with a C is the one who tells the truth. She said my Baby Doll will *always be my little baby.*"

"I'm not quite sure what you mean by *she's the one who tells the truth*, but what your aunt said is definitely an expression," says Gloria. "And you can't flip out about that. No one can stay one year old for five years. She's six now. Look at her hair. Look at her eyes. The two of you look a lot alike."

"Here," says the Other Ginny. "Look again. It's really me."

She holds out the picture and this time I take it.

I see that her face looks *approximately* like my Baby Doll's. Then I bring the picture up to my eyes. I put it back down and look back at the Other Ginny. Then I bring the picture up again and move it to the side so I can see the Other Ginny and my Baby Doll at the *exact* same time.

And I see that they are the same person.

Which means that Krystal with a K is the Other Ginny. My Baby Doll turned into a little girl. Patrice was right.

I can't see anymore because my eyes are wet. "It isn't one year old?" I say.

Gloria laughs. "Nope," she says.

I am confused. If my Baby Doll is six years old then it doesn't wear diapers. It doesn't need me to pick it up and hide it. It doesn't need me to give it human milk. It doesn't need me to take care of it at all.

I look in Gloria's car just to make sure there isn't a car seat in the back. To see if Gloria is playing a trick. What I know and what I used to know keep trading places in my brain. "My Baby Doll isn't in the apartment?" I say even though I already know the answer. Then I don't know it anymore. Then I know it again.

I stand there blinking.

Gloria makes a breathing sound. "I knew this was going to be hard for you. We can talk about it while we drive. Let's get in the car."

"No," I say. Because what I know is still switching back and forth. In my brain I write,

Baby Doll = Krystal with a K = Other Ginny = Six Years Old

and that is way too many equal signs.

My voice won't work but in my brain I say, *It's just an expression, It's just an expression.*

"No?" says Gloria. "What do you mean, *no*? And what are you whispering?"

What all this means is that Gloria told the truth. Does that mean Crystal with a C told a lie? I don't know what to do but I have to figure it out fast. I open and close my eyes. I look down at the numbers on my watch and pull myself up out of my brain. "Are you still going up to Canada?" I say.

"Yes. Of course we are," says Gloria. "We're going to Quebec to stay with my family. They're going to hide us for a while. Why are you even asking that? You know where we're going.

We talked about it and you understood. Now come on. Get in the damn car."

She grabs my arm and pulls. I *recoil* and fall on the cold wet ground. Gloria picks me up and stands me on my feet. When I can see straight I see a man near the gas station standing still and looking at us. Gloria yells at him. "What are you staring at, asshole? She fell, okay?"

In my brain I remember the time Gloria came to the Blue House and peeled out. I remember how she came to school and *made quite a scene.* I remember how *violent* Gloria can be.

But, *We'll be safe with her family,* I say in my head. *We'll be safe.* I write,

Gloria's Family = Someone to Help *Keep an Eye* on my Baby Doll

And,

Gloria's Family = Someone to Help *Keep an Eye* on *Me*

My bottom hurts from where I fell and my pants are wet. I look down at the numbers on my watch and shake my head. No. Gloria is still completely *impulsive* and *unreliable.* We're not going to be safe with her no matter where she takes us.

"Ginny?" says Gloria.

I stop blinking and look up.

"Come on. People are starting to stare," she says. "That guy who just went into the gas station— We have to go."

"No," I say.

"What?" says Gloria.

I swallow. "No," I say again but it doesn't sound like my voice. I don't know if it was me or (-Ginny).

"Why the hell not?"

In my brain I see the answer. I see *exactly* why because:

Gloria ≠ Someone Who Can Run Away to Canada without Getting Caught

Gloria will end up in jail and Krystal with a K will go to a Forever Home. Just like I did.

I hold up two fingers. "There are two reasons," I say.

"Well, what are they?"

"The first is because my Baby Doll is six years old."

"Yes, I'm glad you got that straight," says Gloria. She looks left and right fast. "What's the second?"

"The second reason is that you're going to end up in jail."

Gloria shakes and her eyes get skinny. She is going to hit and so I *wince*.

"You've got a lot of nerve, kiddo," she says. "Look at your sister. Look at her! I raised her just fine, without your help! I know she's skinny, but that's just how we are! And damn it, we can't talk about this now! We can't stay here! Someone's going to come looking for you any minute! Don't you see? Your school is right down the street!"

She points but I don't look. I keep my eyes on her hand. Her knuckles are white. Behind her Krystal with a K points at me and points at the car and makes a smile with big teeth.

Gloria makes a loud breathing sound. "That's it. Come on!"

She reaches out and grabs the front of my coat. She pulls me forward.

In my brain I see him. Donald.

"No!" I yell. I grab Gloria's sleeve and rip her hand away. Then she tries to grab me again so I pull back. I put my hands up to stop her. "Please!" I yell. "Please!"

Gloria stops. She looks at me in a scared way. Then she puts part of her hand in her mouth like she's trying to eat it. "It isn't supposed to be like this!" she says. "It isn't supposed to be like it was before! You aren't scared to come with me, are you, Gin?"

She wants me to say *No, I am not scared* but that isn't true so I don't say anything.

Then Gloria says, "Ginny, I need you. I need to have you back with me so we can be a family again. Don't you see what they took from us?"

I check in my brain. I don't see what anyone took from us. I just see too many equal signs and words that don't add up.

Now Gloria's eyes are wet. "I did the best I could!" she says. "I had a habit! And damn it, we have to go! We're going to get caught! The school will start making calls and—"

She makes a grunting sound and reaches to grab me again. I try to pull away but now she has me. She pulls me to the car. I try to yell but my mouth won't work so I pull, pull, *pull* away. I slam into the car door.

Then Gloria's face is right in my face. I see her teeth and her eyes and then my brain makes me say, "Please no!" like I used to and cover my head with my hands.

She grabs my wrists and pulls me up again. "Ginny," she says, "we have to get out of here! We have to leave! No matter how awful you might think I am right now, we have to leave. *Now!*"

My voice won't do what I tell it so with my eyes still covered I shake my head.

Gloria looks around the parking lot and across the street and when she looks back at me her face is mad, mad, mad. "Get in the car!" she yells. "Just get in the car! I didn't come all this way to relive every mistake I ever made! You think I want to act like this? I came to make things right! Now, are you coming or not?"

While she talks she hits the top of the car. She hits it again and again and each time I jump.

I try to say something but Gloria is making so much noise I can't find a place for my voice. It is hiding deep in my brain again so I close my eyes and pull my hands and arms down and then I *make* a place for it.

"We do not yell!" I say. "We do not yell or hit! We say *I'm too mad to talk!* and then we go get some air! So you just stop it, Gloria! You stop yelling at me!"

Because it's all true. That's how we do things at the Blue House.

When I open my eyes again Gloria isn't yelling anymore. She is quiet. When she starts talking her voice is scratchy and low. "I can't keep going like this." She laughs but it isn't a funny laugh. "It's way past time for me to go. You turned into a real piece of work, Gin. A real handful. We can make it work, if you still want it to. But you have to want it to."

I lower my head. "I don't want it to," I say.

She hits the car and at the same time says my name. Then, "So this is it? After all this, you're just going to call it off?"

Slowly I shake my head but then I start nodding. My brain is scared and it doesn't know what I want anymore. "Yes," I say but the word scares me. Because I don't know what comes after it.

"Krystal?" says Gloria. She bites her lip and wipes one of her eyes.

"Mom?" says Krystal with a K.

"Get in the car."

Krystal with a K gets in the car. She doesn't say *goodbye*. Then Gloria says, "I'm sorry, Ginny. I'm so, so sorry. I love you, but I'm not going to stand here and get caught. Not today."

I don't say anything.

"The cops will be here any minute," she says. "Maybe look

me up when you're a little older, all right? When you're eighteen. We'll be in Quebec. Until then, try to take care of yourself and… and have a nice life. Okay?"

She hugs me and I don't *recoil*. Because I want her to now. Her whole face is wet, wet, wet. She squeezes so tight it hurts but I'm okay with her hurting me now because I know as soon as she stops she'll leave.

Then she stops.

And gets in the car. The engine turns on and the car backs up and the car drives to the edge of the parking lot. It stops for *approximately* one second and then the tires turn so fast they squeal and make black smoke. I cover my ears and crouch down low and when the noise is gone I open one eye and stand.

Gloria's car isn't in the parking lot anymore. I am alone behind Cumberland Farms without my Baby Doll or anyone. I am alone on the other side of the giant equal sign. I don't know if I can get back to where I came from.

I am scared and anxious. Gloria is gone. She isn't going to kidnap me. She tried but I said no.

I said no.

I look to see if there are any cars coming and then I walk across the parking lot. I look across the street and see my school. I could try to go back across but I don't belong there. Where I belong is where I'm nine years old and my Baby Doll is still a baby but now it's six years old. The math I was using doesn't add up. Plus Gloria said I was *a real handful*. Crystal with a C said that too.

I look down at my hands. I am still holding the picture of me and Krystal with a K. Of me and my Baby Doll. Both of them have faces.

I put the picture in my pocket. Then I pull my thumbs out

of the thumb holes in my mittens and start to pick at them with my other fingers.

There's nothing for me this side of Forever and there's nothing for me on the other side either. I'm not Ginny *LeBlanc* anymore and I don't know how to be Ginny Moon. My Baby Doll doesn't need me. No one needs me at the Blue House. I don't belong anywhere anymore.

Because I am (–Ginny).

I'm guessing this is what it feels like to be a ghost. Or not to have a face. No one knows me and I don't even have a house or a car or a suitcase to hide in.

I look across the street. A truck comes by fast. I feel the wind on my face and I *recoil*. But when it is gone I look at my watch and stand up straight again.

I look down the road to the right. There are a lot of cars on it but the sidewalk keeps going. I know that it's safe to walk on sidewalks. So I start walking.

I walk down the sidewalk until I come to a corner. I can go across the street or I can take another right. The noise of the cars is loud and the air is cold and my backpack is heavy. I don't know where I'm going. I don't know where a girl who doesn't belong anywhere should go.

Mostly I think I need to find a place to live. But no one is here to help me do that. I need to find one on my own. I don't know if it will be a house or an apartment. I don't know if it will be in the city or the woods. Right now I'm guessing the city because that's where I am and I don't see trees or the woods anywhere.

The cars are moving fast and I am anxious. So I turn right again. Ahead of me I see a lot of buildings made out of bricks. I see signs that say *Credit Union* and *Books and Jewelry*. There is a church and a store called Boss Furniture and a Chinese food restaurant.

I walk past all of these. Then I see a movie theater and I

remember that I don't have my DVD player with me because I brought a gallon of milk for my Baby Doll instead. So I say, "Well dang!" as loud as I can because no one is around to hear me.

The movie theater has a big sign on it with letters that start at the top of the building and go down to the door. The sign has a lot of colored lightbulbs on it but they are not lit up right now. The letters say *Colony Cinema*. I walk to the door and look up at the sign. It makes me dizzy when I look all the way to the top. I am cold. It would be good to go inside to get warm. I look at the door and see that no one is inside. Plus there's a chain on the door which I'm guessing means I can't get in. So I walk around the corner of the building to see if there is an open window because that is what Gloria told me to do one time when she needed to get into Donald's house to get her money back.

Behind the movie theater a cat climbs over a fence. Papers are blowing around on the ground. I see an old bicycle with no wheels. There aren't any open windows behind the movie theater but there's a black staircase made of metal. It is up in the air but there is a ladder hanging down from it. It looks scary but I really want to get inside because the movie theater looks like a good place to get warm and maybe live and mostly I'm guessing I can watch movies there. There are windows up higher on the building and all of them are near the staircase.

I climb up the ladder and step onto the stairs and start going up. It is like walking on a black skeleton. I can see down to the ground and I feel like I could fall but I know there are windows up higher so I keep climbing. Finally I come to one. It is open so I climb inside.

It is dark in the room but I find the floor with one of my feet and pull my body all the way through the window. My backpack almost gets stuck. When I stand up I see a room with nothing in it except old blankets and black garbage bags and a door that is closed. There are pipes on the ceiling and a broken picture frame on the floor. Everything is dirty and it is hard to see because there are no lights.

Then I see a switch on the wall. I walk to it and flip it but nothing happens. So I say, "What, can't I get some lights?"

But no one answers me.

And I think, *Maybe this can be my room.* I don't like that there are no lights but there is a door and maybe a kitchen on the other side of it. I try to open the door but it is locked. So what I have is a room with no kitchen or bathroom or lights.

I stand in the middle of the room. I turn around and around and around. I see the window again and again as I spin. I hear the sound of cars outside. I do not hear people talking. I do not hear music. I do not hear the sound of someone washing dishes or Baby Wendy playing. And it is cold, cold, cold.

Which means this isn't a good place to live.

Then I feel hungry which means I have to find something to eat. I am good at finding food. So I go to the window and climb out onto the metal stairs. When I get to the ladder I climb down to the ground but then I can't remember which way the front of the movie theater is. I start walking until I come to a street.

And I see a police car.

The police car is not moving. It is parked next to a streetlight and a garbage can. There is no one in it which means the police officer is out of the car somewhere. He might be looking for me.

In my mittens I start to pick at my thumbs. I look up and down the street. I see an old lady bringing a dog somewhere on a leash. I see a man in a long coat go inside a building but I still don't see the police officer which means he's probably hiding somewhere or around the corner asking people, "Have you seen Ginny? She's in a lot of trouble now."

Now my hands are shaking and I am *hyperventilating* and my legs want to move, move, move. So I run.

I run past a fence and some more brick buildings. I run past piles of garbage and garbage cans. I run past cars that are parked and cars that are moving. I run past two old ladies and a man listening to headphones and a man wearing a winter hat with no pom-pom and a lady with a black coat and a black bag and silver earrings. There are loud noises everywhere. Engines and horns and sometimes people talking or the wind. And the air is cold and my feet are tired. I am breathing fast and I still don't know where to go even though I need to find a place to live.

Then I feel wet on my back and my bottom and my legs. I stop running. I am on a sidewalk in front of a big glass window. There are people on the other side of it. I take off my backpack and look inside. The gallon of milk is empty. There are drops of milk on the plastic and all of my things are wet. The milk jug is broken. It has a big crack in it. I'm guessing the milk is what made everything wet even though nothing turned white.

Which means I don't have any milk for my Baby Doll.

Then I remember how big it is and that it is not one year old.

I want to cry but I need to be a *tough cookie*. I want Gloria to come back in her car so I can say I'm sorry for making her mad. And I want to tell Krystal with a K that I'm okay with her being the Other Ginny and replacing me. I will say anything if Gloria will take me back and take me up to Canada with her. Because I need to belong somewhere and where I am isn't anywhere at all.

But deep in my brain I know that I don't want any of those things. I just want to be safe now.

I need to put the broken milk jug in a garbage can because it's a rule that *We do not litter* but I don't see a garbage can. I am still standing next to the big glass window. There is a lady on the other side of it. Looking at me. She is wearing an apron and has a tray in her hands with cups and mugs on it. She looks at me and puts one of her hands in the air and scrunches her face like she is confused and moves her mouth. So I say to her, "Don't you know I can't hear you? You're on the other side of the window."

She looks behind her and then looks back at me again. She makes a funny face and she starts talking.

So I say, "Don't you understand me? I can't hear you!"

Then the lady puts her tray down on a table and walks away. I'm guessing she had to go to the bathroom.

I'm still hungry and cold but I need to find a garbage can to put the milk jug in. My jeans are sticking to me because they're wet and my legs and bottom are getting colder and colder. But there aren't any garbage cans anywhere. There was one near the police car but I don't want to go back there. I look down the street again and look across the street and then someone says, "Are you all right? Do you need help?"

I turn around. It is the lady from the window. She is on *this* side of it now. She is holding her arms like she is cold.

So I say, "Yes, I need help."

"What's wrong?"

"I broke the milk and my pants are wet," I say. "Plus I have no place to live." I'm hoping she will give me a nice warm place to stay.

The lady makes another funny face and says, "Are you hurt? Are you feeling all right?"

But that is two questions at once so I don't say anything.

"Listen," says the lady, "it's really cold out here. Why don't you come inside and we can talk? There's a phone, if you need to call someone."

But I don't know who to call because my Baby Doll is six years old and I told Gloria I didn't want to go with her and if I go back to the Blue House then Maura and Brian might make me live at Saint Genevieve's Home for Girls Who Aren't Safe. I don't belong anywhere and I am not happy about it.

The lady is saying something else now but I can't hear her.

Because I'm still thinking. Then behind her I see a police officer walk out of the door she came out of.

So I run.

I run to a crosswalk. I run straight across as fast as I can without looking. I keep running and running. I run past stores and buildings. Then behind one building I see a Dumpster.

A Dumpster is like a big garbage can except you throw big things in it like old couches or broken chairs. The Dumpster is next to a brick wall. I run to the Dumpster and stop. I know that I need to put litter in its place so I throw the broken milk jug over the top. It is like scoring a basket at Special Olympics. Only there's no one here to cheer. There are no people here at all. I look around to see if I can find someplace to sit down or get warm. There's a fence across from the Dumpster and through the fence I see a big open space with weeds and dirt and snow and some garbage blowing around. And more buildings on the other side of the open space. There are no trees like there are at the Blue House. And at the Blue House there aren't any train tracks.

I stand at the fence for a long time. I see a seagull flying. I hear a police siren far away. I wonder if the police officer saw me and is on his way. Then I hear another noise. A rumbling sound. It doesn't go away like other noises do. It is getting closer. Then I hear a horn that is not a car horn. It is a train horn and it is long and loud and coming faster and faster.

The train tracks are right in front of me on the other side of the fence. The train is coming too fast and there is nowhere for me to go. I run back to the Dumpster and climb behind it and press my body against the brick wall of the building and cover my head with my hands. The train is coming closer and closer and it is getting so loud that I want to kick and yell but there is nowhere to move because I'm in a small tight place. Then the train is here and it is so loud that I *recoil* and throw myself

backward. I hit my head on the brick wall. It hurts so much
and the train is so loud I can't hear the words I'm saying in my
own brain so I scream and I scream and I scream.

There are three ladies standing with me in a small room with one window. There is a table in the room with a cushion top. A scale and some machines hanging from the wall. One of the ladies takes my watch. Another one of them puts a white plastic bracelet on my wrist where my watch used to be. I want to fight her but I'm so tired I can't. Another one says they'll give my watch back when it's time for me to leave. It's a rule that you can't wear a watch or jewelry when you get *admitted* to the hospital, she says. And besides, one of the other ladies says, there's a clock in every room.

Which is true. I know because I remember.

Because the hospital is where you go if they want to see if something's wrong with you. I went to a hospital four other times. Once to this one when Crystal with a C tried to leave me at school. Then to two different ones before that when I ran away from my Forever Homes. What was wrong with me those other four times is that I was stuck on the wrong side of the equation. The wrong side of Forever. I had to subtract myself because I wasn't where I was supposed to be.

But this morning I went back to the *right* side of Forever. I was with Gloria and my Baby Doll but everything was all wrong. I stayed fourteen years old and my Baby Doll was six. So I'm not sure what the problem is. I'm not sure why I'm still (-Ginny).

"Let's go see your room," one of the three ladies says.

One of them puts her hand up to touch my shoulder. Then she puts it down. And smiles. We walk out of the room. The lady with her hand on my shoulder points to a long hallway. All of us start walking.

Because *my room* is the place where my bed is. It's the place where I keep all my things. Which I'm guessing means I'm going to live at the hospital now.

And that doesn't make any sense at all. The hospital is not a place for people to live. You're not supposed to stay. I didn't get to live here before when I ran away and got kidnapped.

I think and I think and I think. I walk and try to think about how this happened.

How I got to the hospital is the police found me. They pulled me out from behind the Dumpster after the train went by. I tried to fight them but my head hurt too much from when I hit it on the brick wall. When they put me in the backseat of the police car they told me that a waitress from a restaurant called them. They asked me my name. I said I didn't know. They asked where I was going. I said I didn't know. Then they asked if I was the girl from the Amber Alert back in October and I said, "No, I'm the girl who went to have a little *rendezvous* with her Birth Mom but her Baby Doll grew up and has a different head."

They took me right to the hospital after that.

"Here we are," says one of the ladies.

I come up out of my brain. We are standing in front of a doorway with the number 117 next to it. I look hard at the number.

So I say, "But I'm only fourteen years old."

The lady smiles. "Come on in. You'll love it."

We go inside. The room has a bed and a chair and a bathroom in it and a giant television. There aren't any pictures of Michael Jackson. There aren't any shelves. Two of the ladies help me sit in the chair and the other one looks at my hair. "Let's get you all cleaned up, and then we'll put a bandage on your head. You have a little bump."

I go with them into the bathroom. In the mirror I see my face but it isn't the face I want to see.

I scowl.

The ladies take my clothes off and stay with me while I take a shower. After that I step out. They give me a towel to dry myself with. They give me a brand-new bathrobe. They help me put it on but I can't tie it.

Because the ties are in the back.

None of this happened the last four times I was at the hospital. I just went into a small room and a doctor looked at me and that was all. Now they want me to live here and the strings on all the bathrobes are on the wrong side. Which means that *nothing* works right anymore. And I am definitely still on the wrong side of Forever.

And the giant equal sign at Cumberland Farms must have been the wrong one.

That's why I'm still (-Ginny) and I didn't get to be nine years old when I walked across it.

But I don't know if I'll ever be able to find the right equal sign. I don't know if I can find a way to get things back to *exactly* how they were before the police took me out from under the sink. And I remember now that I don't really want them that way because I know that Krystal with a K will be safe after Gloria gets caught.

When I come up out of my brain I am sitting in my new bed. The mattress is raised so I can sit up. The sheets are white and the pillow is hard. And Brian and Maura are here. Standing next to me on either side.

I blink.

"Hi, Ginny," says Brian.

I want him to run to the bed. I want him to say *Oh my goodness, we missed you so much!* and I want Maura to hold my hand. Like she used to.

Instead they tell me that Baby Wendy is with Grammy and Granddad.

I look at Maura. Her mouth is a thin tight line.

"Can you tell us what happened?" says Brian.

So I say, "Gloria tried to take me up to Canada."

"Did she try to force you into the car?"

"Yes."

"How did you get away?"

"I said no and yelled."

"You did?" says Maura.

I nod my head yes.

"Why?" she says. Then her voice gets louder. "Why, Ginny? Because we know you set the whole thing up. We found the cell phone outside your window. You've been trying to go with Gloria ever since you found her on Facebook. So why the hell didn't you go with her when you finally had the chance? Why?"

I don't say anything. I try to be calm. Brian looks at the door and then back. "It doesn't matter anymore," he says to Maura.

"It doesn't matter? Of course it matters! I want to know why she didn't go! I want to know why, after lying and stealing and setting the whole thing up, she didn't go through with it!" Then she looks at me. "Gloria still has your Baby Doll, doesn't she? Gloria still has little Krystal, right? So why are you still here?"

My throat is tight and that was two very different questions but I know I have to tell them. "Because my Baby Doll is six years old," I say.

"You saw her, then," says Brian. "Your sister was there when you went to see Gloria."

I nod my head yes.

"But you didn't get in the car with them."

I shake my head no.

"Tell us why again," says Maura. "Explain it."

"Because she's not a baby anymore," I say. "My Baby Doll doesn't need me."

"That's it?" says Maura. "That's why you didn't get in the car?"

I nod my head yes again. "Plus I know Gloria's going to get caught."

"Why do you say that?"

"Because she's completely *unreliable.*"

"Humph," says Maura. "What did she say when you said you weren't going?"

"She said I was a real piece of work and a handful. She said I'm too much and she's just not enough."

"Really?" says Brian.

Maura steps backward. Her eyes get big like Ms. Carol's and a space opens between her lips. "Really?" she says.

And that was the same question twice from different people but still I say, "Yes."

Then Brian says, "It sounds like she was angry."

"She was very angry," I say.

"What did she do after that?"

"After what?"

"After she said you were a real handful," says Brian.

"She told me to *have a nice life.*"

"I don't believe it," Maura says.

And again Brian says, "Really?"

I nod my head yes.

"Then that's it," says Brian. "So it's all over?"

"I wouldn't count on that," says Maura. "Not yet. But right now we need to know where Gloria went. Ginny, do you know? Do you know where they were going? We really need to find out."

I keep my mouth shut tight. Then I shake my head no. Because I don't want to help the police catch Gloria. I don't want to be the one who helped find her. The police can do that without me and then my Baby Doll—Krystal with a K—will be safe.

"Well, we'll let the police figure that out," says Maura. "You'll talk with Patrice about it, too, but it sounds to me like we finally might have some closure here. Some real closure."

"So I'm not going to live here?"

"Of course you aren't going to live here. You're coming home with us as soon as the doctor has a look at you."

I look at the clock behind them. It says 12:42 in the afternoon but I don't really believe that that's what time it is. Nothing adds up anymore.

EXACTLY 10:58 IN THE MORNING,
WEDNESDAY, JANUARY 26TH

Patrice is sitting in her flower chair. We have been talking for *approximately* one hour. I didn't go to school because there is some more *business that I need to take care of.* I am petting Agamemnon. Patrice put him on my lap again. He is purring and that makes me relax.

"Well, that's it, then," says Patrice. "You're going to get another chance."

I reach over to the table next to me and pick up another brownie.

"Now that Gloria is completely out of the picture and you've proven that you don't want to go with her, Brian and Maura are willing to give it another try. Isn't that great?"

"Mmm-hmm," I say.

"Is there anything you're wondering about?"

"Mmm-hmm," I say again. I swallow and take a drink of milk. "Am I going back to Saint Genevieve's Home for Girls Who Aren't Safe?"

"Not yet," says Patrice. She smiles. "Maura was really surprised that you stood up to Gloria. All of us were completely shocked, really. But Maura sees it as a sign that things have changed for the better. In you. She's willing to try now. She's willing to let you stay and see how things go. So, as long as things keep on getting better, you're not going to Saint Genevieve's. You're going to stay right where you are."

I look around.

"At the Blue House," says Patrice.

I pet Agamemnon some more.

"But we're going to have to work hard to get you reintegrated at school. You stole three phones and ran away from Ms. Carol. We'll need to write some 'I'm sorry' letters again. I think everyone will understand. Especially now that Gloria is out of the picture." She drinks her coffee. "But we need to talk a little more about what happened. There are some details that are missing. Everything doesn't quite add up."

I stop petting Agamemnon. Does Patrice know that this is the wrong side of the equal sign? I wonder if the details we'll find will help me get back to the other side of Forever. I wonder if they'll help everything work right again.

"So you went to Cumberland Farms," says Patrice, "and you had a lot of clothes and a gallon of milk in your backpack. It sounds like you were going on a trip. Where was Gloria going to bring you?"

I don't want to answer the question. Because *where Gloria was going to bring me* is the same as *where Gloria went*.

"Ginny?"

"What?" I say. When she says *Ginny* it sounds different like it isn't my name anymore. I am still (-Ginny) because I'm on the wrong side of Forever. I'm still not nine like I'm supposed to be.

"I asked you a question."

"Can you ask it again, please?"

"Where was Gloria going?"

"We were going to drive away with my—with Krystal with a K."

When I think about Krystal with a K my belly hurts.

"It's great to hear you use her real name. But Gloria was going to bring the two of you someplace. Do you remember where it was?"

I stop nodding. I shut my mouth tight, tight, tight and shake my head no.

"That's all right," says Patrice. "That's all right. She'll turn up at some point. But we really need to know so that the social workers can help her out. Remember, they went to visit Gloria a few times to help her take care of Krystal with a K."

"They were going to take her away," I say.

Patrice nods. "Yes, they were. But remember, that's only because they knew she wasn't safe with Gloria. You don't want Krystal with a K to be unsafe, do you?"

I don't. But I know Gloria will get caught soon and I really, really don't want to help make it happen. But that wasn't what Patrice asked so I say, "No, I don't."

"Are you sure you don't know where they were going?"

I make sure my mouth is shut tight and shake my head no.

"All right, then," says Patrice. "So let's get back to the argument you had with Gloria. After you finally understood that the Other Ginny was Krystal with a K, the two of you got into an argument. Is that right?"

I nod my head yes but in my brain the girl who told Gloria not to yell at her feels like someone else. Someone stronger than me.

"What was the argument about?"

So I say, "I told her how we do things at the Blue House because she was yelling. Then I told her her head was still the same and the only reason I wanted to get kidnapped was to keep my Baby Doll safe. From her. Then she tried to grab me and I yelled."

Patrice smiles. "It sounds as though you really surprised her. You told her some things she wasn't ready to hear," she says. "You've come a long way since you were with her, you know. You're learning how to self-advocate and how to express what you want."

"But I wanted to be nine years old again," I say.

Patrice looks at me funny. "Nine years old? Why would you want to be nine years old? A big girl like you can do a lot more than a nine-year-old can."

"Because if I was nine I could still take care of my Ba—"

I stop talking and rub my knees together and pick at my hands. Agamemnon shifts and stops purring.

"Ah," says Patrice. "Now I'm starting to see. That explains a lot. We've known for a while that you were locked into the role of parenting—*parentified* is the word—ever since we learned that Krystal with a K wasn't a doll, but now we're dealing with something a lot more complicated. You feel like you don't have a purpose anymore. Before, you were anxious all the time because you thought your sister was still a baby and needed your help. Now that you know she's not, it's almost like your job was taken away. So this is the aftermath, for you. It's a little like being unemployed, I think."

The word *aftermath* sounds really, really scary. So I say, "Is that why nothing adds up? Because I don't have a job?"

"I think so," says Patrice. "If we're understanding each other. And believe it or not, I can help with that. It's a really easy fix, too, as far as psychology goes. But let me talk with Maura first. It'll be a pretty big step for both of you. For her, especially."

I don't know what Patrice is talking about. I don't want a job. I want to get out of the *Aftermath*. I am more confused than ever so I make a frowning face.

"Listen, Ginny. By now you know that you aren't going to live with Gloria and Krystal with a K. You tried and it didn't work. Gloria wanted you back, but the truth is that she wasn't ready for you, and she probably won't ever be. And that's the sad part. She wanted to be capable, but she knows she isn't. So you need to stay with your Forever Family. They like you, Ginny, and believe me, it's hard to find people like that. It's much easier to love someone than it is to like them. So please, stay put!"

I still don't want to be where I am. I don't understand what Patrice is saying. It's too many words and I am still thinking about how I used to know where I belonged. Because I am still stuck on the wrong side of Forever in the *Aftermath* and I'm still (-Ginny).

"Ginny?"

"What?" I say.

"What do you think about staying put?"

"I don't understand what it means."

"It means you need to keep living at the Blue House with your parents. They want you to stay. So you should stay with them. Because, trust me, the Blue House is a lot better than living with Gloria or at Saint Genevieve's."

By *parents* she means *Brian and Maura*.

"And you've got to stop stealing, but I don't think that will be a problem if you aren't trying to get kidnapped. Right?"

"Right," I say because when someone says *Right?* they always want you to say the same thing right back to them. But Patrice is a *smart cookie*.

"*Right* what?" she says.

"Right now," I say.

"Ginny, what do I want you to do?"

"You want me to stop trying to run away."

"What else?"

"You want me to stay with Brian and Maura."

"Exactly," says Patrice. "But I think it might be a good idea to start calling them your Forever Parents again. And like I just said, no more stealing. You've made quite a reputation for yourself at school. As it is, the parents of the kids whose phones you took have agreed to let the matter drop, but you're going to have to work hard to earn everyone's trust back. And the two of us are going to have to keep seeing each other for a long, long time. We need to keep you safe, young lady. All of us care a lot about you. We need to make sure that you're always in a safe place."

I know that if I stay at the Blue House I'll be in a safe place but it still isn't right. I pick hard at my fingers. Tears come out of my eyes now and I start breathing faster. "I want to live with my Baby Doll," I say. "I'm okay with Krystal being my Baby Doll. I'm okay if she turned into the Other Ginny."

"It's okay to be upset," says Patrice. "But none of those things are true. Krystal with a K isn't the Other Ginny, and she's never going to be a baby again. As long as you understand those things, it's okay to be upset. You have every right to be. But you have to stop stealing, and you can't sneak around anymore. Now, will you please let go of Agamemnon? He's going to get mad if you keep grabbing his fur like that."

Then something jumps in my face.

I yell and wave my arms. It is Agamemnon. He hits my face with his paws so fast that I can't even count. He makes another loud noise and is gone.

"See?" said Patrice. "Agamemnon doesn't like it when you squeeze him so hard. It hurts him, but he doesn't know how to ask for help. So sometimes he just lashes out and surprises us. When you're hurting or angry about something, you need to learn how to ask for help, too. I can see that you've been hurting a lot, Ginny. Now, let's start by promising that we'll stop stealing."

I nod my head yes because there's no reason to steal if I'm stuck here in the *Aftermath*.

"Good," says Patrice. She looks at the clock. "We have a little time left. Let's start writing those letters of apology that we talked about earlier. I've got some paper right here. And then I think we'll be ready for me to have that chat with Maura."

EXACTLY 11:07,
WEDNESDAY, JANUARY 26TH

I am asleep in bed but my eyes are awake. They are as open and as green as the numbers on my alarm clock.

When you run away the police always find you. If you try to fight they pick you up and put you in their car and take you to the hospital. After that the family you lived with comes to bring you home.

But there are times when you don't run away and the police still come. To your house. If you try to fight they still pick you up and bring you to the hospital but then the family you lived with doesn't come. They don't come to take you back. Instead a social worker comes. She brings you somewhere new.

That was what happened before.

I ran away two times from Samantha and Bill before I pooped on Morgan's rug which was when the police came to take me away. Because I didn't want to live there anymore. I was really tired of Morgan. She was *tedious*.

And before that the police came to take me out of Carla and Mike's house. That was because of Snowball. I felt bad afterward and kept saying, "Please, please come alive again," but I was *too late*. And when you hide a dead cat you should never put it under your mattress. People will go in your room and say, "What the hell is that bump in your bed, Ginny? What the hell is that bump!"

So if you want to leave a house forever it's pretty easy. You just have to do something bad. It doesn't even have to be on purpose.

But it can be.

Because I don't belong here. I belong on the other side of Forever where I'm still nine years old and everything adds up. Not here in the *Aftermath*. There's no place for (-Ginny) in the *Aftermath* at all. She doesn't fit in the equation or the sentence and the minus sign means she's supposed to be subtracted. I know that I drive everyone bat-shit crazy. I see the funny way they look at me when I talk. I'm just a cave girl who doesn't belong. I can't do anything right and can barely keep my mouth closed. I can't take care of anyone so I just don't belong unless it's in a cave or like Bubbles in a zoo.

So I'm going to make the police come. If I do something really, really bad they'll come put me in jail. Because jail is like a cage at the zoo. Jail is for people who need to be away from everyone. If I can't be who I used to be and my Baby Doll doesn't need me then I'm guessing I shouldn't be anywhere except behind bars. Because (-Ginny) isn't even a person. She is like an animal or a ghost or a scary, scary statue.

Which means tomorrow I'm going to make Brian and Maura Moon wish they let me get a cat.

EXACTLY 4:35 IN THE AFTERNOON, THURSDAY, JANUARY 27TH

Maura is on the couch holding Baby Wendy. She just finished breast-feeding it.

I am sitting on the floor. I just finished watching.

Because there are three things that Patrice asked Maura to let me do now that everyone thinks I'm staying at the Blue House. The first is to *let me watch when she breast-feeds*. Before Maura used to put a white cloth over her shoulder or a receiving blanket to hide Baby Wendy's head. I wasn't allowed to look. But now I'm supposed to watch because it *encourages attachment*.

The second thing I'm supposed to do is *help out a little more* with the baby. Like getting things ready for its bath or picking out a storybook when it's time to read. So this morning I asked if I could carry the diaper bag when we went to the grocery store. But Maura wouldn't let me.

The third thing I'm supposed to do is *hold the baby while Maura watches*. Once a day. Maura says *we aren't there yet*.

Outside I hear the mail truck coming down the road. I hear it slow down and stop at the neighbor's house. Then it starts up and slows down and stops in front of the Blue House. I hear the sound of the mailbox door open and close. Then the mail truck drives away.

"There goes the mail truck," says Maura. "Ginny, I'm expecting something important, so I want to run outside and see if it came. Wendy is almost asleep, so I'm going to put her down in her crib. Do you think you'll be all right if I go get the mail?"

I look up. "Yes," I say but it doesn't sound like my voice. It doesn't sound like Ginny's. I know *exactly* whose it is.

"Good. Now, just stay here. Get yourself a coloring book or maybe something to read, and just relax until I get back. Okay?"

"Okay," I say.

"Great," says Maura. "Just remember, if Wendy starts crying, everything will be fine. I'll be right back. And if the sound bothers you too much, just go right into your room and shut the door. But really, it shouldn't happen. She just finished eating. She's already asleep. I'm sure I can set her down without waking her up."

Maura stands up with Baby Wendy. The baby's eyes are closed. She walks past me into the kitchen and goes upstairs. She comes down *exactly* forty-four seconds later.

"There," she says. "Now, I'll be right back. Be a good girl, okay?"

"Okay," I say.

She sits down on the bench by the door to the screen porch and puts her boots on. Then she gets her coat. She zips it up and pulls on her gloves and hat. She smiles at me one last time. And leaves.

I stand up.

In summer or spring or fall when there's no snow it takes *approximately* four minutes to get the mail. When it's cold and snowy in the winter it takes five. So Maura will be gone for *approximately* five minutes.

Which means I have plenty of time.

I get up and run into the kitchen and grab a dish towel from the counter. It is white with two green lines around the edges. Two green lines as green and thin as snakes. Maura used the towel a little while ago to dry some baby spoons and a little bowl. Baby Wendy didn't eat the rice cereal and pears she made for it.

The towel is still damp. I hold it with one hand and lift the other one to turn on the stove but then I start to get *anxious*. I put my hand back down again and run into the living room to look out the window. Through it I see Maura in the driveway halfway to the road.

I run back into the kitchen and turn the front right burner on. The same one I used in the Little White House to make eggs. Only this time I'm not cooking. I'm setting the white-and-green dish towel on fire *on purpose* so that it will make the counter and maybe the cabinets start to burn. Then Maura will come in and put the fire out and yell and scream and call the police to take me away and this Forever will end. *Approximately* five minutes from now.

It's all part of my new secret plan.

I stand over the burner. The towel is in my hands in a tight, tight ball. The burner turns orange. I smell hot metal.

And then Baby Wendy starts to fuss.

In my brain I say, *Well dang!*

I step back to listen. The fussing gets louder.

I run back to the living room again and look out the window again and now Maura is standing next to the mailbox talking to someone. Mrs. Taylor. They are talking and talking and upstairs the crying is getting louder and behind me I know the burner in the kitchen by now is red, red, red.

I put the towel on my shoulder and start to pick at my fingers.

Maura said to go in my room if the baby starts crying. Maura said she'd be right back. She didn't say anything at all about stopping to talk with Mrs. Taylor.

I look down the hallway toward my room. I think. Then I run into the kitchen again. I turn the burner off and pull the towel from my shoulder and hold it in front of me. By two corners. I put the corners together and lay the towel flat on the counter. Then I fold it in half again and smooth it out. Nice and even, even though my hands are shaking from the crying. Because I need everything to be *all set* and *ready to go* when I get back.

I turn and run up the stairs.

At the top of the stairs the crying is so loud that I have to cover my ears even though it's on the other side of the bedroom door. I look through the bathroom out the window and still see Maura and Mrs. Taylor talking at the mailbox.

So I push the bedroom door open and walk right up to the crib. The baby's eyes are closed. It doesn't see me yet. I bend down close and say, "Ush, ush, ush."

But the baby doesn't stop. It just gets louder. Its tiny hands are in fists and its mouth with no teeth is open and it is screaming, screaming, screaming.

Then on the dresser I see the bunny. The bunny is small and fat and has eyes that are sewn in thread because buttons are dangerous for babies. The fur on the bunny's ears is flat and thin because the baby chews on it all the time. Maura washes it mostly twice a week so that it doesn't smell. It makes Baby Wendy feel better when it is sad or having a hard time going to sleep. It needs the bunny. Now.

So I grab it and put it in the baby's arms but the baby is all worked up. I know it isn't going to stop. I start looking for somewhere to hide. Outside I still see Maura and Mrs. Taylor talking, talking, talking so I pick the baby and bunny up together and move up and down gentle, gentle and say, "Ush, ush, ush," again even though I'm breaking the most important rule.

And it works.

The baby settles down and is quiet. I take a deep breath and hold it close. Its bottom is in my right hand and my left holds the back of its neck and head. Baby Wendy is little, little, little. It snuggles close and grabs my shirt and starts to suck.

The feeling is warm. Like a hug. Its hands and arms feel like my Baby Doll's. I want to *recoil* because it isn't supposed to feel that way but I can't because I'm too deep in my brain. In the feeling. I can't let go even though I want to.

Then I hear a noise downstairs. Is it the door? I can't tell.

I walk to the stairs to look and listen. I don't hear anything. I turn to look out the bathroom window again but when I do the bunny falls. It falls down three, four, five steps. And sits there.

The baby starts to cry again.

I bounce and I *ush* but this time it doesn't help. The baby needs the bunny. I have to get it but I can't get it because both of my hands are holding Baby Wendy.

Outside I see the mailbox. Maura and Mrs. Taylor are gone. Which means I have to move fast.

I put the baby down on the floor and step over it. Onto *Step One. Two, Three, Four, Five* and I bend down to grab the bunny. Then I turn and lay on the stairs so my chin and arms are on the landing next to Baby Wendy. I put the bunny near her face. "Look! Here it is!" I say.

The baby stops crying. It opens its eyes. It looks sideways at the bunny. Then at me.

It doesn't know what is happening. It doesn't know anything. It opens its mouth and yawns. Then it looks in my eyes like it is surprised. I wonder, *Does it see what's in my brain? Does it know that I am (-Ginny)?*

My mouth is open so I shut it fast. I look at Baby Wendy over my glasses. "The brain is in the head," I tell it.

It smiles and laughs.

Then I say, "I know you can't see inside but that's where my brain is. I don't want you to see what I'm thinking."

I move the bunny closer to her. Baby Wendy is too little to always grab things on the first try. She picks her head up and reaches and falls back down again with her cheek on the carpet.

I move the bunny closer.

I remember doing the same thing with my Baby Doll.

"Ginny?"

Maura is inside the house. I take a deep breath and my shoulders and arms get tight. "Ginny, where are you?"

Baby Wendy doesn't make any noise or sound. It just keeps looking at the bunny. Reaching for it.

"Ginny, where are you? Ginny, what are you—" Her words stop but they are all one word. Her voice is a hole in a window.

She leaps four, five, six times and is past me. I duck. She picks up Baby Wendy.

Now Maura is standing over me on the landing with her lips curled and her teeth showing. "What the hell were you doing?" she screams.

"The baby dropped the bunny!" I say.

Maura looks confused. She looks and looks and looks. At me. At Baby Wendy. At the bunny near the edge of the landing.

"You were trying to get her to *roll*!" she says. "You took her out of the crib and tried to make her roll down the stairs!"

"No, I didn't!" I say.

"Yes, you did! What the hell else could you be doing, offering a toy to a baby at the top of a staircase? What's wrong with you? Why would you do something like this?"

That was three questions all at once and I don't know which to answer so instead I *self-advocate*. I push off the edge of *Step One* so that I'm kneeling on *Step Three*.

"You were outside too long! The baby started to cry! I picked her up and gave her the bunny and she stopped! Then I heard a noise so I went to look but the bunny fell and I had to pick it up! So you stop yelling at me, Maura! Stop yelling at me right now! I did a good thing!"

Maura's mouth opens but no words come out.

It is *exactly* the same look that Gloria gave me when I yelled back at her. It is *exactly* the same look she gave before she told me to have a nice life and left me all alone.

I want to put my head down but instead I look right in Maura's eyes. I look and I look and then I open my mouth and breathe.

"I believe you," she says. She swallows. "Okay. I'm sorry."

I don't know what to say so I don't say anything.

"I still don't think we're ready to have you start holding her yet, though," she says. "There are things you need to learn, no matter how much you already know. And this proves it. You can't put a baby down near the edge of something she could fall off of. But I do think you're probably ready to start helping out with Wendy a little more. How does that sound?"

That sounds confusing but she is not yelling and she is not calling me a crazy girl. She is not screaming or telling me I did something bad even though I was going to set the kitchen on fire. She's telling me I can help take care of my baby sister.

"That sounds really, really good," I hear myself say. It is *my* voice. Ginny's.

Then I stand up and wait because I don't know what else to do.

So Maura says, "Wendy had a nice long beverage before I put her down. She's probably ready for some solids. Do you think you could help me by taking out the rice cereal?"

I do not say *Hmm* or *Let me think about it*. Instead I lean forward. "Do you think it would make her *approximately* happy if we put some human milk in it?"

Maura leans forward too. "I think it would make her *exactly*

BENJAMIN LUDWIG

happy if you put some human milk in it. We'll have to warm
it up first, though."

I look down at the floor again. The bunny is still there. I
pick it up and give it a hug and then give it to Wendy. We all
go downstairs.

In the kitchen I take out the rice cereal. I put it on the counter.
With one hand Maura pulls a chair out from the kitchen table.
She points at it so I sit. She lets out a loud breath. Her smile is
crooked. "All right," she says. "I don't know any other way to
work myself up to this. Ginny, could you please hold Wendy
while I get the cereal ready?"

I am so shocked that I can't answer with my mouth. I nod my
head yes. I put my arms out and cross my left leg over my right.

Maura stands close and puts the baby in my arms. My sister.
Wendy's head rests in my left elbow. I start to breathe slower.
Nice and gentle, Nice and gentle. I am holding Wendy and Wendy
is holding her bunny. The bunny isn't holding anything, not
even a carrot. But when I look up again Maura is holding the
dish towel. The one with the green lines along the edges.

The one I was going to use to set the kitchen on fire.

"Mrs. Taylor says her dog is going to have puppies," says
Maura.

I look behind her at the stove. The burner is cold and dark.

"Brian—I mean *your dad*—was thinking of maybe getting a
dog this summer when school gets out. He thinks it might be
good for you. For all of us. Does that sound like a good idea?"

I think. In my brain I see Gloria's apartment with the two sets
of cages against the wall but the cages are all open and all the
Maine coon cats are gone. I look around to see where they went.

Somewhere far behind me a door opens. Tiny feet scamper
away.

"Ginny?"

I look up. "Dogs like to play Frisbee," I say.

"Yes, I suppose they do," says Maura.

"They like to go in the car with you when you go to the lake."

"Right."

"They like to run through the leaves when everyone is out-side raking. They like it when you throw snowballs for them."

"Right again," says Maura.

"They do not like to be by themselves."

Maura swallows. "No, they don't. You're right, Ginny. You're right about all those things. I promise that I'll do my best to let you be more involved. But you have to try, too. I know it's a struggle, but please try to be less...inward. I know that that's part of who you are, but...you'll try, won't you?" She wipes her eyes and looks away and when she looks back I see that they're wet. "So what do you think? Is it a good idea for us to get a dog?" She closes her eyes and looks sideways and smiles. And puts her finger up. "No, wait—just the second question."

"Yes," I say. "I think that getting a dog would be a very, very good idea."

Maura puts the towel over her shoulder and measures some rice cereal into the bottom of a baby bottle. She pours a tiny bit of human milk into it and stirs. Then she puts the bottle in a pan of water and the pan of water on the stove.

I pull Wendy closer and look over at my watch. The time is 5:08. The date is still Thursday, January 27th. From now on I'm going to spend a lot more time trying to *help out a little more* with Wendy. Because even though I come from a different place and my head is different I still have my first name and my eyes are still green. I don't have to be (-Ginny) if this Forever Family wants me around. I don't have to be (-Ginny) if they let me do things and *help take excellent care* of my little sister. My new secret plan didn't work but mostly that's okay because in the *Aftermath* things never add up the way you expect. Plus *two wrongs don't make a right* and what I was doing with the dish towel would have made me be (–Ginny) forever. So I'll stay here at the Blue House until the cows come home which is mostly safer than looking for giant equal signs or waiting for the police.

Which means, I'm guessing, that I'm finally staying put.

★ ★ ★ ★ ★

ACKNOWLEDGMENTS

I'm an adoptive parent as well as a writer, and so in writing this book I've worn two hats. It follows that I need to thank all the people who supported my writing, as well as everyone involved in my journey in deciding to adopt. And so, in chronological order—

I'd like to thank my mother and father, who always made it clear that children were to be cherished above all things, and welcomed at every stage of life.

Thank you to Claudio and Liz, who read page after page of my work when the three of us were in seventh and eighth grade. You kept asking for more pages and said you were hooked, but it was I who hung on your words.

Thank you to my undergraduate mentor, Professor John Yount, at the University of New Hampshire, who told me, *Don't teach. Wait tables if you have to, but don't teach.* I taught anyway, but your warning showed me that my writing might be just as important as teaching, perhaps even more so. To Professors Margaret Love-Denman, Mark Smith and Sue Wheeler, also from my undergraduate years at UNH.

I'd like to thank my wife, Ember, for her eagerness to explore foster care and adoption, and for reading so many manuscripts so, so many times. Thank you to Ariane, our daughter, whose love of Michael Jackson inspired Ginny's.

Thank you to Karen Magowan and Patricia Pettegrow, and all the other social workers at both Maine DHHS and New

Hampshire DCYF. Thank you to all the foster parents, adoptive parents and parents of special-needs children I've met over the years. You continue to serve as my mentors and role models.

Thank you to Jeff Kleinman, my agent at Folio Literary Management, for responding to Ginny's voice, and for believing in her. To Molly Jaffa, Director of Foreign Rights at Folio.

Thanks to Russell Dame, who read tirelessly through the manuscript, and whose comments were invaluable in its revision. To James Engelhardt at University of Illinois Press, who offered feedback on an early draft. To Justin Pagnotta and Mark Holt-Shannon from Dover Middle School, both of whom offered insight, support and advice at various stages. To Kate Luksha, Jimmy Roach and Jayce Russell, who read short sections in workshop at the University of New Hampshire. To Ann Joslin Williams, our workshop director.

Thank you to Liz Stein, my editor at Park Row, for celebrating Ginny's humanity and championing her dignity. And to copy editor Libby Sternberg, proofreader Bonnie Lo, and Amy Jones, Julie Forrest, Sheree Yoon, Stefanie Buszynski and Shara Alexander in marketing/publicity.

We tend to listen to people who shout the loudest, who demand our attention. With all the noise, it's easy to forget that others aren't capable of making their needs known. Some people—displaced children, and children in the system, especially—often don't believe that their needs matter at all. How could they, considering what society has taught them by their experiences? One of my hopes in writing *Ginny Moon* was to give a voice to people who might, as Ginny does, have trouble self-advocating. I also hope the book inspires people to help kids in foster care. There are an awful lot of them. I'll have some things to say about these issues at www.benjaminludwig.com.

HQ
One Place. Many Stories

The home of bold, innovative
and empowering publishing.

Follow us online

 @HQStories

 @HQStories

 HQStories

 HQ Stories

 HQMusic